FIRST EDITION

Written by **Chris Chau**
Cover by **Ivan Zanchetta - bookcoversart.com**

This is a work of fiction. Names, characters, organizations, places, events, and incidents are either products of the author's imagination or are used fictitiously. Any semblances of actual people, living or dead, or events are purely coincidental.

Library of Congress Cataloging-in-Publication Data
ISBN: 9781791838621 (Paperback)
ASIN: B07LF4PR1J   (eBook)

Like my page on Facebook at Chris Chau - Author, to stay up to date on new projects, Reddit AMA, (Ask me Anything) and random musings. Thank you for reading, enjoy!

PATIENT 3

A novel by Chris Chau

Table of Contents

Prologue

A 1998 NASA photo of "space debris" taken from the STS-88 mission is theorized by some to be the 'Black Knight' satellite that has been lingering in Earth's orbit for thousands of years. Conspiracy theorists believe it to be of extraterrestrial origin, a probe that has been watching over our planet for all these years, sending signals back to an unknown source.

October of 2017, unidentified astrological object, 'Oumuamua' decelerates before entering our solar system and exits in an unpredictable path at increased velocity that defies Newtonian physics. The object showed no signs of a comet tail. It can only be described as an asteroid that may have originated in the Vega constellation by scientists.

March of 2018, footage of a United States Navy pilot's encounter with an unidentified flying object in 2015 is declassified and released to the Stars Academy of Arts and Science. In the video, the pilot pursues the object in an F/A-18 Super Hornet, the encounter is recorded with an infrared camera. The object accelerates at a speed the fighter jet is unable to match to continue the pursuit. The object did not have any plumes or exhaust trails, the pilot and weapons operator aboard the fighter are baffled. The United States Department of Defense has declined to comment on the video since its release.

February 27, 2025, during routine software maintenance at NASA Mission Control, the Mars 2020 Rover, Raider II, and Pathfinder III camera feeds are supposedly hacked by activists. Images of possible alien structures on the planet emerge online and go viral. NASA and the Homeland Security claims it is nothing more than a hoax filled doctored images in a poor attempt at a publicity stunt.

The result of the lost signal was reportedly due to an atmospheric storm that destroyed the feed to the unmanned vehicles. Government officials vehemently deny the authenticity of the images. The activists were labeled as actors who fabricated the images to appear on several interviews posted online as a hoax that went too far... the 'actors' were never heard from or seen again.

June 6, 2028, the last major military battle ends in the Middle East with the exception of small isolated skirmishes throughout the region. Oil is no longer a sought after precious resource as the majority of urban areas across the world are relying more heavily on renewable sources of energy, particularly solar. The world's elite fund all major solar energy projects in the developing world. Humanity recognizes the global threat of increased levels of carbon emissions and work together to reverse its effect.

January 21, 2029, the All Nations Treaty is signed at The Hague in the Netherlands to end all major conflicts including any unresolved ceasefires to officially become recognized as peace treaties. As a result, every individual nation is forced to severely reduce their standing armies by eighty percent and the All Nations Initiative (ANI) is formed as a global peacekeeping force.

Their aim is focused on maintaining the peace and ensuring the safe transport of food and water to an ever increasing population at each of their posts spanning across all continents. The United States, Russia, China, and North Korea are the last countries to sign the monumental treaty.

September 23, 2032, the ANI experiences a change of leadership and undergoes further military spending cuts, from the reduction in force, arms, R&D, and even the health benefits of its soldiers. For the first time in *recorded history, humanity has nearly achieved global peace.*

Due to the global reduction in military spending and rising fears we may outgrow our planet within a century, humanity has pooled its intellectual and financial resources to once again look to the stars. Funds are diverted to the International Space Program to reinvigorate exploration outside of our solar system to learn more about our place in the galaxy and possibly a search for intelligent life and perhaps a new home.

The first manned, international mission to Mars to experiment new terraforming methods is set for the spring of 2034. There have been no new confirmed extraterrestrial occurrences since the 'Oumuamua' asteroid event in October of 2017...

Pins and Needles

"Alright Michael, I'm done with your vitals, the doctor should be with you shortly to go over your test results. Do you have any family nearby?"

"Yeah… My fiancée is on her way over, why?"

"Excellent." The nurse wraps the stethoscope around her neck, gives a nervous smile as she turns towards the door. The chatter in the hallway and the swishing of her scrubs cease as the door closes behind her.

Such an ominous question to ask and have me stewing here, analyzing what it could possibly mean as I wait for the doctor to return. If it were good news, she would have told me then and there, right? I replay the conversation in my head and focus on her body language, stress levels in her speech, and facial expressions while she was examining me to see if I could guess what kind of news I would be getting. There is nothing to glean from our interaction. She was straightforward and didn't say much other than the necessary words to instruct me to maneuver my body to get my readings during the examination.

The silence in the room became deafening once the voices and the footsteps in the hallway faded. I could hear every single drop of water drip from the faucet as each one pools up into a large droplet, dangling from the faucet head until its own weight becomes too heavy to support itself and it releases its grip and crashes down onto the sink's hard metallic surface in a gentle splash, shattering into several smaller drops. The cycle continues as I watch, except now faster; or at least it seems that way as I notice my left foot nervously tapping on the footrest of the examination table.

The next droplet forms and follows the same fate as the droplets before it, my heart beat thumping in my chest feels like it is keeping pace with the drops, matching each splash when it explodes in the sink on contact. I take a look at my watch and come to the realization that only two minutes have passed since the nurse stepped out.

There isn't much to do in here other than stare at the most blandest paintings under the flickering fluorescent lights above. As jubilantly colorful as they are, the pamphlets about washing my hands, covering my face when I cough, or wearing a seatbelt when I get into a car didn't pique my interest enough to pull from the shelf and read. My phone is in my footlocker back at the barracks. Naturally, watching and listening to water slowly drip out of the faucet has captivated my attention as I'm on edge, eagerly awaiting the doctor's return.

I've never been a fan of doctors since my adolescence. Going to the doctor's office if I wasn't sick or hurt either meant it was time to get my physical checkup for high school sports only a few years ago, or what I dreaded most, getting routine vaccine shots when I was younger. I was so bad at taking shots that even bribes of ice cream and candy from my mom and dad never worked. It was always a distraction that got me, where I would have a conversation with the nurse while the doctor hit me with the needle.

It never felt excruciatingly painful, but the thoughts of needles leading up to the shot were the root of my anxiety. The moment the doctor holds up the vial to the light to extract a precise amount of medication is still the most terrifying part to me as it meant impending doom to childhood me.

I look down at my socks as my feet dangle and swing from the sterile table, further reminding me of the presence of my inner child, and dreading the return of the doctor, now, and like I did before. Footsteps outside the closed door start out faint and begin to grow louder as the person walking approaches my room.

The steps sound like they're getting closer and closer until they stop. I can't make out the muffled words the man on the other side of the door is saying to another person down the hall, he finally stops talking, two gentle knocks thud on the wooden door. About a half second delay, the handle twists and the door inches open until a man with peppered hair pokes his head in.

Doctor White walks through the door. Ever since I was a kid, I never could tell from reading the faces of authority if they were going to give me good or bad news. Whether the teacher told me that she wanted to see me before recess, or if the cop would be returning with a ticket after running my plates and registration, or in this case, a doctor looking over my test results. I never knew what to expect.

Today is no different, other than the fact that life as I know it could change forever when he finishes his spiel. After going through the battery of tests, they were definitely looking for something pretty serious and specific. The A.N.I. doesn't willy-nilly send its soldiers to the doctor's office to perform all sorts of expensive tests unless they think something is seriously wrong.

If he gives me good news, I would have a new lease on life, live it to the fullest, and try my best to remember not to take it for granted for the rest of my days. Each time I hold my fiancée Eve, I would be present in each moment I get with her and make special note to the little things that make her laugh and smile; the way she feels when we hug from when our faces touch to the extra little squeeze at the end right before she breaks away.

Without a word, the doctor shuts the door behind him, eyes fixated on whatever it is that he is reading on the clipboard with a laptop tucked at his side. He plops down on his chair and starts typing on the laptop for a few seconds until he speaks, "Sorry to keep you waiting Michael, tell me again the symptoms you were having again, up until you ended up here in my office, in your own words. Start with what was happening a few minutes before the episode started."

I go from being tense to relaxed, my shoulders come to rest. No matter what he tells me, he won't be able to say it until I'm done talking. "Yes sir, we were at the firing range this afternoon. I was prone on my stomach on the ground in full gear, ears, and eyes protection, sending some rounds down range with no issues sir. All of a sudden, my hands crinkle and seize up into a claw, I couldn't grip the rifle, nor could I let go of it, it was the strangest feeling. A few seconds later, I had trouble breathing. I finally got my hands off my rifle but I still couldn't move my fingers to pop off my helmet, so I used my shoulders to swing and roll over onto my back and motioned both my wrists over my throat so that someone or the Sarge could see I was in trouble. I could barely breathe and my legs wouldn't work."

Doctor White stares intently at his laptop as he mashes away on his keyboard while I spoke and a few more seconds after. I pause from my story to have a sip of water to give the doctor a chance to catch up on his notes as I can see the keyboard cursor still racing across the screen and filling it with words from the reflection of his rectangular glasses. He finally stops and looks back up at me, indicating to continue my story.

"Next thing I know, a couple of guys in my platoon are tossing me onto a stretcher and loading me into the back of a Humvee to transport me to the aid station. By the time we arrive, mostly everything is back to normal. I start breathing fine again and I can easily clench my hands into a fist and open them up to spread my fingers as far as they can go. At that point, I was able to get off the stretcher and hop out of the vehicle on my own.

The guard on duty came up to me and asked me for my name to get checked in... but I couldn't remember for the life of me. I remember looking down at my uniform but couldn't make out the words. The guard gave me a puzzled look, glanced at my uniform and scribbled it down on the clipboard and instructed me to follow him. After a few short minutes of examination, the medic sent me here to the hospital. I haven't experienced ANY of those symptoms for at least an hour now."

"Do you know your name now?"

"Michael Walker"

The Doc continues to hammer away on his laptop even though I've already stopped talking for about a minute. I can't contain my nervousness so I start to twiddle my thumbs. My focus is trained on the doctor, awaiting the news he's about to deliver. Finally, Doctor White stops typing, turns his chair to directly face me and places both his hands on his lap. He takes a breath.

"There's no easy way to say this Michael, but after the battery of tests we ran on you and what you've just told me, it is clear that you have Cerebral Nervorum, or CN. It's that rare neurological disorder that you might have heard about over the last few months, we still have no idea what the root cause of it is."

As he is delivering the news, I bury my face in my hands before interlocking my fingers on the back of my head, and resting my elbows on my lap. I know full well what happens to these people.

Doctor White continues, "What you have experienced today is how it starts, which is why you were given priority for all of these tests. Within twenty-four hours of the first signs of symptoms, dexterity and basic motor functions will rapidly deteriorate. Within forty-eight hours you'll experience severe short-term memory loss and basic motor functions will be completely gone. From there, without any breathing assistance devices... complete respiratory failure.

Researchers believe it to be a prion-based disease, similar to mad cow. We are learning so much about this every day that passes. What we do know is that increased brain activity causes the disease to spread and accelerate. About one in fifty thousand of the world's population is getting diagnosed with it, but it's not contagious. There is no cure yet, but there are a few treatment options."

If there isn't a cure, I can only imagine what my options are... things that keep me, "comfortable" when the time comes. I ask the doctor as a formality, "What are my options?"

"I see on your chart that you're a Private First Class, assuming you don't have any millionaire family members that are willing to foot the six-figure cost per month treatment for CRISPR... Clustered Regularly Interspaced Short Palindromic Repeats gene editing therapy... which isn't covered by our insurance due to the spending cuts that were passed a few years ago by the way, you only have three real options.

One, we'll keep you as comfortable as possible with pain medication and let nature run its course given you sign a DNR, Do Not Resuscitate, order that allows us to keep you off of an IV drip and life support. Two, we can keep you in hospice care where your short-term memory faculties will be severely reduced and all of your basic motor functions such as walking, talking, eating, etcetera will be gone within a week, but we'll keep you on a respirator to keep you alive."

"Well Doc, I'm glad you led off with the good stuff, I'm not sure if the third option could possibly be any better than these... please tell me, satisfy my curiosity." The doctor is not amused by my coping mechanism of sarcasm. He gives me a blank stare, without breaking eye contact or blinking, he continues right where he left off.

"The third option, which is the most popular option, is to put you into a medically induced coma. This forces the disease to come to a grinding halt due to the drastic drop in brain activity. This is simply a bandage for the problem; as I said earlier, we are learning so much about the disease that we expect a more permanent and affordable treatment in the near future.

Again, most of this isn't going to be covered by your insurance since this is a new rare disease that insurance companies aren't hopping on board with, especially ours… but the price is much more manageable than CRISPR. What most hospitals are doing to keep costs down is housing the patients in low traffic areas of the hospitals with a nurse on rotation for the whole level to monitor basic vitals, change out IV's, move patients to prevent bed sores, and provide other basic care."

I reluctantly nod in agreeance for option three. It's not even a choice I'm being presented here. Doctor White reaches into his lab coat and pulls out a brochure for Harbor Point Medical Center and tells me, "Page three shows you their treatment packages for Cerebral Nervorum depending on your budget. I'll leave these here with you for you to go over. It is highly recommended that you make your decision within the next couple of hours before the disease spreads any further.

Speak to your loved ones and make sure all of your affairs are in order. When I say we are anticipating a cure, it could mean a few years to a decade which is still relatively quick for a complex, newly discovered disease. Call the number in the brochure and they'll get you set up. There will be doctors and nurses standing by to escort you in so you can skip the line at intake. It's one of the two local facilities that have retrofitted their CN treatment areas to keep costs down. Someone from base will be here shortly to drive you back to your barracks to gather your things and get you to the hospital, good luck son."

I follow Doctor White out of the examination room and use the elevator to get down and exit the hospital. The sinking sensation of the elevator's descent follows my body even after the elevator stopped and the doors have opened. My mind wanders and my body goes on auto-pilot as I continue my way out of the building.

Every single person that I walk by has their own story of why they're here, the sick, the injured, new parents, hypochondriacs, and patients who have had their whole lives flipped upside down. There's no way to tell what anyone's story is from passing by, something I had never thought about until now. I can't even explain what I'm feeling now.

There are several people sitting outside on the benches, waiting for their rides to pick them up at the roundabout. I'm too nervous to sit down, so nervous and anxious that I can feel a numb trembling in my jaws. I move them around and start mouthing words in an attempt to get the trembling to stop, I take a deep breath.

In this moment, I notice a young couple laughing and playing with their infant child in a car seat as they await their ride. This sets off a chain reaction of thoughts, thinking about my fiancée Eve, our future together, what I should do, what I need to do, and what I dread is going to happen within the next couple of hours. Decisions about my life that I never thought I would have to make at the age of twenty-one, going on twenty-two.

My ride arrives, a large armored plated Humvee that sticks out like a sore thumb. I stand and wait as it lurches its way through the roundabout, waiting its turn to get through as other vehicles are picking up their friends and loved ones at the curb. Even at rest, the monstrous roar of the ancient diesel engine is absolutely deafening compared to all of the silent electric cars that surround it.

I hop in and shut the door. With both hands remaining on the steering wheel and eyes on the road as he steps on the gas, the driver greets me. "Hey, I'm Corporal Mathers, a page has already gathered all of your personal belongings on base and has transferred them out to the armory a few miles from here. Your fiancée will be joining us there instead of the hospital. Harbor Point is a hop and a skip away from the armory... I'm sorry about all of this man."

All I can do is muster up a nod in response to this sentiment.

I think back to my days in college, before dropping out last year. The struggles that people went through around the globe, especially third world countries before the All Nations Treaty was signed. People were struggling to live peacefully, not go hungry, getting access to clean water in the midst of civil wars over politics and religion. Those were the types of people to feel sorry for, not me. I should feel lucky that the doctors are able to diagnose me and have these arrangements made for my stay, and the time to plan out what will happen in my absence… but I don't. I can only think about the future that I will be missing out on, how Eve will take the news, and the undue stress that I will be putting on those around me that care about me.

There isn't a moment to spare, every minute and every second counts. Now is not the time to wallow. The more time I spend preparing for what is to come, the more I'll have to say goodbye to Eve, my love. I open up the dark blue brochure depicting a nurse tending to a patient's IV bag on the cover as he lays unconscious. I still haven't accepted that it's going to be me there in that picture in a few hours for God knows how long.

As I flip through, I notice a theme in the treatment packages they offer that are a little off putting. If a patient is willing to part with a few extra dollars a month, apparently they can get "better care." I am picturing a meeting with the hospital's executives where they are drawing up ideas on how to squeeze extra money from patients in creative ways and greenlighting the ones that would be the most profitable.

There are three tiers of plans. The very basic plan ensures that a nurse will check your vitals, change your IV, and reposition you every eight hours to avoid bed sores.

The basic "PLUS" plan includes all of those things as well as some media options. You tell them what your favorite movies, TV shows, and music are, and they will make sure to get you at least three hours of "media" time per day. Doesn't make sense at all considering that the purpose of the coma is to limit brain activity… another way to bilk people I suppose.

The illustrations in the brochure are awful. The "unconscious" patient is smiling with headphones around his ears while musical notes float away from his head. I guess the idea here is that the patient would come up with a list of their favorites and the hospital would throw in the extra service of making sure that they would get to listen to the audio a few hours a day, the theory is that they would subconsciously absorb the sounds... Gosh… I need to stop thinking in terms of "they," this patient is going to be "me."

Reading this page of the brochure conjures a terrifying thought I hadn't even considered during this whole nightmare of a situation. There's a chance that I could be conscious the whole time and trapped inside my shell of a body, unable to move or communicate to hospital staff that I'm alert and confined into the tightest possible space, my own skin. Where my internal screams would go unheard, itches I can never scratch, and an active mind that will remain in solitary for years to come except for the brief one way interactions with the nurse that changes my IV.

I can't think straight as I develop a nervous sweat. I hope the sweating and fuzzy mind is due to these intrusive thoughts and not a symptom of the disease accelerating.

I can't wait to see Eve, she's the beauty AND the brains of our little operation, she'll help me rationalize everything and help me get through it with love, affection, and the part that I love most about her, her silly sense of humor. Honestly though, I want to feel her warm embrace, close my eyes, hug her and wake up to her kissing me and this whole day becoming nothing more than a memory of a terrible dream.

I turn to the last page of the brochure, the third and final treatment option is the "Premium PLUS" option, written in big bold letters. It has everything in the "Basic" and "PLUS" plan, but it also includes some new advances in electroshock therapy. Administered once a day, it apparently stimulates your muscles enough to prevent the loss of muscle mass so my body wouldn't wither away over the years, in addition to a physical therapist that will move my ragdoll of a body around with stretches and workouts… but it costs twice as much as the "PLUS" package.

We arrive at the main gate of the armory, Corporal Mathers' slides his ID under the window to the guard sitting in his booth, after a quick glance at the card and both of our faces, the guard returns the ID and points towards the main lot by the large building. The faded red and white metal arm raises, and we make our way to the armory that looks more like an office building than anything else.

I see Eve standing outside the main structure in the distance, arms folded and motionless, forcing a nervous smile. I raise my hand for a little wave, she responds by putting a hand over her mouth and squints her eyes to hold back her tears.

We pull up closer. I can see that Eve had been crying from her smudgy mascara which in turn forces a few tears to squeeze out from my own eyes. Before the Humvee comes to a stop, I casually dab my tears with the sleeve of my uniform to at least put up a façade of being strong for her in this difficult time. We both try to force a smile to strengthen the other, but it doesn't work, she chokes up, cries some more, and we both cry.

I hop out and immediately hug her as she is now audibly sobbing. I kiss her on the cheek and hug her as hard as I can, so hard and tight that I can almost touch my sides with my fingertips.

I never truly appreciated how great her warmth and embrace felt until this moment, I wasn't sure if it was due to the gravity of the situation, or if she always feels like this. It's now something that I will never forget and something that I may not experience for many years to come. After a full minute without words, we both finally let go, hold hands and stare into each other's eyes.

As I'm about to tell her I love her, she wipes her face one last time with a tissue, looks into my eyes, cuts me off and says, "I love you babe, but we need to get inside and sort some things out right away. We don't have a lot of time." While still holding onto one of my hands, she leads the way into the building and pulls me into an office where all of my things from base have been gathered.

"Michael, I've come up with a budget for us, things will be a little tight, but we can manage, but I want the best care for you."

"You are so amazing babe, but you don't have to spread yourself so thin like that, I'll just be taking a longer than usual nap anyway. I don't want you to worry about me or spend any more than you have to."

I appreciate her lovely gesture, I truly do, but I can't bear to put that kind of financial strain on her. I am so lucky to have had someone like her in my life for so long. She's been my sweetheart since we met at 3rd grade recess during a game of tag. She chased me for a bit, but when she finally tagged me, I lost my balance and fell over and scraped my hands. She put her palms on mine until a teacher came to see what had happened. Despite my pain, I wasn't going to cry in front of her so I smiled and she smiled back. From that point on, Eve was my date to all of the middle school and high school dances, we became inseparable.

We even went to the same college up until the start of my senior year when I had to drop out and join the service to get my parents on my medical insurance when they got too old and sick to work. We hadn't been apart for longer than a few months at a time since we met and that only happened twice; when our folks had different summer vacation plans one year and the second time, when I went off to basic training in Georgia. The thought of leaving her for years at a time is tearing me apart.

I don't care about what is going to happen to me, I worry more on how she'll manage to support herself and my bills without me there to help or cheer her on. My role for this upcoming chapter of our lives is pretty simple, lay there, idly by as she has to do EVERYTHING on her own.

Eventually though, my own selfish wants and needs begin intruding into my head, I know she'll visit my dormant body from time to time, but I hope that maybe, just maybe, while I'm under… I'll get to see her in my dreams.

Until Death

While updating my will and medical release paperwork, I can hear Eve on the phone, frantically bombarding whoever is on the other line with several questions about power of attorney and how all of the major decisions are going to be dealt with in my absence. Her conversation inspires an idea to make things a little simpler for us. It may not be the party we were hoping for, to celebrate with our friends and family, but at least we can still get married.

Eve hangs up the phone looking exhausted and tells me that the hospital will have all of the waivers and forms waiting for us at the hospital's Financial Services wing. As we're both sitting at the table, I hold her by the hand while she is taking notes with the other and ask her, "Do you want to get married right now? It'll save us a whole lot of trouble and paperwork for you to manage everything while I'm gone. We were going to do it anyway. What do you say? The hospital will have a chaplain somewhere in the building. All we have to do is make the call!"

Her frazzled look moments ago, quickly vanishes and morphs into an accentuated smile. Eve immediately jumps into my lap, puts her arms around my neck and gives me a kiss, nods, and smiles in agreement.

We look into each other's eyes and touch foreheads, she hands me a pen and paper and says, "In the meantime honey, you need to give me access to all of your active accounts, passwords, e-mail etcetera so I can handle your bills while you're gone. Also, since we're going to get the premium package, you need to write down some of your favorite music, TV shows, and movies you want to listen to, you'll get a couple of hours of that per day. I'll even throw you in a little something of my own and record some messages when I visit you. That way, you can remember what I sound like so you don't go running off, fantasizing about some other women in your dreams."

It makes sense now… the media package isn't intended for the patient, but more for their loved ones, to provide some sort of comfort and assurance, knowing that there is some sort of possible connection to the outside world.

Before she gets back on the phone to update the hospital that we are getting married before the procedure, she gently dabs me on the tip of my nose with her pointer finger as she walks to the other side of the room. I am so incredibly lucky that Eve has been a part of my life for so long… in a couple of hours, we'll be making our vows to be together forever.

Let's see… music will be easy, I'll need to give Eve access to my playlists and we'll be in business, simple enough. I'm not one to re-watch a bunch of old shows or movies, so I wonder if there is an option for new releases only. That is going to be a ton of TV, but I may as well stay hip with the kids if I will even be able to hear anything in my vegetative state.

Corporal Mathers pokes his head into the office, "It sounds like you two are about done in here? I'll drive you and your fiancée to the hospital as soon as the both of you are ready to go."

"Yup, let me grab my things."

I pick up the small olive green duffle bag containing all of my personal belongings that they retrieved from base and go through it, making sure everything Eve needs is in there before I leave the office that had become our little crisis command center.

An envelope emerges, I am reminded that I started the day being excited. A friend must have entered us into a contest for a dream honeymoon vacation… the letter informed us we were finalists. The contents instructed us to shoot a video, talking about where we would want to go and what we would do. The letter had a large red stamp on it that read, "Submission must be Post-marked by March 19, 2033." I never told her about the contest; it was supposed to be a surprise.

Eve is so creative, I'm sure she would have come up with some hilarious script and we probably would have won. Most couples would want to pick somewhere warm, probably with a beach where they'd be served some sort of refreshing, ice cold, alcoholic beverages to their cabana…

Not us though, we've been talking about our dream vacation for a while.

We want to go to Iceland to see the Northern Lights, relax in the Blue Lagoon, and hike its gorgeous landscape. It's funny how the priority of things you wish could happen can change so quickly. I discard the letter into the trash bin before I leave the room.

I find Eve in the hallway, with her back towards me. She turns her head to face me and leaves her hand out for me to hold as I approach her, we interlock our fingers and make our way out of the main entrance. Back into the Humvee I go, but this time, my bride to be is at my side. I open the door to the backseat for her; toss my bag in the front seat and follow her into the back row before I shut the door.

Even though the ride to the hospital is only ten minutes, I live in the moment and appreciate every second of my waking breath, the drive becomes surreal. I hadn't ever thought about the beauty of my environment, how the striking greenery that the trees and the lush green grass compliments the backdrop of a state of the art city skyline. It resembles something you would find in a utopian science fiction movie, filled with tall glass buildings, run completely by solar energy that the windows and rooftops absorb.

Come to think of it, it's our military presence in this lush state that is the ugly but necessary thorn to the city's splendor. Most of our machines of war are run on arcane, limited, and antiquated resources like fossil fuel and coal. This is evidenced by the loud growls of the engine's rev from our very own vehicle burning this fuel and releasing a visible stench into the air.

The rationale behind the top brass I'd imagine is that it's what's been used for over a century and dependable in any given situation. Even the cars that are currently sharing the road with us show the juxtaposition of the two technologies. There's us in this monstrous vehicle and there's the gaggle of silent electric cars, swarming the highway. Funny how you don't notice these things or ever stop to appreciate your everyday surroundings until you're facing your own mortality and know that you will miss the simplistic beauty of everything in front of your eyes.

I turn and look at Eve as she is staring out the window, I attempt to absorb the whole experience; the way she smells of sweet lilacs to the way she looks as the sunlight turns her dark brunette hair into a dark auburn. She catches me staring and admiring her beauty as her voluminous long hair covers a third of her face, but not enough to cover her smile, she lets out a snicker, "What?"

"Nothing, I'm appreciating how beautiful my bride to be looks."

Without a word, Eve unbuckles her seatbelt, leans over to my side of the vehicle, grabs my arm at the elbow, closes her eyes, and rests her head on my chest. The harsh reality of going under for years at a time finally strikes me. I don't want this moment to end, I'd give anything to live in this perpetual state forever. Our ride comes to an abrupt stop as we both jolt forward and are parked at the emergency entrance of the hospital.

"Here we are." Bellows Corporal Mathers. He and I catch eyes in his rearview mirror and nod.

Eve and I hop out of the vehicle; I open the passenger side door to grab my bag. The corporal sees that we are both clear of the Humvee and gives me a lazy salute or a wave before he drives off. I pause for a second, make a deep sigh as I survey the entrance of the plain looking hospital. This will be my new home for years to come.

Before I cross the threshold of the entrance, I turn around to have one last look at the cloudy sky with hints of blue beyond the trees, and breathe one last breath of fresh air, trying to take in the whole experience. We walk hand in hand through the hospital's automatic sliding doors.

Before we even make two steps beyond the second set of automatic glass doors, we are greeted by a plump old blond woman, wearing a brown pantsuit. She shakes my hand and introduces herself, "You two must be Michael and Eve, my name is Darlene, we've been expecting you. I'll be your liaison throughout the intake process, if you have any questions, feel free to ask. First thing's first though, let's get you married! Do either of you have any friends or family that will be joining us to witness the ceremony?"

Eve responds for the both of us, "Nice to meet you Darlene… unfortunately, we don't have any friends or family that will be joining us. From the time he was diagnosed and the time I was notified, it's only been a couple of hours. No one we know is able to make it on such short notice, especially coming from outside of the city."

"I don't mind being the witness for you two if you'll have me."

"Thank you Darlene. That would be fantastic." Eve replies.

Hospitals are such funny places. In the same building there are people that are sick, injured or dying, there are newborns that are taking their first breath of life into this world, and today, people getting married, all under one roof. We follow Darlene as she waddles her way to the elevators.

"Father Mark will be conducting the ceremony. Eve told me over the phone that you two are Catholic."

"Yup!" Eve quickly replies.

With Darlene's back toward us as we wait for the elevator to reach the chapel level, I immediately shoot a look at Eve and give her a bug-eyed look while attempting to raise a single eyebrow. She responds by giving a fake smile, pursing both of her lips back, and baring her front teeth, shrugging her shoulders, hands palms up to shoulder level, and mouths the words, "Looooove you."

Darlene plays along by remaining silent and acting oblivious to any of our interactions despite our close proximity and our blurred reflections from the metallic elevator door.

We exit the elevator and make our way to the chapel. All I can do is laugh at this point, I guess I'm Catholic today. I'm not religious at all, but Eve's family is a bit more traditional and would be more offended than my parents if the wedding were not performed according to their wishes and belief system. I guess a Catholic priest was always bound to marry us from the get-go, we just hadn't gotten that far into our wedding plans yet.

As we turn the corner down the hall, it is obvious which room is the chapel. At the end of the hallway stand two large brown wooden doors with opaque, colorful, stained glass windows off to each side. The contrast of the most sterile and plain looking environment is a little amusing. As Darlene walks us through the chapel doors, the white walls, linoleum floors, and drab lighting disappear behind us as the doors close as if we had entered a portal to another dimension.

Inside, it's a quaint little chapel with only three pairs of rows of pews that couldn't seat more than twelve people in total. The room is still and serene, you would never be able to tell that there is a hospital on the other side of the doors behind us, running its day to day operations.

The violet carpet, the wooden pews, fake flowers, regular old-fashioned tungsten light bulbs in the chapel creates a convincingly strong illusion, not to mention how perfectly silent it is in the chapel.

Darlene stops in front of us and motions us down the aisle to greet the priest that is already standing at the altar waiting for us. We make it up to the altar, a short, stocky, bald, bearded man in black pants and shirt, wearing rectangular glasses and a priest's collar greets us. "Hello there you two, I am Father Mark, I wish I were performing this ceremony under different circumstances, but here we are. Let's get started. We are gathered here today to…"

Eve and I both zone out and squeeze each other's hands tight, my fingers over hers, pressed into my palms as we stare into each other's eyes while the priest is performing the ceremony. He could have been singing a nursery rhyme for all we knew. I am so entranced by Eve's beautiful eyes, I can't believe after all these years of knowing her, I am now just noticing that one of her eyes is brown while the other is almost green.

I become lost in her eyes and my own thoughts and start picturing us living out our days in the suburbs, sitting out on our porch in the evening of a warm summer day. Eve is reading a book to our youngest baby girl, rocking back and forth on the chair while I lay on the deck, pushing a little toy truck around with our toddler son. The auditory exclusion is overwhelming, or my imagination is so powerful that I can't hear a word the priest is saying while seeing this moving picture in her eyes.

For now, we save our tears for later. The imagery quickly fades away as the priest clears his throat for the second time, my eyes are still locked with Eve's as we are both still standing before him at the altar. Father Mark coughs once more while tapping his ring finger and I snap back to the present.

The Father gently coughs again, "Ahem… the rings?"

The phrase doesn't register with me and what I'm supposed to do, so I give Eve and the Father a puzzled look. Luckily, my perceptive bride is quick on her feet. Eve looks down at her hand and removes the engagement ring I got her when I asked her to marry me and places it in my hand and takes another ring off of her thumb and keeps it in her palm…

I proposed to her over Christmas break, during our junior year of college. I took her to the site of our first official parent chaperoned date back when we were kids and I ordered the same dinner that we had over ten years ago for the both of us. She laughed at the order until I reminded her that it was the same meal we had on our first date together several years before. When we got back to the car, I had her blindfolded, at that moment, she knew what was going on, but she didn't know where it was going to happen.

We parked outside of the old elementary school's gates and had to walk a bit until we got to the playground. The very playground where we first met as kids, I had her take off the blindfold and asked her if she knew where she was. It took her a moment for her vision to get adjusted to the night that was lit by a single light post. Eve looked around and started to tear up as she nodded, before I could even say anything or get the ring out, she shouted, "Yes!"

"Now, it is time for the vows."

"I, Eve, take thee Michael, to be my lawfully wedded husband, to have and to hold, from this day forward, for better for worse, for richer, for poorer, in sickness and in health, to love and to cherish, till death do us part."

She places the ring on my finger.

"Michael, your turn."

"I, Michael, take thee, Eve, to be my lawfully wedded wife, to have and to hold, from this day forward, for better for worse, for richer, for poorer, in sickness and in health, to love and to cherish, till death do us part."

I place the ring on her finger, for the second time and the last time.

"You may now kiss the bride."

I kiss her like I've never kissed her before. I gently grab her by both cheeks as she grabs me by each arm, I hold her face near mine as I try to take in the whole experience, to be present in the moment with all of my senses. The way she looks, the way she smells, the way she sounds, and the way her presence makes me want to smile.

From the deafening silence we had experienced, comes some loud clapping that pierces the quiet room. It came from Darlene. I didn't realize how awkward a single person clapping would sound, but there it was. "Alright you two, let's get to the basement level to sign those papers and prep you for the procedure. All of the paperwork should be smooth sailing now that you two darlings are married."

Before we go, we thank Father Mark for performing the ceremony, he says a little prayer for us before we leave.

"Let us bow our heads and say a prayer for the journey that you are about to embark, we pray to the Lord for your safe return, and for Eve to remain strong and to persevere through this dark time in your lives. Oh heavenly father, please bless this young and lovely couple and the men and women that are working on a cure for these two to be reunited so that they may one day raise a family of God's children, amen."

We shake his hand and make our way back to the elevator, the elevator that will bring us down, down into the belly of my new home. We're less than an hour away from a bad dream that will last several years for my wife... and a blink of an eye for me. Eve is my wife now, but I will be absent from her life for years to come, none of this is fair for anyone, especially her.

Going Under

I make my mark on the last form. My life is now signed over to Eve, the woman I've been madly in love with for over a decade, the woman that will take care of things while I'm gone, the one I trust most, my best friend.

A freckled young nurse with poofy red hair and a smile to match enters the room, "Michael and Eve, we're ready for you, put this on and I'll be back in here shortly." She tosses a white hospital gown and an empty, clear blue plastic bag onto the chair near the door before she leaves and shuts the door behind her.

To lighten the mood as I'm minutes away from becoming comatose for the next several years, I tell Eve, "Well, you can't make fun of me for not being trendy with my outfits, technically, I have the freshest and newest gear out of any of the other patients in this building."

She forces a fake laugh at my contrived attempt of a joke.

I didn't get the genuine laugh I wanted, so I tell her to turn around while I get undressed. Even though she has seen me naked before and is only a couple of yards away from me, I extend my arm and put my hand in between my face and hers in an attempt to obstruct her view, not really providing any privacy and hiding nothing but my face. This makes getting undressed and putting on the gown exponentially more difficult using only one hand for the sake of a silly joke.

Eve giggles, "You are so stupid, I can't believe I'm married to you."

I got the laugh I wanted! More importantly though, the words she uttered sent chills down the back of my neck as I was tying the last knot on my gown.

Last week, we started the early stages of wedding planning to celebrate with our friends and family, perhaps a year from now. With the snap of a finger, I'm now married and essentially on my death bed where my wife has to do everything a married couple would do… without the support, and presence of her life partner… an unsettling cloud over what was planned to be one of the happiest days of our lives.

The only thing she'll have of me that she can always keep with her is the fact that she knows I love her. I'm going to miss the simple things, like going grocery shopping with her, watching our favorite shows together, and cuddling until we both fall asleep… or my arm. My side of the bed back home will remain cold and empty for years at a time.

I throw all of my clothes I had been wearing today into the plastic bag. I tighten up the drawstrings, write my name and birthdate on it with a black marker and toss the bag in the corner of the room by the door.

I sit back down on the side of the bed, face to face right in front of Eve. Our knees are interlocked, side by side. We hold hands and try to soak in these final moments in silence. I wish I could tell her that everything is going to be OK, but I can't, I don't know that, and she's too smart to be comforted by an empty sentiment.

A knock at the door; we both turn our heads towards the interruption. Before entering, a woman's voice asks, "Michael, are you changed in there? Or do you need more time?"

"You can come on in."

The poofy haired nurse re-enters with a cart full of medical devices in tow. From what I can make out, there is a heart monitor, an IV pole, some plastic tubes, vials, and of course, the thing I've dreaded the most since I was a kid… a syringe.

I remember my parents always telling me that all it feels like is a little pinch and every time they told me, I never believed them… it doesn't feel like a pinch! Even to this day, whenever I have to get a shot or get my blood drawn, I have to look the other away before the needle hits my skin.

The nurse clips my finger with some sort of wired device, the heart monitor lights up. I can see my heart rate at a calm sixty beats per minute. She asks me, "Michael, are you squeamish at all? Or do you pass out at the sight of your own blood?"

"Ummmm… why?"

"Well, we need to hook you up to the IV drip and saline to keep you hydrated with electrolytes and nutrients… we also need a line into your system for the drugs to keep you unconscious to limit your brain activity. I'll need you to hold still while I make the insertion, at least until I tape the tubing in place."

The heart monitor begins to beep at a more rapid pace, "92" beats per minute reads the screen. I'm visibly nervous, the nurse takes notice. All I'm doing is lying down perfectly still on the hospital bed, not exerting any energy. Eve can also see that I'm freaking out, she pulls her seat closer to me and gently strokes my forehead with her hand and says with a smirk, "I can't believe you are afraid of needles, this is hilarious, I love that I'm still learning about you after all these years." She giggled.

I give her a fake frown and bring my upper lip down as low as I can. My heartrate is still increasing despite attempts on both our parts at bringing some levity to the situation.

"I'm not afraid of needles babe, I've never been knocked out before, yeah… that's why I'm scared." I don't think she's buying the story I'm trying to sell.

The way the nurse is watching us as she put on her gloves, it would seem that she is appreciating the dynamic between Eve and I and is getting involved with some of the banter herself.

While looking me dead in the eyes, the nurse stretches the glove wide open to get her hand in and lets it "SNAP" to her wrist as loud as possible, she cracks a smile as she snaps the last one on. The nurse reaches back over to the tray and grabs what appear to be towelettes wrapped in little packets, she tears it open. It looks like she is taking Eve's side in ribbing a man whose scared inner child comes out when the needles do.

"This is an alcohol wipe that I'll be using to disinfect the injection site." She tells me as she's rubbing the top of my hand with the cold and damp wipe.

My palms start to get overly clammy and I can feel a single bead of sweat roll down my forehead. I act as if I'm stretching out my arm out and quickly dab the sweat with my bicep. My little ploy doesn't work, despite everything on the surface indicating a calm, cool, and collected man, the beeping on the monitor indicates otherwise.

The monitor now reads, "115" and continues to intensify. It never gets that high unless I'm exercising.

The nurse opens the plastic packaging for the hypodermic needle and tells me, "Remember, don't flex your muscles or clench your hand, if you break the needle while it's in there, we'll have a whole new host of other problems today."

She places a large red band over my arm, gives me a wooden dowel to squeeze, and the blue veins in my hands and wrists immediately raise.

"Oooh, you have good veins, this should be easy. I'm going to begin insertion now, try to relax and look away now if you need to."

I turn away and look at Eve while I hold her hand. I feel the pinch and some pressure where the needle had entered. I allow my hand to stay relaxed and go limp, but at the same time, I can feel every other half of my body tense up… my back arches a little and is evidenced by the scratching sound the paper bed sheet makes as it slides around on the fake leather. "You're doing great, I'm almost done, all I have to do is place the tube, andddddd… done."

I look at my hand to inspect her work as if I even know what to look for. I hear the screeching of tape being pulled, "zzzzzziiiiipt," a clip, another "zzzzzziiiiipt," another clip. The nurse tapes down the tubing on my hand to keep it in place.

I look at my wrist again and realize that I have a ton of hair where the clear tape is placed. I guess the pain of taking it off will probably be the least of my worries for the foreseeable future.

The nurse tells me, "You can relax now, the needle isn't in your hand anymore, it's only a plastic tube. The anesthesiologist is going to come in any minute to start the IV drip and put the medication in to knock you out. If you two want to say anything to each other, now is the time. The medication will kick-in in about three to five minutes once it's in your bloodstream. From there, they'll start the procedure to put and keep you in the induced coma. I'll let you two be… good luck. I'll see you in there with your new roommates, you'll love them, they're really quiet and are pretty good at keeping to themselves." She winks and smiles as she exits.

I laugh and look at Eve, "How long do you think she's been working on that joke to tell each of the new patients? Seriously, she's definitely made that joke before, it sounds like something you'd hear in a sitcom, I was honestly waiting for the audience laugh track."

Eve's face and demeanor turn solemn.

"Michael can we be serious for a second, I want you to go in there knowing that I'll be alright. Between both of our families and friends, we have a great support network. We'll try to visit you whenever we can okay? You and I both know you're not good with meeting new people, I hope it doesn't get too awkward when it comes to socializing with your new neighbors even if they're quiet and keep to themsel…" Before Eve could finish the sentence, her straight face vanishes and we both erupt into laughter.

This girl totally gets me. Underneath my smile and laughs, I worry that this back and forth we have with one another will change years from now and we'll have to be strangers, having to get to know each other all over again… her, a husband whose been gone away for years, and me, a wife who has lived a life on her own, with years' worth of stories to tell.

Two subtle knocks interrupts the laughter. A man with a serious face in a white lab coat enters. He introduces himself, "Hi, I'm Doctor Schneider, I'll be your anesthesiologist."

We nod to acknowledge his presence as our smiles are wiped away.

Doctor Schneider puts on his glasses that are suspended from his neck, snatches the clipboard sitting in the sleeve at the foot of my bed, and reads my chart intently. Under normal circumstances, me or Eve would throw in a joke, or make small talk when meeting a new person to break the silence.

This time though, without saying a word or even making eye contact with one another, we both know not to distract the man from his job, his responsibilities are some of the most important in a hospital, it's where the most complications occur in any medical procedure. Too much medication and the patient's heart stops, too little, the patient remains half-awake and moves during a procedure… both are nightmare inducing scenarios.

After a minute of going over my chart, he grabs a vial from the tray and opens up another hypodermic needle from a sealed plastic pouch. The doctor presses the needle into the vial, holds it up to eye level and carefully extracts a precise amount and tosses the remainder back onto the metal cart causing a couple of "clanks." Doctor Schneider flicks the contents of the needle and gently depresses it until a little squirt of clear liquid flies out and nose dives into the blanket on my lap.

"Michael, what I have here in my hand is a dose of pentobarbital, it's the chemical agent used to put and keep you in an induced coma mixed with a cocktail of something that will calm your nerves. I will be putting it directly into your IV line… you will start to feel its effects within a few minutes. During that time, we will wheel you into where we are holding the other 'sleepers' and where you two can say your goodbyes before you go under."

The doctor injects the medication into the line; I can feel the cool temperature of the chemical, course through the veins of my hand and into my arm. I'm not sure if I'm imagining it or if I can really feel it making its way through the rest of my body. I immediately start feeling woozy. Two large orderlies in maroon scrubs enter the room and open up the second of the split doors to the room so they can wheel my bed through.

In a deep voice, one of the orderlies says, "Excuse me ma'am, can you clear the way? We're going to be pushing and pulling the bed through that doorway over there to get your husband into his new room if you can clear the way."

Eve stands up, pushes the chair she was sitting in up against the wall and waits over me by my side. The orderlies crouch below the bed for a second to release the brake levers on each wheel. One of the orderlies pulls the bed while the other pushes with one hand and pulls the heart monitor and IV pole along with the other.

My heart rate has dropped down to "53," but each beat feels like a thunderous pound that I can almost hear, trying to burst from my chest, but not in a painful way.

My eyesight gets slightly hazy, as if each source of light has a glaring halo around it that won't focus, and each blink becomes heavier, I can't find Eve but I can feel her hand on my shoulder as the men are wheeling me through the hospital's hallways.

Each set of fluorescent lights comes into my field of vision only to fade away until the next set appears in increasingly rapid succession. I arch my back and neck to look up past the head board, there she is, looking ahead at where we're going as tears run down her face. I place both my hands on the back of hers, give her fingers a kiss, close my eyes for a couple of seconds, and rest my face on her hand.

I look down towards my feet to see where we're going as we slow down and approach two shiny metal doors and come to a complete stop. An orderly grabs a card clipped to his waist and waves it at a rectangular black keypad with a thin red light near the top. A faint "beeeeeep" rings out as the red light turns into spearmint green, the doors begin to slowly swing open on their own.

Once the doors open as far as they can go, we continue rolling forward into the chilly room. I turn my head to the side to look around with no luck, the lighting is as grim as a morgue and the space is about half the size of a basketball court with a low ceiling. There are two other patients already in here, lying motionless in their beds as a nurse is checking on their vitals and making notes into each of their charts.

As the two orderlies are wheeling me in and positioning my bed, I survey this sterile, uninviting looking place that will be my new home for the foreseeable future. I sneak a peek at the other patients; one of my new neighbors is a pale red headed fellow and the other is a lean African American man. Both of them have accumulated a substantial amount of facial hair, they must have been the first wave of patients with the disease.

The bed finally comes to a stop, I notice that despite the large room, they have placed each of us within a few feet from each other, if my arm were a foot longer, I swear I could reach over and high five the pale man next to me. I'm only the third patient in the city so far, they must be anticipating more.

My eyesight continues to get progressively blurry after each blink. Even my body feels heavier like I'm getting swallowed into my bed. I groan to Eve, "Honey, I think it's kicking in."

She grabs me by the hand and puts her face right up against mine. "It's going to be okay sweetie, next time you open your eyes, I'll be a little older and to you, it will only feel like waking up from a good sleep. I love you babe, everything's going to be okay."

We kiss, I squeeze her hand with what little strength I have left. She shushes me as I struggle to barely mouth the words, "I--- lo---ve yoooou..."

Tears well up until there is nowhere else for them to flow but out. The first drop leads the way for a steady stream to pour down her cheeks, I can barely lift my hand to rub away my own. I try to fight off the medication for as long as I can, but it keeps pulling me under. I feel my body sinking further into the bed. I stave off the urge to close my eyes as my mind is overcome with a sense of peace and serenity. Eve kisses my forehead as the light in the corner of my vision slowly fades to a blur with my eyes still open as I try to remain awake.

The Tablet

Seven years and several months later…

Slipping in and out of consciousness, I sit on a cold metal bench, waiting for the train to take us to the eastside, about a half hour outside of the city… where Eve's parents live. They offered to help care for me until my full recovery. I don't remember how I got here, but with Eve by my side, holding me up with my arm around her shoulders and her other hand on my side reassures me that everything is going to be fine.

With each and every restless blink, I get a glance of Eve's for a few seconds at a time until I have to rest my eyes once more. In each of those few seconds, I am reminded of the promise I made to myself, to relish each sweet moment with her for the rest of our days, the promise I made the day at the hospital.

She doesn't say anything, nor make any eye contact with me as her gaze is fixated on our ride to arrive. Still, seeing her with my own eyes and smelling her scent gives me an indescribable tranquil feeling, like the weight of how ever many years have passed since we last spoke is slowly being lifted off of our shoulders. With a brief glimpse of her face, she hasn't aged in the slightest. I continue watching as she stares down the tunnel, waiting for the train to arrive.

I look down the tunnel and see a faint headlight approaching in the distance. The next few moments become an out of body experience as I watch us waiting for the train... I notice that there is not a single soul around us that can be seen or heard. The train, nearly silent as it slows down and enters the station. No bells or whistles to indicate its arrival, only this persistent beeping from the loud speaker on the intercom system, where normally, a voice would be announcing the train's arrival.

The lights in the station shut off into pitch black and becomes darker than dark. I can no longer see or feel Eve beside me. The sounds of constant and sporadic beeping envelope me in a cacophony of my own heavy breathing, water bubbling in a puddle like the sound of rain splashing out of a gutter... and that incessant beeping.

The repeated beeping brings me back to full awareness and puts a churning feeling in my stomach that turns into a reality check that makes my heart skip a beat or two. I'm not waking up from any ordinary night's sleep; I remember I'm in a room, probably filled with strangers, strangers that are hooked up to medical devices, just like me.

My eyes are sealed completely shut and I don't sense any light in the room. I can't quite get my eyes open, I remain still and silent, attempting to listen to my environment. Some of the beeping is closer than the others and at differing speeds. Hearing their presence but unable to see any of them becomes unnerving… I need to get my eyes open.

I slowly raise my hands to rub my eyes and am reminded that the tubes are still attached to one of my hands. The additional weight and feeling the IV tubes rise with my left arm is enough to deter me from using that hand at all for fear of scratching my retinas. I use my right hand to carefully rub off the crust that has formed over my eyes.

My eyelids are still sealed shut, but I know I'm making progress as I rub, I can hear the light crackle of the little specks of dried mucus and skin landing on my hospital gown like light rain landing on a jacket, I continue gently rubbing my eyes. Almost there, I can almost open them. The entire room shakes, the ground, the water, and the cabinets and drawers violently rattle.

I stop rubbing and stay as still as possible. I can hear a loud vehicle hover not more than thirty yards overhead until the loud exhaust slowly fades away and the ground gradually settles from the shaking. Impossible… the roof of this building is at least fifteen stories high, and commercial planes are much faster and shouldn't be moving that low and slow… it didn't make the rattling and chopping sound of a helicopter either. They must have moved me to a different facility.

I finally get my eyes open; the room is darker than I remember. This is the first time in a long time that my pupils have been exposed to any kind of light. Objects are still a bit blurry and have a fuzzy cloud around them, the darkness isn't helping any.

I sit upright from my bed and look around, my eyesight slowly comes into focus. All I know is that it's significantly darker in the room than before and there are some faint, scattered bits of green light all over the floor.

I look at the bed to my right, one of my neighbors is still asleep, and I look to my left and notice a few more patients that are still incapacitated. These are all new patients; I don't recognize any of them. Why am I waking up? Am I cured? How long have I been out?

There are no signs of hospital staff nearby, perhaps the nurses already made their rounds. I stretch my arms up and prop myself up with my palms on the bed to test out my upper body strength, a little weaker but not too bad.

A water bottle rolls into my wrist; it must have been next to my hip on the bed. Staff must have left it there for whenever the medication eventually wears off so that we could hydrate ourselves. They are expecting us to wake up, finally, a good sign.

My throat feels so dry and sore that my own voice might scratch it if I tried to speak. I take a few gulps of the room temperature water and let it sit in my mouth and throat for a few seconds before swallowing it down for the soothing sensation.

I lay back down on my bed, patiently awaiting the nurse or a doctor to unhook me from all of these tubes and monitors and tell me that I'm cured. My mind starts racing, thinking about all that I have missed out on over the years.

I can't believe Eve isn't here to greet me, sleeping in a nearby chair, waiting for me to wake up. They had to have told her when they would be waking me up, maybe it's the middle of the night right now. I look around on my bed as my eyesight is nearly restored; I notice that there isn't a nurse call button on my bed. I mean, why would there be in the CN ward?

I sit upright again and look at the floor once more to scan my surroundings. My jaw drops and I begin to breathe a little heavier and the beeping on my heart monitor ramps up once I notice what those fragments of green light on the ground are… military grade Cyalume chemical glow sticks that I am all too familiar with. Back at basic we would train with them in night time maneuvers. Why are they using those here at the hospital instead of the normal lights?

I focus on the furthest light stick in the corner of the room to my left. I get a sinking feeling in my stomach, I gasp, and my heartrate doesn't get faster but my heart begins to pound harder.

More than two thirds of the room is caved in with some concrete piled up ceiling high with several bits of rebar exposed and several portions of that side of the wall cracked open. There appears to be a pile of rubble where they were planning to place new patients. If memory of the layout serves me correctly and if this is the same hospital… those poor souls underneath the rubble didn't stand a chance, at least their minds weren't present when it happened.

Other than the patients to my left and to my right, I can only see the silhouettes of three other patients in the room, all of whom are still unconscious as well. I think the worst, there's been a terrible earthquake and we are buried alive here in the basement of the hospital.

Eve is probably outside waiting for a rescue team to dig us out along with other family members of staff and patients. The plane I heard overhead must have been a search and rescue team, I pray they haven't forgotten us down here.

The chem lights aren't all lying flat on the floor, some are half submerged in large puddles of water, covering most of the floor… the water doesn't appear to be rising at all but I can see and hear water dripping from various parts of the ceiling and leaking through the cracks in the walls giving off a faint green glow.

All hope for any nurses or hospital staff to greet us is abandoned, if we're going to be getting out of here, we're going to have to do it ourselves. We're in the middle of a major disaster, we can't rely on the help of a search and rescue party in a major metropolitan city. We have to find a way to let them know we're still down here, alive and breathing.

I slowly peel away the tape on the back of my hand that's holding the IV tubing in place and carefully pull the line from my hand, exhaling as I do so to ease the discomfort. I toss the tape and tubing on the floor, causing a splash when it hits the ground. I peel away all of the nodes that have been attached to my chest, my heart monitor goes silent.

Strange, each of us has four IV bags rigged onto each of the poles and a couple of them have been depleted. I imagine a scenario when the earthquake happened, they decided to wake us up, and somehow, the nurse that was taking care of us ended up underneath that pile of concrete while waiting for help to arrive. I start to panic and yell at my fellow patients, "Wake up!!! Help!!!"

Nothing. I'm yelling at no one but myself. No movement, no response from any of them, and no changes in their heart rates. All I can say for sure is that they're alive. After the initial shock and bewilderment of my surroundings wear off, I sit up from my bed and stretch my arms once more and let my feet dangle from the bed as I contemplate my next course of action as I reassess the situation with a slightly cooler head.

As I'm stabilizing myself with my arms on the bed while I swing my legs, it would appear Eve paid for the package with the electro muscle therapy. My muscles haven't lost too much mass or definition, but the real test will be in my ability to stand and walk.

I set my feet onto the wet ground, splashing on impact, and instantly drenching my socks. I hang onto the rails of my bed in case my center of balance is off. I let go and everything seems normal so far, strength isn't an issue but getting reacquainted with using my body becomes more about stability as my blood rushes to areas where it hasn't been in a very long time, causing a lightheaded sensation.

My hospital socks are completely soaked, I pull them off, wring them dry as best I can, and toss them on the bed to dry out and attempt to walk around without the aid of latching onto anything for balance.

Everything is strewn about, from the looks of this room alone, there is strong evidence pointing to the theory that the building was destroyed by an earthquake. But why would they leave us here and not bother to wake us up or evacuate us? They had the sense to give us water and light up the room with these sticks, why not get us out of here?

These questions are answered and my theory as to what happened is quickly dismantled. In the corner of my eye, I notice a couple of chem sticks that aren't on the ground or in the water. They're crisscrossed sitting on a counter illuminating a few large backpacks and what appears to be a rifle and a couple of sidearms. What in the hell is going on?

Each step I make towards the light on the counter is methodical as to not slip on the wet floor and make the situation any dire than it already is. As I get to the counter, I can see the words, "PLAY ME!!!" written on some masking tape stuck to a tablet sitting on one of the duffle bags next to the firearms.

I look around to see if any of the other patients are awake to share the experience with me, alas, it is still only me. I fumble around the device to locate the power button... I turn it on and see the hospital's logo of a blue cross wrapped in a stethoscope pop up. After the tablet loads, it reads, "Please Sign in with PassID or Continue as Guest."

I tap, "Continue as Guest."

The screen loads with only one video file on the screen to open. I touch the filmstrip icon on the tablet to play the file.

A computerized voice begins, "Entry number one, date, August 10th, 2040."

The computerized voice stops, some loud banging, static, and explosions on the screen ring out. A woman's voice comes on with some indiscernible speaking off camera, her voice is trembling... The video comes into focus as some sparks fly behind a woman with fair complexion and some dirt on her cheeks and around her eyes.

The majority of the screen is covered by her face in a green night vision tint as she is filming herself with the tablet. It looks like she is here in this very room with unconscious patients behind her in the background.

"If you are watching this, it means you are still alive and we are one or two days ahead of you. We are on our way to the underground camp beneath the city... Wait, hold on, I'm getting way ahead of myself, let me... let me start over...

Less than two weeks ago, our planet fell under siege by an unknown lifeform from out of this world. They crushed all of our forces in a matter of days, they are technologically superior... we lost.

We don't know how other nations fared as communications went dark right before they started their attack, but if they went up against what we did, it is likely that they suffered the same fate, it's not about fighting and resisting anymore... it's about hiding and surviving."

The woman steps away from the camera as it points up at the ceiling in the dark room, she can be heard sobbing off camera as well as some men barking random orders in the background.

She returns to focus and recomposes herself,

"I'm sorry, we've lost so many people. The ones who haven't been killed are getting ripped from the ground and disappearing into the sky and God knows what is happening to them, they are hunting us down one by one.

On the first day of the attack, they laid waste to most of our structures and vehicles with a bombing campaign, anyone caught above ground more than likely didn't make it. Those of us that have survived here at the hospital happened to be checking in on you folks here in the lower levels.

A handful of soldiers searching for survivors arrived here a couple of hours ago and offered to escort us and a few others to an underground encampment filled with other survivors if we leave this instant.

We can't bring you all along with us nor do we have enough supplies to feed the soldiers along with a dozen other survivors that were with them… we couldn't' wait around for you all to wake up, I'm so sorry.

We pulled you all off of the medication that is keeping you unconscious, it takes anywhere between twenty-four to forty-eight hours for you to wake up. We're sorry, but we can't pass up this opportunity to be rescued, I hope you understand.

We injected you with some adrenaline in the hopes of speeding up the waking process. We also removed several other medical devices that you were all hooked up to. This should save you some time to get going to catch up with us.

We're rigging up extra IV bags for each of you before we leave, if they're all empty when you wake up, be sure to hydrate yourselves, the food supply in the backpacks should get you the proteins and electrolytes you need for the trip ahead of you over the next day or so.

The next part I'm going to tell you is important, so pay attention. Seven years have passed since the first lot of you entered our hospital, although there isn't a full on cure yet, there is a bandage that has been developed. It's a suppressant shot you can inject that keeps the disease at bay, much like the CRISPR therapy that wasn't widely available.

There are a few catches for these shots though; they need to be constantly stored at thirty-five degrees Fahrenheit, injected every twenty-four hours, and taken within fifteen minutes of leaving the refrigerated environment for it to work effectively… they are also in very limited supply. This means don't use more than you need in case anyone that passes through needs a dose too.

You will start exhibiting the early symptoms of Cerebral Nervorum within a few hours if you don't keep up with the daily dosage. Once you reach the encampment, according to these soldiers, there should be medical staff that will be able to put you back under to stop the disease, if not, we'll setup a station when we get there, remember, those syrettes are extremely limited and are not a long-term solution.

It is imperative that the first person to wake up and play this video, grabs the syrettes from the refrigerator in the overhead cabinets above the counters, and inject yourself and the other patients anywhere in the neck. It was originally intended for people that received the diagnosis and needed more time to get their affairs in order and say their goodbyes, but none of that really matters now does it?

All of the hospitals are on a solar grid and should have enough juice to power each facility for at least a couple more weeks, even if the above ground portions of the building are destroyed, the solar batteries are usually housed in the foundation and should keep the medication chilled.

The next part is also important… the injection site is the neck because the nanomites in the syrettes need to be as close as possible to both the brain stem and the spine for it to work effectively. Injected anywhere else, you could greatly reduce the duration and effectiveness of the suppressant. You guys will be traveling by night, so you'll need every minute you can get.

Every major clinic should be stocked with these syrette shots, ready to go. They should all be clearly marked as "CN Syrettes." The standard procedure for most healthcare facilities in the area is to house patients with CN in the basement levels, so these syrettes will hopefully be and hopefully not the pharmacy areas above ground.

Remember, you'll need to take these shots every twenty-four hours and there's no need to be gentle with the needles, really get it in there and squeeze the fluid through after you break the skin. The needles are short enough to not cause real damage.

Even though the encampment is only a few miles away, it will take you a few days to reach the destination since you'll be traveling by night to each waypoint that isn't exactly a direct route, the sergeant will explain it further.

Last thing before I go, your personal belongings that you and your loved ones stored here at the hospital are still in the shelves underneath your beds. I'm going to hand you over to Sergeant Myers who will be telling you about these alien beings and how to survive, good luck."

A middle aged man in military fatigues donning a helmet with night vision goggles strapped to the top comes on camera with a stern, serious face, and a voice that sounds a little rough from years of smoking cigarettes.

"Thank you misses. Sergeant Myers here, I'll get right to it. The encampment is only a few clicks away, but you will want to travel only under the cover of darkness and you'll want to move carefully and slowly to evade detection from these things.

According to military intelligence, the line of sight for the enemy is similar to ours. They see the same light spectrum as us as far as we know; travelling by night will increase your chances of survival.

We've plotted points on this map for places where you'll be able to find the health clinics and hospitals that should have the syrettes available for you all to use. It should take you a few hours to get to each location with a couple of hours until dawn to spare.

The enemy has sporadic, aerial, and ground patrols, use the city's cover accordingly, shadows are your friend. Don't believe for a second this means you can make a mad dash for it at night, they have these search lights that turn night into day that can cover an entire football field.

If you hear or see any of these patrols, and trust me, you'll know it when you hear them; find shelter as fast as you can! It won't be dark for long when they show up.

We left you some MRE's in the rucksacks that should keep you fed for at least a couple of days, we're also leaving you with first aid supplies, some cyalume chem light sticks, sleeping bags, water, a rifle and a couple of handguns. Do not shoot at anything unless you absolutely have to, they'll send in reinforcements that will swarm you within seconds.

A warning when you get outside, things won't look the way you remember it. It's mostly a wasteland of dirt, concrete, and metal rubble of where our buildings used to stand and our streets used to run.

DO NOT use any radio equipment that you may come across, I repeat DO NOT use them. Intelligence determined early on that these things can monitor radio waves and can trace transmissions to its source. Also, there have been some unconfirmed reports that these things can look and act like us, our unit hasn't encountered any ourselves, but just be aware of that if you come into contact with anyone outside of your group.

There should be enough juice in the solar batteries to power whatever you want in the buildings that aren't completely destroyed, but these things… they quickly snuff out anything brighter than a small fire and anything louder than a whisper, it is vital that you maintain noise and light discipline. They crushed our conventional weapons and vehicles in a matter of days, do not engage the enemy unless you absolutely have to, the name of the game is stealth and evasion. There are ten of you, work and stick together and you will make it out alive, we'll see you when you get there, Myers out."

The man's face and fingers blot out the screen as he fumbles with the camera for a second to stop the device from recording… the video finally cuts out.

I look around and only count a total of six of us in the room, the section over there must have collapsed sometime within the last day or two after the convoy left. I'm not sure why, but the gravity of the situation hasn't hit me yet, my mind and body go into autopilot and I start thinking about and doing things that will increase my chances of survival. Perhaps subconsciously, I know that my survival means a chance at finding Eve.

I examine the three weapons on the counter that were left for us. I release the magazines in each of the guns for an ammo check. After un-racking a round from each of their chambers, each weapon is at full capacity. However, it looks like that is ALL the ammo that they provided us, no extra rounds or magazines can be found nearby.

The only other items I can find around the packs are several MRE's, boots and fatigues. The fatigues look used, either dirt or dried blood are caked onto them. I dare not think about the fate of the previous owners.

I locate the refrigerated medical cabinet to search for the syrettes. I can't tell which vials are the ones we need from looking outside through the glass.

I open the cabinet, the lights don't come on, but cold air rushes out to my hands and face, assuring me that the cabinet is still functional. Found them, they are pouches of clear fluid labeled, "CN Syrettes" with a needle on the end covered by a plastic tip like the nurse promised.

I walk over to my fellow patients to administer the drugs. The lady on the tape said not to be too gentle when injecting the medication and to jab it anywhere into their necks and squeeze the cold liquid through after the needle has penetrated the skin. I'll do myself last after I get some "practice" with the others.

I stand over the first patient. The first thing I notice is that he doesn't have massive facial hair like someone who had been asleep for years at a time. I realize that none of the patients do, I raise my hand to feel my own face, nothing but maybe two or three day old stubble.

I head over to the sink and examine my reflection through the cracked mirror. My face in the faint green light confirms the minimal scruff and that my face is still my own, but only a little older, no wrinkles but a little more rugged and a hairline that has receded a scosche.

The first patient is male, about 5'10", curly brown hair with rosy cheeks. The name on his chart reads "Charlie," and if my math is right, he's 27 years old. I do the math for my own age and realize I entered this hospital as a twenty one year old and am now a twenty eight year old man without gaining any wisdom or having the experiences of my prime. Years of my life that are now lost and have been spent without Eve.

I'm not a religious man, but I pray to God that Eve is alive and waiting for me at the camp. If I were able to talk to her during my slumber, I would have told her to go on ahead without me, and I would eventually catch up to her. But knowing Eve, she would have tried her damndest to stay by my side until dragged away by force.

"Focus Michael!"

The video didn't mention any alcohol wipes, but I find some in the drawers and rub the injection site before I twist off the cap of the first syrette. The cap provides a lot of resistance like a tiny pickle jar until I get it going, it comes off with ease. I plunge the half inch needle into Charlie's neck and squeeze the fluids out of the pouch and watch the clear liquid make its way into the needle, and eventually into

Charlie's neck. He didn't flinch nor did his heart rate change, he's still knocked out cold. One down, four to go.

The second patient is female, about 5'4", a fair skinned brunette with several light freckles on her face. She kind of reminds me of Eve, but she's got a pointier nose. The name on her chart reads as Ellie, 26 years old. "Okay, same thing as last time." I tell myself.

I clear away her wavy hair from the injection site and rub her neck with the wipe. This time, I'm gentler when I press the needle into Ellie's neck. I don't know why I was a little more careful this time, is it because she faintly reminds me of Eve? Or is it simply because she is female? At any rate, I finish flushing the remainder of the fluid from the pouch and into her neck. Three to go.

The third patient is a mostly bald, Asian male with some hints of gray hair around his temple, about 5'8". His chart says his name is Brian and he is 47 years old, if it weren't for the few patches of gray that remain on his head, I would have guessed he was in his early 30's. I repeat the procedure, unscrew the cap, wipe the site, press the needle into his neck and squeeze the medication into his bloodstream.

I look at the patients that I've already injected, they are still lying there, asleep, and motionless, no changes in their breathing or heartrates. I continue on.

The fourth patient is male, about 6'2", a light skinned, heavy set African American with a shaved head. His chart reads, Shawn, 38 years old. I grab one of the remaining two syrettes from the tray and inject the dose.

Finally… the fifth patient. White male, maybe mid-twenties, about 6'0" tall, muscular build, the jawline of a guy that would want to fight you if you looked at him wrong. His chart is missing, no name, nothing, odd... I look around on the floor and don't notice any clipboards nearby or submerged in water. It's fairly dark in here with only the glow sticks strewn about on the floor to light up the entire room. The chart could be anywhere. He wouldn't be down here if he weren't a CN patient though; I stick him in the neck.

And now, it's time for the main event, my turn. I unscrew the cap of the syrette and rub my neck with the alcohol wipe. I'm more hesitant to jamming the needle into my neck like I did for the others, so I hold my breath and gently exhale as I slowly slide the needle in until it stops from the plastic base coming into contact with my skin and cannot go any further.

With a shallow breath, I squeeze the near icy liquids in the pouch to release the medication into my bloodstream. The cold temperature immediately numbs any pain or discomfort I'm experiencing and allows me to squeeze the remainder of the medication with ease. It feels like a gentle cold burn, much like putting an icepack on bare skin. I grab the flimsy metal tray with all six of the used syrettes and caps and slide them into an empty sink.

In that moment, I am captivated by the sounds the syrettes and caps make as I tilt the tray down, listening, and hearing each one individually slide as it gently scrapes against the metal surface, clips the raised edge of the tray before leaping, and crashing in the sink.

It's true what they say, when one of your senses is dulled or gone, all others are heightened to near super-human levels. Seeing objects in detail further than five feet in front of my face is difficult, but with the sound of the syrettes sliding off of the metal tray, I feel like I can see them with my ears and can pin point the moment they go airborne before crashing into the sink... the act of hearing becomes a surreal experience.

This brief moment of Zen and reflection is interrupted by a moment of clarity. After injecting each of the patients, I come to the realization that none of these people are the same patients that were next to me when I went under. Those patients must have been shuffled around to other facilities over the years or heaven forbid, were moved to the collapsed side of the room. The heart rates of all five of the patients steadily increase in frequency. Between pulling us off of the medication and the adrenaline they hit us with before they left, the extra little pain stimulus to the neck must have done the trick to get everyone else to start coming to.

Rise and Shine

It is done. Everyone in the ward has been hit with the suppressant and is good to go for a day. I sit, idly waiting for these strangers to wake at any moment, eager to greet these people who have experienced the same turmoil that I had gone through, having to leave everyone they loved and knew behind. Thirty minutes pass, still nothing.

To kill some time, I find some clothes, fresh socks, and shoes from the rucksacks sitting on the counter that fit my small frame. I bring them back to the bed and set them in the very middle of the mattress to ensure that none of it falls over the edge onto the wet floor. I dry my feet off as best I can with an unused part of the bedsheet hanging off to the side. I remember the nurse in the video mentioning that our personal belongings are stored in the shelving underneath our beds.

I hang upside down from the side of my bed and locate the handle, I slide the drawer open. As it rolls out, I am reminded of the things that were on my person when I was admitted to the hospital. Items include; my cheap digital watch that appears to have run out of batteries, phone, empty wallet, and keys to my apartment on base.

Sitting in the middle of the drawer is a reminder that I am missing my love and that she isn't with me, my silver wedding band, dimly shining from the ambient green light.

It was the ring that Eve removed from one of her fingers and gave to me the day I went under which in turn became mine for our impromptu wedding in this very building a few floors up. I swipe it from the drawer and slip it onto my ring finger as a reminder of what I'm fighting to survive for.

There are also some new items… earphones, a tablet similar to the one with the nurse and sergeant's message, memory cards that are labeled, "Movies & TV," "Music," and one with a handwritten label, "Eve."

My curiosity piques with the memory card titled, "Eve." I insert the card into the tablet. The screen starts to populate with several audio files. Goosebumps raise on my forearms as well the hairs on the back of my neck at the idea of being able to hear her voice for the first time in a long time. I place the earbuds in, but before I could tap the screen to hit "play," I hear some gentle shuffling from one of the hospital beds furthest away from me. I stand up and wrap the earphones around the tablet and place it on my bed. It's time to greet my roommates from the last several years.

The shuffling intensifies to the point of almost sounding violent until there are two or three loud jolts, someone is awake. I walk over to the furthest bed, it's Brian, the middle-aged Asian fellow. I pull up a stool at the foot of his bed as he is rubbing his eyes. His vision is still adjusting as it was for me and he still doesn't notice my presence. He continues to look around and scan his surroundings, he notices that he is still hooked up to the IV bags.

I whisper, "Brian…"

He gives me a deer in the headlights look, still facing towards me while his eyes are slowly scanning his immediate surroundings. Brian can barely see me in the miniscule amount of light in the room in addition to never using them for several years. I reach down and pick up a glow stick from the ground, shake the water dripping from the stick and hold it to my shoulder so that he can see my face.

Brian clears his throat and asks, "Where am I? Who are you? Where are the nurses and the doctors!?"

I try my best to remain calm despite the gravity of the situation to avoid any trembling in my voice, I tell him, "My name is Michael, I am a patient here just like you and the others." Brian rubs his eyes once more and looks around at the other patients who are still asleep.

I point to the ceiling. "Something terrible has happened out there. The doctors and the nurses woke us up. Everything there is to know is explained in this video. It'll be easier if you just watch it." I hand him the tablet and he watches in fearful curiosity.

I can tell from the abrupt changes in his facial expression as he watches the video that he understands the implications and accepts the likelihood that several if not all of his family and friends are dead. The initial shock and horror on his face quickly changes to one of acceptance, as he is watching, it makes me wonder... if there were another conscious person or a camera in the room when I watched the video, was my reaction the same? To be honest, the only thing I could think of when I woke up was why Eve wasn't at my bedside; everyone else in my life had faded to the backseat of my thoughts.

Brian nears the last few minutes of the video, I hear what only can be described as a female voice having night terrors, "Ahhhhhhhh!!! Ahhhhh!!!" It was Ellie. I race over to her bed as she continues to scream and her feet begin running in place, pulling the bedsheets up towards her back as she continues trying to run, causing the sheets to bunch up underneath her.

I cover her mouth with one hand and put my pointer finger vertically over my lips, hoping that she can see me motioning her to be quiet. I say as tranquilly as possible in a whispering voice, "Shhhhh... calm down, calm down, you're safe, no one is going to hurt you. But we need you to stay quiet so those things don't hear us... I'm going to uncover your mouth now, nod if you understand me."

I can barely see her face, but feel her head nod as she acknowledges my request and I slowly remove my hand from her mouth and use it to point towards the ceiling as the three of us can hear a loud aircraft hovering over us, high in the air.

"My name is Michael, once Brian over there finishes watching the video explaining our current situation, he'll hand it over to you to see for yourself." Brian raises a hand to wave while staring into the tablet.

His face is the only thing in clear view at the moment, the lights from the tablet illuminates his face and brightens the room barely enough to see where each wall begins and ends. I guess I never noticed how bright the device was considering everything around me seemed to disappear when I put it directly in front of my face.

The remaining three patients are a lot less dramatic as they are coming to, only some minimal shuffling and waddling in their beds. They know where they are, the only questions that are asked are, "What day is it?" "Where is everyone?" "Why is it so dark?"

I get off my stool and move myself toward the counter with the best lighting, near the supplies. "You all can watch the video that's being passed around to see what's going on, but I'll give you the cliff notes version for inquiring minds. I don't know when you all went under, but it's now 2040, something awful has happened. Some kind of alien race attacked Earth and nearly wiped us all out in the span of a few days. The handful of remaining survivors here at the hospital, high-tailed out of here when a military escort came by to lead them to an underground human sanctuary a few miles away."

A collective gasp comes from those who have not yet seen the video.

I point to the collapsed wall of rubble to the right side of me, "Supposedly there were ten of us when they left… the other four are probably buried under that pile of concrete over there. There isn't a cure for our disease, but there IS a suppressant that we have to inject ourselves with every twenty-four hours to keep us alive until a long term solution is figured out, I already injected you guys for this first go around when I woke up."

The bewildered patients begin feeling around their necks, near the injection sites.

"There's a limited supply of these injections, we need to make a few stops along the way to the sanctuary to find more meds. If the situation isn't already totally impossible, these meds also have to be stored at a cold temperature, so we can't hoard a bunch and use them when we need, they become useless if left too warm for too long. Apparently it's advised that we travel by night for the best chance of survival… any questions?"

Still lying in his hospital bed, a curly haired man raises his hand.

"If memory serves me correctly… your name is… Charlie?"

Charlie nods but responds in a combative tone, "First of all, why aren't you lying in bed with all these tubes still attached to you like the rest of us? How do you know so much already? And how do you know our names???"

The rest of the group nods and turn their attention back to me. I reply, "I happened to wake up before you all and waited for help. When none came, I looked around this room for clues as to what is going on and how to get out of here. I came across that tablet that our friend Brian passed around, it should be with one of you and it explains everything that's happened. If you watch that video, you will know as much as I do at this point. As for knowing your names, my job before all of this was that of a fortune teller."

Not a single laugh or smile in the room. All I could say at that point to comfort my own anxieties of telling a joke that fell flat on its face was to come clean, "Tough crowd I see… I looked at your charts." In the corner of my eye in the poorly lit room, I see some teeth indicating a smile; Ellie has a small grin on her face. At least I made one person smile with my dumb joke.

Out of nowhere, the tall muscular man bellows out, "Who put you in charge!?"

I reply, "I actually don't know your name since I couldn't find your chart, but I'll answer your question with two words… 'Military experience.' I am the best chance you have to getting out of here alive in one piece, I can show you all some survival tactics and navigation using minimal light and noise."

To put an exclamation point on my statement, I direct everyone's attention to the firearms sitting next to the large backpacks right next to me on the counter. "I'm also handy with the steel… do any of you know how to properly operate and maintain a firearm?"

They didn't have to know that I was a terrible soldier; an average shooter at best, one of the last ones in the platoon to finish runs and marches, and only joined because my parents needed health insurance. Though, what they needed right now was an assertive leader with some basic survival skills.

Everyone looks around, only one person is raising their hand, Shawn, the plump black man.

"I used to be a cop before all this, but survival and combat is your wheelhouse, I'll defer to you man."

I nod and acknowledge his statement and finish off my diatribe by confidently saying, "Besides, you are all free to go your own way if you want, in fact, it would be easier for me to get to each rendezvous point on my own since I am trained for this and one person is much harder to detect than a group of six, it's up to you."

Remarkably, my voice didn't tremble during that speech. Everyone looks around again, complete silence, so I continue.

"But you make a good point Mister Muscles; we don't know each other, so let's go around the room and say a little something about ourselves. Since the spotlight is already on me, I'll start us off. My name is Michael. I was in the All Nations Initiative before all of this went down. I'm married to a wonderful woman named Eve and would like to get to our new home as soon as possible and look for her there."

I have no choice but to show confidence and bluster to lead these people, of course we're all scared, some show it more than others. In my own head, I'm still the young, unsure, twenty-one year old that joined the military out of necessity rather than duty, a twenty-one year old that just got married ahead of schedule because of a disease, a husband that can't find his wife, and is terrified of the situation outside.

But now, to them, I have stepped up to assume the role of a leader as a seasoned twenty-eight year old military veteran who can bring this group to safety, not because I know I can or because I want to, but because they need me to. It was by chance I was the first to wake up and learn everything before they did.

"Who wants to go next?" I ask.

The short brunette woman raises her hand, in a soft voice, "My name is Ellie and I was a third grade teacher. I'm not sure if I'm more scared now or the day I found out I was diagnosed which seems like yesterday."

With her head tilted down in a shy manner, Ellie stops and looks around at everyone, waiting for the next person to tell their story.

The portly, light-skinned African American man raises his hand next. "My name is Shawn and I'm a cop here in the city, I have a wife and two kids who I hope are OK and made it to the survivor's post in the video."

Brian, the middle-aged Asian man starts as soon as Shawn finishes, "Hi everyone, my name is Brian, I was a software developer, I've never fired a gun before, so I'd rather not have to hold one if I don't have to." He ends his sentence by turning his head to face the remaining two men.

Charlie, the curly haired gentleman with rosy cheeks raises his hand and chimes in. "Hi, my name is Charlie. I was a solar energy consultant and also worked as an adjunct professor at the university.

"That leaves you mystery man… what's your story?" I ask.

"I'm Lance, I was a recovery agent for a bail bonds company. I'll take a weapon, assuming you and the cop have the other two."

I look around and reply, "It's all yours. Let's spend another day here so we're all on the same sleep schedule. This will also give everyone a chance to run around, stretch, and get re-acclimated with using your bodies again. The electro therapy only did so much for us, I'm not even sure if everyone here got that package. We'll use the buddy system so no one gets lost, pair up with someone if you need to leave the room. I'll start looking for a way out of here and scavenging the hospital for tools and supplies other than what they left us in those bags. Once you're done stretching and running around, get some sleep, we're leaving at nightfall tomorrow."

The remainder of the group who had not seen the video gathers around the tablet to watch. Each of them has a different facial expression while watching, whether it is because they all process their emotions differently or perhaps some are quicker than others at truly grasping the predicament we are in and how lucky we are to be alive as it is.

I can tell which ones have accepted what has happened by how down and out they look. The ones that appear optimistic are the ones that still believe that none of this is real, or have yet to come to terms with the fact that their loved ones are more than likely gone. Ellie and Shawn are amongst the hopeful and optimistic while the others know the reality that we face. I guess I fall under the category of optimistic, we all have someone important from the before time and we are holding out hope they are still alive, patiently awaiting the time to be reunited.

Tomorrow night, we'll begin our journey and hopefully avoid any unwanted encounters with this lifeform whose main directive is apparently to either capture or exterminate us... I'm not so sure that any of us will be getting much sleep.

Eve's Audio Journal: Part 1

Spending much of the early morning searching for an exit, Brian and I finally locate a ventilation shaft that leads to the outside world. It becomes our only viable option as the stairwell is completely sealed off by large immovable chunks of concrete and the elevator doors are nowhere to be found. Some faint daylight reflecting through the metal ducts grow weaker as each beam is redirected from each panel as we look up. This probably leads to what used to be the main entrance of the hospital.

The hard part will be to create some kind of pulley system to move up the vent and to lift our gear up through the shaft, something we can't really test out until the cover of night. It's been a few hours since we've heard a patrol buzzing by our area, but we can't take any chances.

To pass the time, I play the messages that Eve recorded as part of my media package. If they played these messages for me while I was out, I don't remember them, I am anxious and excited to hear her voice. I feel a tingling sensation go up my spine as I play the file.

==================================

February 19, 2033 – Time 1430hrs
-Begin Message-

Hey there sleepy head. It's kinda weird talking to you when you're unconscious like this, I don't even know what to say in these things... I can't believe we've been married for a full week so far! I already miss you, but at least I get to hug you right now. In case you can actually hear this recording when they play it for you, I'm hugging you... right now! You seem a little cold; let me put this blanket over you!

I missed you on Valentine's Day, I guess we're not going to be able to talk to each other for any of the holidays. I wish I could wake you up, just for an hour on the days that I really miss you, uggggh, that's not realistic nor is it productive to even think about... come on Eve, get a hold of yourself woman!

Let's see, what has happened this week. Oh... to save some money, I moved back in with the folks. I know my parents won't admit it, but they love having me back around the house. It's like I'm back in high school all over again, doing homework in my room and eating supper with the parental units. Except you won't be there to join us from time to time...

One more quarter until I graduate from college though, that's exciting! It's a little scary that I still don't know what I want to do when I graduate. I know, I never admitted this to you, but you can't say anything about it... though I wish you could...

I'm gonna go now, I miss and love you. (Smooch) In case you didn't feel that… I gave you a big fat kiss hubby. I'll see you later.

-End Message-

May 7, 2033 – Time 1725hrs
-Begin Message-

I'm so sorry I haven't been able to come in sooner, school's been so busy but the end is near! I have great news! I got a job offer to be a financial analyst for this pharma company's headquarters downtown. The pay is pretty decent so I'll be able to get my own place in a little bit and still afford your treatment.

My parents are kinda sorta getting on my nerves. Though I appreciate them letting me crash their place for these last few months, I am starting to remember my justified teenage angst against them. Anyway, I start this new job a week after graduation, I'm so excited! Yay me!

Ugghhh…. Some annoying news for you in case you were curious about current events. More and more people are being diagnosed with CN, this includes celebrities. Guess what, they are actually making reality shows of celebrities going through the "harshness" of CN treatment. It is so absurd, it pisses me off that you're here in a coma, like everyone else who isn't a millionaire.

These celebs go on TV talking about how difficult it is to go into the doctor's office for a few hours a month for the gene therapy in ice cold baths and how uncomfortable it is. For God's sakes, they get to go back to their normal, everyday lives with their friends and family after a short monthly appointment. It's so frustrating… these reality shows are so stupid." Eve's voice trembles and she is audibly sobbing.

"Sorry, you probably didn't want to hear all that, but I love talking to you, even if you can't respond. This is the part where you would tell me that everything is going to be okay or at least make a stupid joke to make me laugh, but it's so hard for me to feel like things will actually be okay when things are so unfair and they're unfair for no reason.

Let's see, I can't leave you on a note like that… Happy thoughts Eve, happy thoughts… What's the difference between a hippo and a zippo? One is really heavy and the other is a little lighter, buh dumm pssst! Okay, I gotta go work on my paper, I'm almost done! Love you honey.

-End Message-

================================

I have a minor panic attack at the end of that last message. Despite hearing her voice and despite it feeling like yesterday that we got married… it finally dawns on me that Eve is more than likely dead along with billions of others. I very well could be a widower, listening to the words of my dead wife. I guess I'm in the category of being a cautious optimist now. Only nine more entries remain, I'll save the rest for later.

En Route

Between the fears manifesting itself in our minds of what awaits us outside these walls, the loud intermittent air patrols passing over us, and the sunlight peeking through various cracks in the ceiling, I don't think any of us got much rest during the day. I look around at our group, either sitting or lying in their beds, their eyes wide open.

Brian looks on edge, deep in his own thoughts, rocking back and forth on his bed sitting cross legged; Charlie and Lance are chatting up a storm and becoming fast pals. I clutch the tablet containing Eve's audio journals, debating whether to play another entry; I hear some gentle splashes make their way towards me and getting closer.

The daylight piercing through the cracks in the ceiling are obstructed by the silhouette, making it difficult for me to see who is in front of me. I put my hand up to block the sun's bright rays and notice it is Ellie approaching. She gestures her hand at the far side my bed and asks.

"May I sit here?"

"Sure."

"What are you up to? What are you listening to?"

"It's a bunch of recordings my wife made for me while I was under. The hospital staff supposedly played them for me so I could hear her voice from time to time. If I'm being honest, I still miss her even though it feels like she and I were just talking yesterday… I wanted to hear her voice. I was thinking about playing another entry, but maybe I'll save it for later."

"Awwww… that's so sweet! The only man that was in my life before all of this was my pup-pup. I left him with my sister before I went under a couple of years ago. It kind of hit me this morning when I was trying to sleep… that they more than likely didn't make it."

Ellie takes a deep breath, gently exhales, and wipes a couple of tears from her eyes.

"We can't think like that, if there's the tiniest of chances that your sister, your pup, or my wife made it out alive, there is still a chance! So… you became a 'sleeper' pretty recently huh? Were there any notable events in the five years leading up to your hibernation? I only ask because I went under during the first wave of infections."

Ellie starts swinging both of her feet from the bed and her eyes look up to access her memories.

"Um… let's see, the United States converting completely to clean energy was a big deal. I know it was probably mostly already noticeable here in our city, but everywhere else in the country has been converted and upgraded, with the exception of you people… the military. Uh, the last game of professional football was played a few years ago until it was ultimately banned after more research was published about brain injuries related to the sport. Oddly enough, boxing still existed."

"I actually kind of remember that… they banned tackle football for kids, up until they entered high school anyway."

"Miller was probably the president when you went under? Yeah, he won it the second time around by running on the same platform of continuing to fix the disasters that were created a couple of decades before. There are now five international space stations in orbit, not sure how many there were during your time."

Shawn and Brian return from searching the accessible parts of the hospital for supplies. Covered in dirt and dust, they return with what appears to be several laptop bags.

"What have you got for us?"

Shawn replies. "We emptied out the computers from these bags and loaded them up with bottled water and some clothes we found in the employee lockers… don't tell my sarge about these thefts though!"

"Nice work!"

"Thanks. Yea, it'll be good for moving supplies and keeping our hands free."

The sunlight that was previously illuminating the room through the cracks in the ceiling a moment ago, gently fade away. I can tell there is still daylight out, but the sun has definitely set. My eyes start to readjust to the minimal amounts of light in the room. The chem sticks that are on the ground which were barely noticeable moments ago become more prominent in the dark.

"It's been great talking to you Ellie, but it looks like it's almost time for us to head out." She nods, grabs one of the bags filled with some street clothes and walks back to her bed.

In a firm voice, I bellow out, "Listen up! Before we head out in a little bit, we need an inventory of our supplies, do our injections, and throw on the clothes you want to wear from the rucksacks or the clothing that Shawn and Brian so kindly found for us. The sun is setting, be ready to go within the hour. According to this map, we will be traveling about a mile to the first point, make sure you're rested if you aren't already."

I make my way over to the counter to search the rucksacks and backpacks to create a mental inventory of my own. After digging through the bags, I estimate we have enough food and water to last us two days without resupplying. Worst case scenario, we can always find some IV bags at the clinics along the way. The backpacks also contain some basic first aid materials, a small hand shovel, more chem light sticks, some rope, a watch, socks, a hammer, and ponchos. This is plenty to get us to the encampment.

Redistributing the supplies in each of the bags is a guessing game in the dark room. I find that shuffling around how much water goes into or out of each bag to lighten the load is the best method. The load in each bag is important; I want the stronger and more athletic looking members of the group to carry a slightly heavier load so that we can all move quickly and effectively in the event of an encounter with the enemy. We are only as fast as our slowest member is my rationale.

Any natural light coming from outside vanishes sooner than anticipated; it's time to rally the squad and move out. I crack six chem sticks and hand them out to each person and keep one for myself. Charlie grabs the syrettes to distribute them and the group starts injecting themselves in the neck.

After removing the cap, I pause and hold mine up, "Do any of you have any medical experience and want to do me?"

Ellie scoffs, plucks the syrette out of my hand, and slides the needle into my neck. I try to relax as I feel the ice cold fluid, rush through my neck once again.

I give Ellie a puzzled look. "Wait, I thought you were a teacher."

"I am, but I have experience working with frightened children." She winks at me and the whole group chuckles.

In a blatant attempt to recoup my masculinity after Ellie's dig at my ego, I firmly say, "Next shot will need to be taken in twenty-four hours… that means we have to hit the first waypoint by 9:07pm at the latest."

The group nods as they are still snickering at Ellie's remark. I can't help but smile.

We make our way to the ventilation shaft that will lead us to the outside with supplies in tow. It's only a one story climb but it's completely vertical. We will have to shimmy our way out by spreading our legs and pressing our hands and feet up against the walls of the shaft, moving slow and steady, alternating between using our upper and lower extremities as anchors points, inching our way up until eventually getting to the top.

We couldn't come up with a pulley system to haul up our supplies, our solution is for the first few people to climb out to do the heavy lifting. The group still in the shaft would be responsible for tying ropes to the supplies and those of us up top will pull them out. Primitive, but it'll work.

I'm the first to head up. I begin my ascent, the first few steps in the vent result in some loud metal crashing like the initial strike of cymbals every time my boots collide with the shaft each step of the climb, a good way to get us all killed or buried alive.

I slowly and quietly make my way back down. "This isn't going to work."

My fellow survivors watch me as I slip out of my boots. Wearing socks for the climb would keep things near silent, but the lack of friction would make it an impossible feat, so I remove them too. The only items on my person for this attempt are my clothes and about 20 feet of rope wrapped around my hip and shoulders. I start my ascent again, this time each step only causes a quiet and deep grumble from the walls of the vent popping outward as it absorbs my weight and pops back in place when I move my weight to the next step. It's a noise that can be heard a few feet away, not a mile.

A few more steps up until the vent goes horizontal, almost out. The cool night air greets my face through the grate blocking my exit. I crawl a few yards to get up close to the grate to peek through, the other side of the grate is actually a room, a room that has at least one wall and a ceiling missing. I gently press on the grate in an attempt to move it, it's not going anywhere and would appear to be secured tightly in place. After lacing my shoes back on, I curl up into a ball to reposition myself so that my feet are to the grate.

I crawl back towards the part of the vent before it drops down and I whisper to the group, "Hey… there's a grate blocking our exit, I'm going to wait until a patrol flies near us. That's when I'll try to kick it through, hopefully the ship will drown out the noise, standby."

A man's voice whispers back, "Good idea."

I didn't have to wait long. Not more than two minutes later, the ground begins to rumble and sounds of the ships exhaust reverberate even louder in this tin box. I consider plugging my ears but I want an idea of how far away the ship is. It sounds like it is at least a couple hundred yards away, not too close. I lie on my side, fully extend my arms up and press my hands into the ridges of the shaft to anchor myself. I take a deep breath, raise both of my knees right below my chin and stomp out the grate as hard as I can with my bare feet.

"CRASH, CLANK, CLANK, CLANK."

The grate was secured only by a few small screws, it doesn't feel like my feet are cut, maybe some small scratches at the worst. The panel went flying several feet onto the ground outside, finally rattling to a stop. I lower the rope back down the vent.

I whisper loudly as the ship stil hovers above, a little closer to us than before but still not in our immediate vicinity. "I'm through, tie the rifle to this rope, I'm going scout the area before we start moving people and supplies up… make sure the safety is on!"

I feel the weight of the rifle on the other end of the rope, it slides an inch or two before I catch it. A couple of tugs and a few seconds later I pull up the weapon, stock first, and re-maneuver myself to crawl out into the world face first. I press the thumb lever to release the magazine to make sure I'm locked and loaded with a round in the chamber before I step out.

Not taking any chances, I wait for the sound of the spacecraft to grow even more distant, I flick the safety switch off while simultaneously remembering what the man in the video said… not to engage the enemy unless absolutely necessary.

The roars of the ship fades further into the distance and the gravel that was once vibrating on the ground come to a stop, I crawl out. I stay in a crouched position surveying the area, my rifle pointed down range with my finger resting outside of the trigger guard to prevent any unintentional discharge.

I look to my left… immediately to my right, nothing. I swing my gun all the way around to see if anything is behind the vent… nothing but a wall left standing in the room that used to be the main lobby if my bearings are correct.

After the quick scan, I realize how severe my tunnel vision is and couldn't believe I didn't immediately notice… the hospital has been reduced to piles of rubble with only a few interior walls left standing in precarious positions.

You would never be able to tell that this building was once over fifteen stories high encased in tall glass windows. What's left of the windows are empty frames that are barely intact themselves. The portions of the walls that remain standing measure no higher than two or three stories while dirt, concrete, and piles of debris in the area are not much taller than me.

Full moon… this does not bode well in our cause to remain undetected when the enemy owns the skies. The only bright side is that we'll be able to see where we're going. There are some charred letters of the hospital's insignia, dangling while others are completely scraped off. This must be part of the brick wall near the entrance.

A metal sheet lying over the wall forms a right triangle about 20 yards away from the vent, perfect cover. It will be our makeshift staging area as we get everyone else out. I throw my glow stick as far as I can towards the wall to direct the other five on where to move once they've climbed out.

I creep back towards the vent, some light chatter emanates from the group down below. While still outside, I stick my neck in and whisper loudly, "Hey! Quiet down, I can hear you all the way up here. Listen up! I found a good staging area once you get out of there. Head towards the fallen sign draped over the brick wall. It'll be straight ahead of you when you crawl out of the vent. Keep your heads low when you make your way to the wall and you'll be fine. I chucked a chem stick over there to light the way for you."

A quick look around, I don't see or hear any ships in the area. The rope starts to wiggle back towards the vent in two short jolts, I pull up the first backpack up the vent, coiling the rope around my hand and elbow until I see the pack above ground, Lance is following shortly behind. He exits the vent.

We nod at each other before he grabs the backpack, pulls out his sidearm from the back of his waistband, stays low, and runs for the wall. I unwind the rope from my arm and toss one end back down the vent and whisper, "Next person."

The rope is taut, I start pulling up the next backpack. The ground starts vibrating and the loose gravel rattles on the ground, a ship is approaching fast with intent. The ship's spotlight is getting closer to consuming the darkness in our area. The noise gets louder and the ground shakes violently, it has got to be headed straight for us. I yell down the vent, "Get down! Everyone down!"

I hear two loud crashes of metal down the vent, presumably the pack and someone falling back down into the base of the vent. I lower the rope back down until there is no longer any tension and only the weight of the rope itself. I shimmy back into the vent feet first until I completely conceal myself from aerial view and hold as still as possible.

I can't quite make out the shape of this spacecraft due its blinding light, but I can see that the ship is closing in on our position and slowing down. A bright light engulfs the whole area as the ship creeps its way over us, hovering, moving what seems to be, inches at a time.

Lance, still outside at the staging area underneath the large sign, ducks down and points his pistol toward the sky. I wave my arms to get his attention, unaware if he can even see me in the darkened vent. I try my best to communicate to him not to shoot as he keeps the pistol trained on whatever it is that he sees.

His position is completely shielded from the ship's line of sight as well, there is no reason for him to shoot, he could get us all killed. The ship is now directly over us, I think about trying to get a glance of what the ship looks like and what we're up against, but the light on the ground is as bright as day. I refrain from sticking my neck out for the sake of a curious glimpse.

The ground continues to shake and the noise from the ship's exhaust remains deafening, blowing dust, dirt, and debris everywhere, and sounds as if it is suspended over our position. I can barely see Lance amidst all of the chaos. I hold completely still, bracing the sides of the vents to prevent from any unwanted motion and rattling.

I'm not sure if he saw me motioning to him not to shoot or not, but he's now lying flat on the ground, taking refuge, hugging the corner of the wall under the collapsed metal sign.

Three loud consecutive pops from the sky, I pray to whoever will listen that whatever that sound was isn't live ordinance dropping from the ship. "THUD… THUD… THUD…"

I couldn't see, but there are three heavy, distinctive objects that have fallen from the sky and crashed into to the ground. Larger chunks of dirt and debris splash on impact and shower the vent with pebbles. I open my eyes and I'm still here… they weren't explosives. It sounds like they impacted to my left, maybe twenty or thirty yards away, it's hard to tell from the metal box, I'm trapped with no view of anything but Lance and the staging area. Do they know we're down here?

I look at Lance as he stares at whatever it was that came from the sky. Whatever it is, it's got him spooked. I can see the whites in eyes, jaw partially hanging, and not a single blink. He breaks down, buries his face into the ground and puts both of his hands over the back of his head, partially covering his ears.

The objects make a hydraulic compression noise in each step as they march towards us. Three pairs of metallic-like legs walk past me and Lance. I can't see anything but their legs as the top of the vent is obscuring my view. I hunker down, trying hard not to move or breathe as they walk right past us, almost close enough for me to grab their mammoth sized legs. They are closer to my side than Lance's; he would have a better line of sight on the enemy if he weren't still in the fetal position.

With each step, they crush the ground beneath them, each step sounding mechanical and menacing as they continue walking, searching for something. Eventually the steps grow; they're finally moving away from us. Our area is no longer lit by the ship above. We wait for what feels like five more minutes until there is complete and utter silence and the cover of darkness returns. I err on the side of caution before making any movement.

The others climb out of the vent with the supplies without any issues. I look back and marvel at where the hospital once stood at more than fifteen stories of shimmering glass and steel… It's been reduced to five to six feet of rubble with a handful of interior walls left standing, much like the rest of the surrounding buildings in the area.

As far as the eye can see in the moonlight, the rest of the city has suffered the same fate and is no longer recognizable. I was dropped off at the hospital, near where Lance is still curled up against the wall, still not blinking, and just staring at the ground in front of him.

We all reconvene between the charred remanence of metal skeletons that used to be two parked cars to look at the map to determine which direction we need to head to get to the first medical center.

Lance is still shaken up, he has upgraded to squatting up against the brick wall with a dead stare. It's not a good sign when the toughest looking one of the bunch looks terrified to his core. Ellie jogs over to him while staying low to check on his status and to console him with inaudible words while she puts her hand on his shoulder, the teacher in her is really showing. She eventually convinces him to rejoin the group.

Charlie and Brian have the map in hand using a small flashlight. They both turn their heads, looking down each street, searching for landmarks to determine which way to head to get to the first batch of medicine. Charlie looks at the map, glances up at the street and says, "Look over there, that's Market Street, we need to get on Market Street, then head north."

"North is that way!" Points Brian.

"Psssst. This is exactly what I mean about noise and light discipline. We have no idea what their sound and light detection capabilities are, when we're out in the open, keep the chatter to a minimum and next time you boneheads need to look at the map with a flashlight, sit down, tuck your head into the collar of your shirt and look at it in there to conceal the light. Otherwise, use a chem stick!" I scold the two in a stern whisper.

Brian nods and puts the map and the flashlight back into his pocket.

The first couple of blocks of our expedition have us all on edge after the near encounter. We make deliberate steps to carefully sneak our way down the streets, moving from cover to cover, not spending more than a couple of seconds out in the open at a time.

Each of our bags weighs in at around twenty five pounds which becomes a heavy burden to our unconditioned bodies. We can't all help but stop to gasp for air in that short period of time.

The electro therapy helped with our muscles but didn't do any favors for our lung capacity. Despite being in the A.N.I. and finishing basic which only feels like a few months ago, my body knows and is telling me this is the first time in seven years it is exerting itself.

Those two blocks were grueling, but we must continue, the less time we spend on the streets, the better. Our lives depend on getting to shelter as soon as humanly possible.

During our march, I surveil the area for enemies, I make an observation that the city I once knew is completely leveled and looks like a foreign warzone from the history books that has been relentlessly shelled, a warzone that has been raging on for years with no respite.

All of the cars on the street are charred to a crisp, most of the buildings are flattened with the exception of a handful of walls barely standing, absolutely none having any roofs, and the concrete streets and sidewalks are crumbled into uneven chunks on the ground like a massive earthquake struck the area. Even an off-road vehicle would have trouble traversing this landscape.

Every step we make causes a crunching sound as if we are walking through a gravel pit, our weight sinks us a bit until the ground compacts, and we track tiny pebbles into our next stride. Whatever attacked our world definitely hit us hard with a bombing campaign that wreaked havoc on our infrastructure and caused major devastation to anything standing or living above ground.

Up a few blocks ahead of us, I see what looks like the top of a stryker turret, visible due to a small nearby fire. An armored personnel carrier used by the A.N.I., they were starting to phase those things out by the time I had joined… our resistance must have gotten pretty desperate. I hold up my hand and ball it up into a fist and lower myself to one knee, signaling everyone behind me to halt and to stay low. They follow suit.

"Michael, what do you see?" Ellie whispers.

"It looks like a friendly unit up ahead and it looks to be in one piece. Everybody listen up! For the next few blocks, we need to go back to utilizing cover and maintaining noise and light discipline. Got it?"

I look back at the group and they all nod, except for Lance. Lance is still wearing a distant, blank stare on his face, he doesn't acknowledge what I said or even reacts to it at all. I debate with myself whether I should confiscate his weapon; though it's probably the only thing that is giving him any sense of security after whatever it was that he saw. Besides, no one else but Shawn and I have any experience with firearms.

"Lance! You still with me buddy?" I whisper.

He snaps back to reality from his daydream and nods after hearing his name.

We make our way towards the stryker, our heads on swivels scanning our surroundings with each step, filled with a full dose of cautious optimism that we may have some friendly firepower left in the field. It's got to be a good sign if one of our units is still intact after a battle with the supposedly superior enemy. We are within ten yards of the APC posted in the middle of the intersection.

Ellie, Shawn, and I walk up to the stryker as the others stay behind to cover our flanks from the corner of a dilapidated wall. The remainder of our approach is no longer shrouded in darkness, the light from the small fire illuminates our movements from here on out. Ellie lets out a little whimper and starts sobbing into both of her hands… Shawn and I see firsthand the cause of her reaction.

Three dead soldiers, lying on the ground, dried blood showing through their uniforms around their chests and mouths. Some with burn marks around their wounds indicating a lost engagement with the enemy… their sidearms have been removed.

These soldiers are wearing helmets with microphones attached to them… these aren't infantry guys. They must be a part of the stryker unit crew over there. I see a separate trail of blood, leading to the edge of the intersection and it disappears without a trace. Someone or something picked him up.

Ellie retreats back to the group taking shelter beside a scorched minivan as Shawn and I creep up closer to the stryker and continuously paint our surroundings with our eyes and the barrels of our weapons. We'd be ready if any enemies are lurking around to ambush us.

After a closer look at the soldiers, they are wearing the patches of the second armored division on their shoulders, an all-black patch depicting a man on a horse wielding a sword with lightning bolts around it. They are based out of Joint Base Anderson-McIntyre, the same as mine.

I don't recognize these men, though, they look my age... but I remember, they do look my age... when I served seven years ago. These kids were probably in middle and high school when I started my hospital stay... Why did they leave the stryker?

We see the evidence for ourselves, the sheer overwhelming power and advanced technology these invaders wield over us. The stryker from a distance looked whole and untouched unlike the cars, buildings and everything else... however, upon closer examination, there's a clean cut hole through one side of the hull to the other, the diameter of a hula hoop.

The trajectory of the hole can be traced going through to the nearby car still containing small flames burning the interior. This skirmish probably happened less than a day ago judging from the bodies and the fire.

Whatever the projectile the aliens used, pierced through the stryker's armor like a hot knife through butter and left no trace. The inside of the stryker looks like it was in an intense fire as evidenced by the molten metal, these kids must have been burning alive in there.

This has to be the work of enemy ground forces with such a deliberate, surgical shot to neutralize the stryker unit like that.

The only thing we can do now is scavenge the area for weapons and supplies. Maintaining noise discipline as we are still securing the scene, I tap Shawn and Lance on the shoulder and hold up two fingers, point them to my eyes, point up, and whirl them in a circle around me to tell them to cover our position so that I can hop inside to search the vehicle.

I flick the safety switch back on the rifle and swing it around by the sling to have it hang over my back barrel up. As I put both my hands on the APC to climb in the hatch, I hear a man's voice yell out from the distance. "NO! NO! NO! Don't! Don't touch it! Don't!"

Muscle memory from my training or perhaps simple self-preservation and survival instincts kick in. Before my mind can even process what is happening, I find the grip of my rifle already in hand with the safety off, weapon pointed towards the incoming unidentified voice.

Shawn and Lance have their weapons drawn and pointed down range towards the voice as well. I whisper as loudly as I can. "Quiet! Show yourself! Show me your hands!"

My gut had me yell those words, but the reality of the situation is that every human left on this planet all share a common unworldly enemy… any human SHOULD be considered a friendly, at least initially.

I'm not sure if it is due to the environment we are in, where we would shoot our adversaries first and ask questions later, or if they teach something different in the police academy for trigger discipline these days. But I notice Shawn, the former cop, having his finger resting on the trigger instead of the slide while his weapon is pointed towards the incoming potential threat. I quickly shake it off as we have more pressing matters that require my full, undivided, and immediate attention.

The crackling of the gravel with each step gets closer and closer until a silhouette appears in the moonlight sprinting towards us with his hand waving above his head and rifle held high by the stock in the other. The man, dressed in a dark trench coat stops to catch his breath as he leans forward with his hands over his knees. He looks to be a man in his fifties with gray hair and beard, though older, he's built like someone who can handle himself.

The three of us lower our weapons.

"Get away from here… I rigged the vehicle with explosives. It's meant for those damn Ladrones."

The old man pops his head into the large hole in the stryker and disarms a trip wire that is set to go off if anything steps into it or attempts to move the vehicle, he also extinguishes the small fire in the charred car with a large rag on his hip, perhaps the fire was used as bait for the enemy.

"Ladrones?" I ask.

"Yeah, where have you all been?"

"Long story… you'll have to give us the rundown of what's going on. Let's get to safety first and continue our conversation there shall we? Know of a place?"

As we move from the intersection and make our way towards the nearby fragments of buildings, the man begins to speak. "Ladrones is Spanish for 'snatchers'… their ships were first spotted in South America. Before they attacked, they floated in the sky off the coasts for a few hours at dusk. A young journalist was filming a story about them. I'll never forget the look of terror in her face, like she didn't even want to be there in the first place with her back turned towards the fleet of ships.

Mid-sentence during her report, a light shined down on her like a perfect spotlight, just enough to cover her body, she couldn't move, whether it was paralysis from fear or something in that light, it didn't matter. A few seconds later, she got snatched from the ground and sucked up into one of their ships that was like a half a mile up in the sky.

The cameraman captured the whole thing and mutters the word, 'Ladrones.' A few seconds later, anything connected to the internet, cable, or satellite went dark. That was the moment we knew they weren't here for peace, they destroyed our cities and defenses with these particle bombs that caused what you see all around you.

Rumor has it that the initial strikes all happened moments later at the same time around the world in populated areas until our planet was bathed in fire. They were already in position to attack, but they must have been cloaked or something, waiting for the perfect moment, we never knew what hit us. Our conventional fighting forces didn't stand a chance. Follow me. I'm in the basement of that little shop over there, I've been holed up the last couple of days. Let's get you all armed so we can get back into the fight, it's only a block from here."

I decide to wait until we're in shelter before I tell him about our time sensitive situation, we could use a break anyhow. The six of us follow our new friend for more information and perhaps some more supplies. He wasn't joking, his spot isn't even a block away, he was probably watching us the whole time we were creeping up on the armored vehicle.

As we're walking towards the shelter, we can hear him mumbling to himself. "We should have been prepared for this (indiscernible grumbling), the government knew and they didn't say anything, they were hiding it... (more inaudible mumbling) we could have been ready, they killed us..."

The old man lifts two wooden doors into the basement and holds it open while we all walk down, he follows us in.

The doors shut and everything goes pitch black for a moment until he hits the light switch. Ah, the all too familiar buzzing before the lights fire up.

The basement is nice and wide with a musky smell to it. It can't be much more than six feet high down here, Shawn and Lance have to duck their heads before they find a spot to set their packs down and sit. We don't have much time to spare so I make sure not to get too comfortable. There isn't much down here besides a few weapons, a couple of benches, and a sleeping cot.

"I've been scavenging weapons and supplies since those things hit us, I can get everyone in your outfit a rifle to get back in the fight and we can hit them back hard and fast, and out before they know what happened.

Retired Specialist, Bill Roberts at your service, served three tours in Afghanistan decades ago in EOD, Explosive Ordnance Disposal, did you serve too son? I was watching the way you moved out there. Who are your friends?"

I introduce myself and point out the others as we're all huddled together on some makeshift benches. "I was actually a private years ago in the first infantry, A.N.I., my name is Michael, that's Shawn, Brian, Ellie, Lance, and Charlie.

We're actually on kind of a schedule here. You see, we're all traveling together because we all came from

Harbor Point Medical a little ways back... we all have CN and need to get to the next clinic to take our injections before the disease does its thing. We're ultimately on our way to the underground survivor's encampment, you should join us."

"Oh my.... I'm sorry to hear that. How much further do you have to go and when do you have to get there by?"

I hand Bill the map and point to the first waypoint the nurse in the video circled for us.

"Ideally, we'd get there before dawn; we're trying to travel by the cover of night to give us a better shot at avoiding those things."

Right on cue, we can hear one of their spacecraft hovering in the distance, the ground isn't moving, so they aren't too close. I'm thankful that we're indoors and underground, it's funny to think about the people with the most money lived in the upper levels and penthouses before all of this happened... now, the further underground you are, the more valuable of a shelter you have.

"You only have about eight blocks to go, you guys are right here. It won't be a straight shot because that whole street is blocked off by a collapsed high-rise. Hang a left here on Martin and head up Pacific for the remaining six blocks and you're good to go."

"Wait, you're not coming with us? There's no fight left here. They have us outmanned, out-gunned, and they own the skies… you and I both know we don't have any tactical advantage over them. Come with us to the sanctuary."

"As long as I can stand and breathe on my own, I'm gonna stay in the fight… you guys go on ahead, grab what you need. I'm staying right here. Someone needs to show these bastards that they'll have to suffer some losses if they come after us.

Throughout history, small guerilla forces have been proven to be effective in stopping a technologically advanced and superior fighting force dead in their tracks. This is OUR land damn it! You have to be prepared to die, and if you do, take as many of those things down as you can with you. I've brought down two of those mechs myself you know! You gotta shoot them in their faceplates when they leave their ships, it's their weak spot and I don't think they can breathe our air."

"What do they look like under their mech suits?"

"I never stuck around to find out, whenever one of them goes down, you have less than a minute to get the hell out of dodge before reinforcements arrive… I disappear at that point."

We shake hands.

"Alright Specialist Roberts. I'm sorry that you won't be joining us, good luck out there. I think we're good on supplies unless you can spare an extra mag or two of nine mill or five-five-six, we could use some. We'll be on our way, it looks like everyone has caught their breath."

Bill reaches into a bag of an assortment of ammunition, more than likely scavenged from soldiers who have fallen... he finds the right magazines for Lance and Shawn's pistols and finally one for my M4. I store it in my side pocket.

Bill leads us back up the stairs to the door in which we came and stops shy of the door and stares at Charlie. A few seconds pass until Charlie realizes that this is a signal for him to switch off the lights since he is the closest to the switch before we can begin our exodus.

The lights go out.

Slowly, Bill raises the door open to make a peek to the outside. Once he is satisfied that the enemy is not nearby, he opens the door just enough for all of us to exit.

He nods at each one of us as we walk past him, he throws in a smile for Ellie when she walks by and she thanks him for his hospitality. When I make my way out, he salutes me with his rifle in hand while his other is clutching the door open. We part ways and he hops back into his shelter and we continue our journey.

Seven

Three more hours until sun up and a few more blocks to go... As we get closer and closer to our destination, I point out the dozens of charred metal car frames, symmetrically lined up in tight proximity of one another. "Look over there, by those cars, that's gotta be the parking lot. The front entrance to the building is the only wall left standing." Not too promising when this facility is supposed to house our life-saving medication and provide shelter during the day.

The entrance isn't the only thing that's visible under the glimmering moonlight ... Other than Lance, who has yet to talk about them, this is the first time we've seen one of them for ourselves. A mech appears before us, just one, it's about ten feet tall, some kind of metallic armored exoskeleton, and some hydraulic movement in its legs as it moves closer to the entrance of the clinic from the right with devastating weight in each step.

The arms are bent into an "L" from its shoulders, where the hands would be are what looks to be the business end of its primary weapon. The mech crushes any bits of debris in every step it takes and can be heard from our location about thirty yards away.

Charlie whispers, "Michael, what are you waiting for? We got the drop on him, shoot him! Remember what that old man told us, shoot it in the dome! That's the weak spot."

Furrowing my brows, I look back at Charlie, "The man also told us that a world of hurt will come down on us if any of those things are attacked. We have plenty of time until dawn, we'll wait him out unless we absolutely have to engage. We don't need patrols buzzing around in the air and the ground forces marching around the area when we're trying to move in undetected. Everyone hold and seek whatever cover you can."

Admittedly, we are in a bad spot, out in the open with a few mounds of rocks and debris between us and the mech. If a foot patrol comes from our flank or a ship flies through overhead, we'd be sitting ducks, if we get any closer to our destination, we risk the giant mech seeing or hearing our approach.

I give a directive to the group, "If an aerial patrol is inbound, we might have no choice but to rush the mech, secure the building, and find the basement entrance right after I put a few rounds into that thing."

Back in the A.N.I., we were trained to hit targets from 300 meters away that size. The difference here though… the target is randomly moving, it's dark, I technically haven't fired my rifle in several years, and if I miss… we die… or worse. Not a good combination of factors and pressure for taking the shot.

I quickly realize how small the target is when I line up my sights. The mech isn't facing us head on and the faceplate isn't as exposed as much from the side profile, making the target that much smaller. I can feel the moisture in my hands as they clam up, fingers sliding around the grip, enough to make me miss if I decide to fire. Perspiration starts rolling down from my head and temples. I take a few deep breaths and the straps to my backpack tighten up as my chest expands with air. I can feel the eyes of the group on the back of my head, counting on me to hit the shot if my hand is forced.

The mech stops its advance and rotates its upper torso, scanning the terrain for any nearby threats. Great… it's blocking our path now. I debate with myself as to whether we should backtrack and reroute to a wider angle and to approach the clinic from the rear.

"Quiet, I hear something." Shawn whispers.

The sound of gravel crunching is slowly approaching our position from our flank, too slow, deliberate, and light to be one of those things. Shawn and Lance have their weapons drawn and trained on the shadows behind us, I turn my attention back to the mech in the event I need to dispatch the thing and lead the group on a mad dash to the medical site.

Whatever it is that was creeping up on us has stopped. It's definitely still there, whatever it is.

A voice whispers out from the darkness, "Michael... is that you?"

I recognize that voice. I turn around.

Gun drawn at us, the shining barrel slowly reveals itself until the figure comes into the moonlight, it's Bill! He quickly lowers his weapon the millisecond he confirms that it's us. We all lower our guns and return our attention back to the mech guarding our destination. Bill crouches and duck walks past the others as they all greet him with smiles, he joins me at my forward position.

While keeping my sights on the enemy, I say to Bill, "Glad you could join us. We could definitely use you and your expertise here and I'm sure the people in charge at the sanctuary wouldn't mind having you around either. What made you change your mind?"

He looks back at the group and returns his focus back towards the mech, "That gal back there, Ellie. She reminds me too much of my daughter. My little one died of cancer years before any of this happened. I imagine that's what she would have looked like if she had the chance to grow up into a young woman. It didn't feel right not getting you all to where you needed to go without my help."

"I'm sorry to hear that, but I'm not gonna lie, I'm glad you're here."

I'm not any good with words. That is all I could come up with to say. Eve was the singer and the songwriter in our little duet. She would have said something more profound and comforting to the distraught old man recalling a painful memory.

"It's okay. That was a long time ago."

"What should we do? That thing is standing in the way of where we need to get to. We probably have two more hours until the sun rises. We haven't heard any patrols since we left your place either, so we might be due."

"Well, if you bring that thing down, there will definitely be a patrol right on top of us in no time, so I would highly advise against taking that course of action."

The group is getting restless sitting here in this position, I can tell from the nervous chatter behind me. At this point, we now only have an hour until sun up. When I woke up a day ago, I never imagined I would be traversing a decimated landscape that I used to call home and having to make life or death decisions for a whole group of people.

Eve was supposed to be there by my side when I'd come to and we would go home and catch up on everything that I missed. I don't know what to do, but a decision has to be made soon before we're exposed by sunlight and before our deadly disease tightens its grip over our minds.

Patience is a virtue and inaction pays off I suppose, our prayers are finally answered, at someone else's misfortune. Automatic small arms fire erupts about a half a mile from our position towards the opposite side of the clinic.

The mech rotates its upper torso to line up the turret forward with its hydraulic legs and begins to sprint away. If it weren't a deadly killing machine, designed to hunt us down, it is almost incredible to watch how quickly it moves without altering its height after each stride. The upper torso remains at a constant height while the legs are pumping and it's probably traveling about 40 miles per hour before it disappears from our view.

Those poor souls don't even know what's about to hit them. The gunfire continues for a dozen more seconds like distant firecrackers until three loud booming thunderclaps can be heard... silence follows. We see one of their spacecraft zooming from the east towards where the mech was headed, shining its spotlight on the suspected area of gunfire.

"Let's go everybody, on your feet! Now's our chance! Move it!" I blurt out.

We do not move from cover to cover, carefully inching our way forward to gain ground this time around. We all make a dead sprint for the front entrance of the clinic. We are moving so fast with our gear that none of us bother to slow down upon reaching the clinic's front entrance and we all slam into the wall and felt it budge a little on impact.

"Alright everybody, spread out and look for the entrance to the basement, that's where the meds will be and maybe other survivors."

We all scour, looking for the entrance under pieces of rubble.

Charlie yells out, "Check the corners of the foundation here, that's where the stairwell would be!"

Makes sense, most staircases wouldn't be in the middle of a building. Lance and I pick a corner and lift up some chunks of concrete with no luck... nothing but solid ground underneath the debris. It shouldn't be that difficult, if memory serves me correctly, this isn't that large of a clinic. Maybe one or two stories at most, there's got to be a lower level somewhere if the nurse sent us here.

Brian bellows out, "I think I got something."

With all of his might as his face becomes scrunched in the ambient light and the veins around his temple start protruding, he attempts to lift a metal door with some concrete debris piled on top. Shawn jumps in to help. This might very well be the door that once led to the stairwell. Sure enough, when they lift and set the door off to the side, stairs appear down into a pitch black basement level. I crack a chem stick and drop it down to light the way. I wait for everyone to hurry down. As the last one to go down below, I lift the door up and pivot it over the stairwell to conceal the entrance. A short corridor leads us to a large room where the CN patients would have been held, not a soul in sight.

Bill flips a light switch to illuminate our surroundings... a few flickers and buzzing, the lights come on. Exhausted body language from my fellow compatriots, a few empty hospital beds, medical monitoring equipment… and a clear refrigerated cabinet!

The solar batteries for these buildings are designed to hold up for a few weeks for life support systems, I hope to God that our medication is still cold in there. I open up the cabinet and a light inside activates and I can feel the cold air crawl up my hands and face. There are about fifteen syrettes remaining, perfect.

We breathe in a sigh of relief and set our weapons and equipment on the floor.

"Alright, rest up, we gotta do this all over again tomorrow night and we have to go a little bit further."

There were six… and now there are seven. Not only that, but now we've added someone with years of military and combat experience, perhaps Bill can assume the role of the leader now since he knows the layout of the battlefield and has fought these things before.

The only drawback I can foresee is whether he can mentally be up to the task if sees his daughter in one of our fellow squad mates. Will he be too focused on Ellie's safety and not have the best interest of the group as a whole? Thoughts reserved and shelved for tomorrow after a day of sleep.

We're still reeling from the journey today and trying to unpack and process everything that has happened… our adrenaline is still at peak levels… no one is getting much sleep around here. To everyone but Bill, we all went into a deep sleep knowing everything other than ourselves in this world would be fine for the most part and woke up to whatever this is, perhaps a collective nightmare?

We all try to calm ourselves and wind down by socializing with one another as we have shared a traumatic experience of waking up to a strange world that isn't our own where we are constantly running for our lives.

We are social creatures, it is part of what makes us human, having to talk through these experiences. Our brains are focused on forming the words to maintain conversation with one another instead of wondering why our hearts are still racing, why we're still breathing hard, wondering if our friends and family made it... These kinds of thoughts are counterproductive and won't allow our minds and bodies to settle down.

It's funny, I can see this human phenomenon in action around me... Charlie, Brian, and Shawn are huddled up, chuckling and talking about God knows what. Ellie and Bill are off in their own part of the room, deep in serious conversation.

If you didn't know everyone had met each other for the first time last night, you would think that they'd all known each other for years, which is good for morale I suppose. Then there's Lance, in his own corner of the room, sitting with his feet crossed and his arms crossed around his knees... thousand yard stare into the wall across the way. This can be poison to morale for us to do what we need to do to brave our way to an objective with a mysterious and terrifying enemy hunting us down.

There is no better time than now to go ask him what exactly it is he saw that is obviously still affecting him.

"What's up dude? Is everything alright? We're all shooting the crap over there, you wanna come join us?"

"No thanks, I'm good."

"Alright, that's your call… but I guess I'll hang out over here if you don't mind."

He nods and glances at a spot on the floor beside him.

I squat down on the balls of my feet, elbows resting on my thighs as I lean up against the wall before I continue the conversation. Lance is such a mysterious character, the man didn't' even have a chart and seemed like the archtype of a tough guy when we introduced ourselves back at the hospital. The more I can get him to talk, the more I can learn I suppose, I'm baffled as to what he saw last night that has him so shook up.

"I'm just going to ask you straight up man, when I retreated back into the vent when those three mechs fell from the sky, and you were up against the wall under the metal sheet, you had the closest view of them walking past you… what did you see that has you so spooked?"

Lance turns, gets uncomfortably close to me and puts a hand on my shoulder, pulls me in as he looks me dead in the eyes as I try to lean away.

"I saw them... their eyes, their faces…"

"Oh man… the Ladrones? What did they look like?"

He moves his hands from my shoulders and grabs me by the collar of my shirt.

"No… I saw the eyes and faces of people… their heads were piked onto the shoulders of those mechs… like a trophy. I can still see the look of fear and terror in their eyes that are frozen on their faces at the moment they were killed! Michael, you owe it to us… if they're about to take any of us, you need to promise us… promise that you will gun us down and put one right between our eyes if it comes to it. Promise me!"

I maintain my composure and give him a somber look as I don't know how to respond to his morbid request. Lance returns to his isolated state and keeps a blank stare at the wall across the room. In a world where we are trying to prevent the extinction of the human race, every life counts. I understand his sentiment though; we have no idea what these things will do to us if they capture us alive.

I nod… not because I know for a fact that I would be able to keep this promise, but simply to get him to let go of his grip on me. He finally releases his clenched fist where the collar of my hoodie unravels. We're making a scene for the rest of the squad as they all pause their conversations to stare at the commotion. Would I really be able to pull the trigger if one of us was being captured by those things?

I stand up and walk back over to the rest of the group. I overhear Ellie and Bill's conversation, it sounds like she is telling him her life story as he sits there with attentive ears and listens to it all. I guess we all need some sort of return to a sense of normalcy after the things we've all seen today. None of us could have imagined or have been prepared for the nightmare that we have woken up to. It's time to get some sleep so we can do it all over again tomorrow.

Eve's Audio Journal: Part 2

Everyone is fast asleep before noon. No more talking, no more laughing, only some intermittent snoring fills the silent room. Like the living room of a party where all the guests have returned with the exception of a few stragglers that have found a makeshift area of the house to slumber.

So many thoughts are running through my head that I can't shake and fall asleep. Restless, I reach into my rucksack and fumble around to find the tablet to play more of Eve's messages, my only source of familiarity in this unforgiving world that is now our lives. If I can fall asleep to the sound of her voice, I can trick myself into believing that she's right here with me for a brief second of euphoria.

===================================
June 24, 2033 – Time 1345hrs
-Begin Message-

Great news babe! Yours truly is officially a college grad! My parents threw me a party a couple of weeks ago, yours were there too! They told me to say "Hi" for them and for me to tell you that we all love and miss you. Everybody here does. This is still a little weird for me to talk to you like you're not here when you're lying down right here in front of me.

The bed next to yours is empty by the way. I was told that he died. His family ran out of money and couldn't afford care anymore. It's such a scary thought. I guess they woke him up to say their goodbyes for one last day and gave him an injection so that he would go peacefully before things would make a turn for the worst... it's so sad.

Anyway, I'll be starting work for that pharma company I was telling you about in a couple of weeks. I'm excited and scared. I hope everyone there is nice. I'll start looking for my own apartment closer to you and work in a month or so, stay tuned!

Not much else to report on, the weather is insanely beautiful, I almost kinda want to bring you outside to get you a tan... you are in desperate need of one! *Eve's snickering is interrupted by indiscernible chatter.* The nurse is telling me that they're about to start your therapy for the day so I'm going to let you go to start your gym session. Love you, see you next time!

-End Message-

September 7, 2033 – Time 0530hrs
-Begin Message-

I thought I'd pop in here on my way to work. It's been a few months at my new job, still haven't made any new friends, though it looks like you have some new ones. You have eight other roommates now. I imagine you all joking and chatting with one another when no one else is here... as soon as someone walks into the room, you all pretend to be asleep; I know... I have the most random thoughts. Speaking of new roommates, last time I saw you, I told you I was getting my own place... Well... I got my own place! I can't wait for you to move in with me!

It's small, really nice, and in a brand new building. Though, in a slightly rough part of town, but yeah, everything in there has brand new everything, I feel kinda fancy. My parents are about thirty minutes away, not so far that if I get homesick I can't go visit them for a home cooked meal, but not too close to where they would be dropping in a ton.

Alrighty, gotta go, I just wanted to stop by to say hi, miss you tons!

-End Message-

December 25, 2033 – Time 1015hrs
-Begin Message-

(Eve can be heard sobbing). Michael, I need you right now more than ever. I'm not here to visit just you this Christmas... Mom and Dad both got diagnosed with CN the other day. They're upstairs off of life support. I left their room a few minutes ago to come down here.

The day they were diagnosed, they told me that they had lived a good life and would hope that you and I continue to live ours to the fullest. I could tell that they actually don't want this but they don't want me to struggle with both you and them in the hospital. They don't understand that I could work two jobs and sell their house to keep you all here. They refuse to be treated and want to pass naturally.

If I could go back in time, I wouldn't have moved out, I could have at least spent a few extra months with them. This is awful, I feel guilty for living Michael! I can already see it taking a hold of them, they didn't even recognize their own daughter let alone do more than turn their heads to hear me speak to them today (Eve continues to sob). I can't see them like that. Why do things like this have to happen? It's not fair.

I don't know where else to go today. Scoot over, I'm going to snuggle with you on your bed until they kick me out. (Eve is heard gently sobbing into the microphone for about ten seconds until the journal entry cuts out).

-End Message-

January 7, 2034 – Time 1437hrs
-Begin Message-

A few days ago, Dad died…. Mom followed within minutes, it's almost like she knew he was gone even though she couldn't move, speak, and was incapable of knowing what was going on around her. It's time to move on and be glad that they're in a better place now.

I just got back from the funeral. It was good to see lots of their old friends come out. I can't deny it, I could have used a hug from you when their lifelong friend Paul performed the eulogy. It was beautiful and saddening at the same time, hearing him talk about them in the past tense.

It occurred to me, what if I get it? I'm not sure what I'll do babe. Who would pay for our bills? The only thing that's keeping me sane about these thoughts is coming here, talking to you, and a little hope that scientists will come up with a cure soon.

If you can hear me in there, try not to worry about me. Money's a little tight after the funeral, but remember, I'm the beauty, the brains, and the brawn of our relationship, I'll figure something out. I should be able to apply for some kind of hardship grant with you serving in the A.N.I. and Mom and Dad gone. Love you, see you soon.

-End Message-

February 12, 2034 – Time 1730hrs
-Begin Message-

Hey there hubby! You know what day it is today? Yup, you guessed right, it's the one year anniversary of us getting married. Your favorite wifey bought us our favorite cheese cake. I'm going to put a tiny piece on your tongue… open wide…

I hope you found that delicious! I mean, all you've had for breakfast, lunch, and dinner every day for the last year has been whatever they're putting in your IV.

Anyway, work has been a little better, I made some new friends and we do happy hour every other Friday, so that's been fun. Your girl also got a small raise! It's been a little helpful with the money situation. Though, there's this new guy that's a jerk that no one likes. He has the same job title as me but is so full of himself and acts like he's going to be the CEO of the company or something. You win some and you lose some I guess.

It's been a whole year of us being apart, still nothing in the news about a cure yet unfortunately. But there is this new suppressant that came out. It's a shot that's designed to keep the disease at bay for at least a day so people can get their affairs in order, instead of scrambling like we did last year. That's got to be a good sign that they're getting close to a cure right? I sure hope so, I don't know how much longer I can be in this world without you. I almost want to wake you up, just for a day, and use this new drug so we can spend a day together, but they're too expensive.

I love you Michael, one year down as a married couple and we haven't had our first fight yet, that's something to celebrate! I don't know if I'll be able to make it back here for Valentine's Day a couple days from now, so happy early Valentine's Day in advance if I can't make it! Later babe, hugs and kisses.

-End Message-

Holding Pattern

I slowly open my eyes, there's some light coming from the hallway but I'm unable to move. The more I try to roll my shoulders to shake myself awake, the less my body physically moves. Each attempt becomes more feeble than the previous. Did the medication not work? Has the disease finally taken hold of me in my sleep? What about the others!?!?

The moment of panic is overcome by a wave of relief. A familiar presence is felt right beside me, followed by a familiar scent while the back of my hand is being caressed by soft gentle fingers. Still in a state of paralysis, I'm unable to turn my head from the ceiling or even fully open my eyes to get a clear picture of what is going on around me. It's got to be Eve.

I can hear her voice right next to me but can't make out the words. All I know is that my face reflexively curls into a smile. I don't want this moment to end. I know I'm not dreaming, this feels all too vivid and real... I can't speak, I want to talk to her, tell her I miss her. My mouth opens but nothing comes out. I give up, I let it happen and make the most of the experience, I may as well enjoy it until this half-awake dream-state wears off.

....

A loud thud returns me to the present and I spring up to a sitting position, still in a fog of confusion. I pause for a second, hoping against all odds of probability, I look and feel for Eve to my right, she's gone, nothing but the linoleum floor, she was never there. It may have happened years ago and my brain is replaying the memory of her voice and touch while I was unconscious.

I remove the earphones in a dizzying haze, my mind and body still trying to wake up. Looks like the ploy to listen to the journal worked a little too well, I fell asleep to the sound of my love's voice. I look at the display on the tablet, all of the entries had been played.

For a few brief moments, I tricked myself into believing she was right here next to me, cuddling with me, and talking to me. That feeling of relief and happiness will have to be replaced with the real thing when I find her. For now, I'll have to make due with digital recordings of her voice.

The sounds of backpacks being zipped open, stuffed with supplies, and boots shuffling about on the floor become more prominent. The audible groans from the group would indicate collective muscles aching and sore bodies... I can feel it too.

My legs feel like they ran a marathon yesterday. I stand up to stretch my arms and legs and Bill approaches me with purpose while I'm still trying to settle into consciousness, "What's the plan boss? Where we off to? When we leavin?"

I show Bill the map and the course that's been plotted for us to get to the next medical facility. He points at an intersection on the map and marks it with a big 'X' with a pencil, "We won't be able to start there boss, it'll leave us exposed for far too long anyway. A skyscraper went down and it's blocking the street for at least two blocks, that's roughly where I was when all of this started. We'll need to head at least two blocks that way to get around it."

"Perfect. Good to know. It'll probably make our little journey a little longer, but much safer in the end. We'll head out in about an hour, there's still a bit of daylight out."

The next place will be a little interesting... we might encounter several other survivors with CN if they haven't already waken up and evacuated the facility yet. It's a larger building that was repurposed to house patients like us in bulk according to a little footnote scrawled on the map, anyone still drugged up in the basement has a good chance to be alive. We might be making some new friends later tonight.

We run the same routine as before, stocking up on any supplies that we can find, strap on our bags, and prepare to move out. The six of us each grab a syrette to inject ourselves ahead of our journey. Before I even have a chance to grab one for myself, Ellie grabs one and doses me in the neck, I didn't have time to react. I try to relax and hold as still as possible until she retracts the needle from my neck. "You're welcome" she says with a smirk.

I touch the injection site to make sure any bleeding has subsided, she plunged it in pretty hard it seems... no blood though. I guess the appropriate response would have been to say thank you, but I felt myself laugh and smile like a teenage boy whose crush punched him in the shoulder. A stoic response may be warranted here.

Ellie clearly likes me, but I will never give up hope for Eve, even if there's a one in a million chance she's out there, still alive. A chance is still a chance and inside the realm of possibility. I shake these thoughts out of my head and make sure the squad is ready for departure.

We have four guns with us now, an addition of a well-trained one at that. The seven of us line up in the stairwell and ensure our weapons are locked and loaded. I look back at the group, everyone is ready and the lights are off. We are ready to leave our newest home behind us and move on to the next one.

I let my rifle hang around my neck by its sling. Both of my arms fully extended over my head, I press up one side of the large metal door. Each step up the stairs raises the door inches at a time until there's enough room to peek outside. No visual contact of the enemy on the ground and no signs of any nearby aerial patrols. I make it near the top of the stairs and hold the door up, allowing everyone else to stream out of the stairwell.

This is only our second exodus on our way to what's left of civilization, but I feel like our group is becoming a well-oiled machine. Shawn and Lance use their weapons to provide cover as the others follow the lead like ants in a colony on their way to an objective.

Each person plays their role as if they had rehearsed this hundreds of times, without using any words or making any sounds, they remain in sync with one another's movements. I witness this phenomenon while I hold up the rear, covering our exit as I gently set the door back down.

The stairwell is concealed, enough to remain hidden from the sky, but cracked open enough for another group of humans that happen to be walking through here to locate the entrance and use the lower level as shelter if need be.

Bill assumes point while I watch our flank and to make sure that no one lags behind during our trek. We have quite a ways to go. He's naturally taking the reins to lead the group. The role suits him well and takes all of the pressure off of me. Plus, I'm still that lost, unsure twenty-one year old, college dropout who had no business being in the military to begin with. I shouldn't be in charge, I happened to be the only option, but not anymore with Bill around.

Bill gets ahead of the group by about 40 yards before he realizes he's moving too fast. Despite being older, his body is nowhere near as fatigued as ours. He stops to kneel near a 30 foot high mound of rubble of what used to be a tall building identified by its window frames and metal beams barely holding up. He waves his arm at us to tell us to hurry it up.

The all too familiar sound begins with the ground rumbling but more violent. The sound of a ship is near, and not originating high in the sky. The sound is coming from the other side of the mound of debris near Bill. The shaking intensifies and now we can see the top of the ship as it lifts off vertically over his position. Without its blinding light, shining in my face, I can see the ship in its entirety.

This particular ship is the size of the fuselages of two large airliners in length and width, in the shape of a jagged horizontal raindrop. The rear of the ship appears frayed with several ore-like spikes. I can no longer see the ship as I shield my eyes from the bright lights once the ship quickly gains altitude over the mound.

Noise discipline is no longer a priority, we have never been outside at the same time as these ships, let alone being this close to one. I shout to the group, "Displace! Displace!"

We all scatter, finding any cover from cars or piles of rubble as long as it is tall enough to create a shadow while we are prone. No one moves a muscle, I find myself hiding behind a car that has been burnt to a crisp except for the trunk space.

I watch the monstrous ship levitate from the ground, nearly blinding me as night has turned into day around Bill.

We have nowhere to run and none of us are in ample cover to avoid detection from these things. It's only a matter of time before they send in those walking machines to shred us to pieces. Our only chance is to remain still and hope they haven't spotted us right under their noses. Hope… not exactly a battlefield tactic.

"No one move! We don't know if they can see us or not!" I yell, not knowing if anyone can even hear me amidst the chaos.

Bill's circumstance is exponentially more hopeless than ours; his cover is rendered completely useless as the ship is hovering about fifty yards directly over him. A blue spotlight begins to emanate from the ship and focuses directly on Bill. I shield my eyes from the ship's light in the hopes of seeing some kind of escape route available for Bill.

The light brings him to his knees as his rifle falls to the ground and his hands come to rest, bound to his sides. His hands look like they are tied to his waist by the wrists. It doesn't look like anything is physically restraining them though. His eyes are fixated on the light as his neck whips back, his face directly looking into the light with his chin to the sky as the ship gains more elevation, and his back becomes arched while he is still on his knees.

Lance's voice echoes in my head, my thoughts run wild at the promise I made… to put anyone out of their misery if any of us ever gets snatched. I train the scope of my rifle on Bill, center mass, not knowing if I will have the fortitude to pull the trigger and kill a fellow human being. As his arms remain locked to his sides, his jacket opens up, enough for me to catch a glance at what he's got underneath; it's covering his chest and stomach...

He's wearing a vest with several rectangular blocks wired to it. It reminds me of something we were trained to spot back in basic. An old barbaric tactic used by an inferior fighting force to demoralize a technologically advanced enemy at great cost.

This brings back memories of my training in IED (Improvised Explosive Device) identification. The Sarge told us new recruits decade's old war stories when he was deployed in Afghanistan, stationed at a checkpoint. There were two stories he used to tell where he could feel the imminence of a suicide bombing attack that raised every hair on his body. The first was when a vehicle was approaching slowly, weight displaced to the rear trunk like something heavy was in the back, and another time where an individual was approaching the checkpoint by himself, wearing unseasonably heavy articles of clothing for the weather.

However, in both instances he was able to notice these irregularities and the look in each man's eyes like they had seen a ghost during their approaches on the checkpoint. He and his fellow soldiers recognized the threat in time and raised their weapons early enough to dissuade the potential attackers without firing a shot.

To confirm my suspicion, I focus in on Bill's hands, and sure enough, despite his arms somehow being restrained to his sides, and his head craned up looking into the light, I see his fingers fumbling around for a remote wired to the vest.

He's going to try to bring them down with him! I lower my rifle. Bill erupts into a maniacal laugh as he finally manages to get the remote into the palm of his hands.

I scream out amongst the chaos, "BACK TO THE CLINIC, NOW! NOW! NOW!"

Without hesitation, everyone makes a dead sprint back to the basement of the clinic, a block away from our current position. I hold up the rear, running but looking back at Bill every few steps to witness his fate.

The ship continues to rise, Bill's body immediately becomes a ragdoll as he gets sucked up from the ground at high speed into the sky towards the bright light and his laughter turns into screams of terror.

His silhouette shrinks smaller and smaller until his body is engulfed by the ship's blinding light and I can no longer see him without burning my vision, his screams can be heard overhead during his ascent until the sound of the ships' exhaust drown hims out.

The ship's spotlight is now centered over us as we run back to shelter. The spacecraft races towards our position at high altitude. The distance between us and the ship is closed in the matter of a second or two. As the ship's engine can be heard winding down and decelerating to match our pace, a small explosion is heard at the rear of the ship.

Some tiny metal fragments and hot ash shower down on the back of my neck like a gentle mist with sporadic peppering of pebble sized fragments raining down on us.

The explosion creates enough damage to the ship causing it to hurl past us and overshoot our position by about one-hundred yards. The smoke trail drags across the sky and screeches off in the distance in a fiery blaze until finally it crashes beyond our view causing a minor tremor at impact and can be heard skidding for a few more seconds.

The old man took one of those things down single handedly, I have got to hand it to him… but this is no time for mourning or celebration. According to Bill's own words, that ship will have backup and they will pounce on us any minute now.

I make sure that everyone gets down the stairwell by performing a quick count. Five of them plus me equals six, once a few feet into the stairwell, I let gravity do its work and let go of the door as it crashes down above us masking the entrance from any curious onlookers above ground.

I instruct the group to keep the lights off and to use chem lights if they need to see where they're going. I remain at the top of the stairwell, lifting the door high enough to see through the cracks if anything is following us. I can't tell if we're being too loud from all of the heavy breathing or if it is actually that quiet outside. My survival instincts have kicked into high gear giving me a heightened sense of sound as my line of sight is limited.

I don't hear or see anything outside, no ambient light from an inbound ship, no sounds of them coming our way. Perhaps Bill exaggerated their capabilities. I lift the door a few inches higher to get a better view, nothing. At least two minutes had passed since the explosion; I'll give it ten more before I make the call to restart the journey.

Charlie asks, "What did you see? What happened? Did something shoot that down?" Additional voices chime in, "Yeah, what's going on?"

I keep one hand on the door and put the other toward them, hand clenched into a fist, to get them to quiet down. A little late to the party, about fifteen minutes after the ship went down, the ground in front of me is illuminated, I can see the immediate terrain in full detail. The ground violently shakes and causes the door to rattle. I set the door down and get everyone to go further into the basement and back to the patient beds and treatment area.

This time is quite different, the sounds of a ship hovering directly over us had become familiar at this point, but now there are at least three of them nearby, swarming the area in search of the culprit that downed one of their own.

Who knows how many troops each of those ships are carrying? We would have no chance of evading one of them that's on alert let alone multiple bogeys right on top of us. We have to stay here for at least one day; hopefully they'll be gone by tomorrow evening. There are only enough meds in the cabinet for one extra night here. Regardless of what happens, we must continue the journey tomorrow.

Everyone gathers around in front of me on the floor, eager to hear what happened. The last thing they saw was their new friend getting sucked into the sky all the while screaming for his life. In a quiet voice, I tell them, "Bill is a hero. He never planned on getting captured alive by those things, he was prepared to bring them down with him. He rigged himself with explosives and you know the rest. He saved our backs out there."

Ellie stands up, walks up to me and pounds my chest with her fists, "Why didn't you save him? You could have pulled him out of there! It wasn't too late."

She starts to sniffle and cry with her face buried in my chest as her clenched fists open, she puts her arms around me and squeezes tight. I put one arm around to console her as best I can with my rifle still in my other hand. It would serve no purpose to tell her that even if I were able to pull Bill out of the ship's invisible grip, they would have immediately seen all of us and sent ground units to sweep in and round us all up for who knows what. I maintain my silence as anything I would say explaining my decision would be counter-productive.

Bill's sacrifice is the only thing that allowed the rest of us to get out of there in one piece. I have no qualms of being the bad guy to let her vent, all I say to her is, "I'm sorry." I set down my rifle and hug her tight until she doesn't need me to.

Despite billions of people dying during the initial invasion, this is the first casualty we've witnessed during the conflict and it's someone we all know, the war with the Ladrones had become real for us.

Though highly unlikely, we all want to believe that the people we loved and cared about before all of this are out there defying the odds, and still alive. However, now, we know with full certainty that Bill is dead. I have to believe that Eve is still out there, waiting for me to make it to the camp… it's the only thing keeping me going.

Eve's Audio Journal: Part 3

A couple of hours pass and the patrols are still buzzing overhead, keeping us on edge all night. If they locate the stairwell and make their way down here, we're sitting ducks with nowhere to go with our backs literally against the wall. I can't let my mind wander down that road as to what we'd have to do if that moment comes.

I can see the whites in Shawn and Lance's eyes, staring at the hallway leading to the stairs while Charlie and Brian are both looking at the ceiling and listening intently, as if to track each ships' movements by echolocation. Ellie is sitting beside me, holding my arm by the elbow and leaning her head on my shoulders. Her anger directed towards me had washed over. She merely needed a shoulder to cry on.

There isn't much we can do but wait those things out and hope they don't find us. I reach into my pocket to grab the tablet and unwind the earphones to play the rest of Eve's messages, I can't believe there are only four more left. I must have missed a few chips somewhere back at the hospital.

================================

December 13, 2034 – Time 1730hrs
-Begin Message-

Hey you… I know it's been awhile, work has been awfully busy. Though, I will say, people have been a lot nicer to me recently once they learned about us and our situation. They understand what we're going through, even that jerk Dan who I told you about before has been less abrasive. Even though the reality shows showing all of the famous people having CN are absurd, at least it's bringing some awareness to people who aren't having their lives turned upside down by this disease.

I can't believe it's almost been two years now since we held each other and the conversation wasn't one sided… Money is still tight, I was able to sell Mom and Dad's house to keep us afloat for now, but that disqualified me from those hardship grants I was telling you about. Michael, I'm scared. I hope things are going better for you in there than it is for me, I miss you.

-End Message-

November 28, 2035 – Time 0607hrs
-Begin Message-

Hey. I don't know how else to tell you this and I don't even know if you can hear me in there… but here goes. There's a reason I haven't been visiting you all that often lately and I have to get it off of my chest. I've been seeing someone, it doesn't matter who, but I just can't do this alone anymore Michael.

You've been in here for over two and a half years with no end in sight, and both my parents are gone... I couldn't do it by myself anymore; it got to a point where I didn't think you were ever coming back... I'm too weak... I'm so sorry.

We met and were together since we were so young, but we never had the chance to meet other people, grow as different people, or know exactly what we want in a partner, we only knew each other. Michael... you're such a great guy, whenever you wake up, I know you'll meet someone great and you'll both love each other, share fun memories, and I'm sure that she'll even help you learn more about yourself.

I don't even know if I should have recorded this, I had to tell you, even if you can't hear me. I'm sorry Michael, maybe in another lifetime this could have worked out.

-End Message-

I try my best to hide from the group that I'm crying my eyes out which shouldn't be too difficult being that only one chem stick, weaker than a night light is illuminating the entire room. Ellie is the only one who might catch me in the act, she is still on my arm and I don't want to get her attention, I try my best not to sniffle or wipe my eyes... I cry in silence as my tears stream out in a continuous flow onto my shirt as every interaction I ever had with Eve flashes in my head, the good, and the bad.

I can no longer contain it, two consecutive sniffles to prevent the mucus from streaming from my nose and I can barely control my breathing, the secret is out.

Ellie looks up at me; she can see the tears on my face reflecting that soft green light. At this point she can probably feel the damp areas on my shirt with her hands. She knows that I received some kind of bad news in the recordings. She holds my arm a little tighter and leans her head on my chest as she closes her eyes. We're both distraught, her from a friend she just met and lost, and I from the devastating words I had endured that were uttered almost five years ago.

I look down at the tablet and see that there are two remaining files. Dare I listen to the remainder after everything I've just heard? The timestamps are years apart. I have to... this can't be the way that me and Eve's story ends. I trudge on and tap the screen to hit "play."

January 19, 2037 – Time 0705hrs
-Begin Message-

So much has changed since the last time I came here and spoke to you. It might be hard for you to hear, but it's something you'll eventually need to come to terms with since it is reality. Michael, you and I are officially divorced, the paperwork was done a few days ago and it was simple since I have power of attorney.

I'm getting married in a few weeks, even though Dan doesn't know you, he loves me enough and is caring enough to foot the cost of your treatment, you won't have to worry about that. If it weren't for the situation we are in, I think you'd like him, he's a good man Michael, I guess all I can say again is that I'm sorry and there is officially no "us" anymore.

Hopefully there's a cure soon... I hate the fact that I have to leave you a message like this. Goodbye Michael, I'll always have a place for you in my heart as my first love.

-End Message-

July 27, 2040 – Time 2016hrs
-Begin Message-

Hey stranger... I don't know why, but this was the first place that came to my head to visit after all the stuff in the news that's happening. I'm scared.

There are hundreds of large objects, the size of a few football fields, hanging around Earth's orbit the last couple of days. No one knows what they are or what they want and they haven't tried to make contact with us. I have a daughter now Michael, her name is Emma. Dan is a wonderful husband and father but he has no idea on what to do in these situations or even the right things to say to keep me calm... so here I am.

I shouldn't even be telling you all this since it's not fair to you, I have this whole new life without you, and you deserve better. Hopefully this is all nothing and we can go back to our regular lives and maybe one day, whenever you're ready, you can meet my daughter. (Eve begins to sob).

I have a confession to make, another reason I'm here is to apologize to you if things don't get back to normal if those things don't leave... I feel awful for what's happened to you... and to us. If those aliens aren't here peacefully, I wanted you to know that there are no words to describe how terrible I feel for everything that's happened over the years. Maybe in another world, where none of this had happened, things would have been different, and the two versions of us would still be together.

-End Message-

Any air in my lungs is immediately forced out like a bench press crashing down on my stomach. I want to vomit but my diaphragm is only filled with emptiness.

All those years spent together, side by side, gone like it didn't matter... I try to convince myself that the only logical move now is to move on… she left me… several years ago at that.

Accepting the strong possibility that she's already dead like so many others on this planet just got easier, at least for now. My emotions wear me out until I eventually fall into a dreamless sleep.

Onward

I awaken to my eyes sealed shut, a buildup of dry skin from tears formed over my eyes and down my cheeks and around my nose. I rub them until my vision becomes clear. The sweet sound of silence greets my ears, no indication of patrols on the ground or up in the air lingering in our area, a positive start for the day after the deluge of one unfortunate event after another last night. We're not dead, I have to be thankful for that.

It would be safe to assume that they didn't find us or breach the hallway. In the process of waking up, I notice that I have a woman in my arms who isn't Eve, a completely foreign concept. Even if Eve is alive, she has her own family now. The faster I can come to terms with it the better.

My emotional health aside, the group once again needs its default leader. I was warming up to, even embracing the idea of no longer having to play the role since a natural and experienced leader had emerged less than a day ago. As quickly as Bill had appeared, he was taken from our lives almost as fast.

I hardly knew the man, none of us did. But out of the whole group, Ellie appeared to have had the closest connection with him. They spent several hours speaking, reminiscing of the times of before. He took her under his wing like a father to his lost child who left the world too soon... but for this "daughter," he would be in the driver's seat to save and protect her, not the doctors.

The man I came to know and respect is different from Ellie's version… he was a trained fighter who wanted to fight and wasn't going down without one. His sacrifice has allowed us to continue on, and for that, we are grateful.

She must have felt me stirring, Ellie is awake as well. The whites in her eyes are visible as she stares at the sliver of light peeking through the empty stairwell. The others remain fast asleep, Shawn is snoring as loud as the roar of those ships, Brian is sleeping with his mouth gaped open with some drool rolling down his chin, Charlie and Lance are both sleeping on their backs with their fingers interlaced over their stomachs.

It looks like none of them got much sleep last night or this morning, we still have a few hours until sundown, they'll need the rest for nightfall.

Ellie and I make eye contact while I'm lost in my own thoughts. She starts stroking my forearm with a finger and asks, "Is everything OK? I saw your earphones in and guessed that you were listening to those recordings again? It's OK to be sad you know?"

"I don't really want to talk about it. Those things I heard on there are from years ago and are inconsequential to what we're trying to do here now. Thinking or talking about it doesn't help our current situation. How about you?

How are you doing? I didn't realize that you and Bill had gotten so close in that short amount of time."

"Yeah, I think I'm fine now... I'm sorry for the way I acted last night, there's nothing you could have done. I guess I've been lucky all my life, up until all this has happened, no one in my life had passed away. I know it's silly to still think that now, since the chances of the ones we knew and loved before all this are still alive."

"You know Ellie... I'm starting to come around to thinking that now myself, the six of us have to stick together if we're going to get through this. There's no guarantee that anyone else is out there but us, even if we make it to the encampment."

"Oh God... I'm so sorry, I didn't mean that about your... I mean... there's a chance she's still out there, that's why we need to keep on trucking to get to her, she's probably waiting for you at the sanctuary!"

"You better knock it off with your verbal jiu-jitsu teacher skills! No, it's OK, I have to accept that she's more than likely gone. All we can do right here and now is work together and survive."

Ellie got me to open up about Eve, but I keep my guard up, I didn't want to tell her that my wife had left me years before any of this had happened. Why? I don't know. Is it because I didn't want the group to think I was emotionally compromised? Is it embarrassment? Or is it because I like this girl and my brain is all flustered? While these thoughts are running through my head, the sound of silence ceases and is now joined by the sounds of shuffling as the others wake up.

Ellie immediately let's go of my arm and shoves off and slides away from under my elbow. Apparently she doesn't want the rest of the guys to know that we were snuggled up together for the duration of the night and the morning hours in emotionally fragile states? Probably for the best.

I need to clear my head of everything that I had heard in those recordings or at least try. There's no room for distractions if we want to maximize our chances of getting to the next site unscathed... easier said than done. The only love that I had ever known left me for another man. This kind of despair is poison and is counterproductive to the task at hand, I have to bottle it up for later.

We gather our things, make our injections, and prepare to leave. It's a little eerie this go around as we all line up in the stairwell, awaiting to make our exodus... it's deja vu but not quite. All is quiet; everyone knows we're down a man from the last time we were here in this exact same position. We're down an experienced gun and for Ellie, a friend she was getting to know.

Charlie makes note that a patrol made a flyby around here about fifteen minutes earlier, now is better than anytime to leave our position and make our way to the hospital. Not only is the next location further, it's a larger facility where it might take a little longer to find shelter and the medication. After the unexpected delay, we're a full day behind. The odds of other CN survivors still holed out at the hospital are that much slimmer than they were yesterday.

Using one hand to push the door up and the other to point the rifle out into the unknown, I make my way up. This time I don't wait for everyone to exit to hold up the rear, as soon as I see that Brian has hold of the door behind me, I make my way out into the darkness.

We make our way through the street without much distance in between each person with me at the front. A chill comes down my neck as we pass by the intersection where Bill was ripped into the sky.

No one else but Lance and I know that this is the exact location where Bill stopped to wait for us to catch up to him. Lance and I make eye contact for a split second and quickly turn away as to not share the experience of reliving the horrible memory. It was all just terrible timing, there's no way Bill could have known that there was an enemy ship docked on the other side of this mound.

I pick up the pace and the rest of the group still on my hip as we pass the area to minimize the amount of time spent there in the event we happen to catch more bad luck.

We're about halfway through our march to the hospital with no encounters or sightings of any patrols. It's still too early to relax, but might as well count our blessings compared to the start of our last maneuver. The group looks exhausted from our brisk pace. I spot a location of what used to be a diner and is now barely recognizable. I used to eat there every few weeks while I was in school.

I sprint up ahead to a pickup truck to cover our approach. After scanning the surroundings, I wave everyone on; they all sprint in a line towards the entrance. We didn't even have to open the door, the glass entrance is completely smashed... even the bottom is completely shattered.

The charcoaled bell hanging over the door rattles off a dull clank as each of us walks through. Our bags or a piece of our clothing catches the frame enough for the doorframe to move. After carefully navigating through the fragmented glass, we all situate ourselves behind the counter. I make my way in, trailing the rest of the group.

Once in, we stop for a small break to catch our breath and drink some water.

"Alright, take five everyone. We'll go the rest of the way after this little break."

The concrete pebbles on the ground and the bell over the entrance clanks on its own. An air patrol is nearby, this time is different though. We all hug the counter a little tighter but our eyes still peering over to see the cause of the commotion.

There are no large lights illuminating the sky. Judging from the sound of it, this patrol is also flying at least twice as fast as the other ships we have seen or encountered thus far.

The ship pulls into our view streaking across the sky about a half a mile in front of us going right to left… there's a second one trailing not too far behind with dim lights pointed horizontally at the lead ship and oddly not down to the ground.

Instead of ducking for cover, we stick our heads up higher over the counter for a better view of the spectacle outside. The sky becomes illuminated only for a quarter second accompanied by a thunderous boom, quickly followed by a smaller explosion coming from the lead ship.

It's not the same type of searchlight that we've seen before. The trailing ship is in pursuit and firing at the ship in front of it. We all duck our heads low but our eyes are still drawn to the action outside, trying to catch a glimpse of what is happening before our very eyes. The ship in front has a small fire on its hull but is still traveling at high speed and the one in the rear is quickly closing the distance.

Dark purple laser beams fire twice from the rear ship, creating two additional loud booms during each strike, causing two smaller explosions from the lead ship creating smoke and debris in its wake. The lead ship has taken more damage than it can handle, it begins its descent with a trail of fire and smoke behind it, plummeting into what's left of three tall buildings in the remnants of the city skyline. The pursuing ship peels off and out of our view.

"Holy crap! Did you guys see that!? You think one of those things is on our side?" Asks Brian.

No one else says a word as all of our jaws are still hanging from what we had witnessed. None of those ships are in our arsenal, at least not since I was in the service.

Are there multiple factions of the alien race fighting for control for our planet or using it as a battlefield? Are they here to rescue us or are they vying to assert dominance into who is going to control the surviving members of the population? Is there a liberation force looking out for our planet? Questions we will not have answered tonight, possibly ever.

Either way, we need to get a move on it, we have no idea if there are going to be multiple ships and ground forces inbound to search the wreckage of the downed ship and we're in the middle of nowhere, still a few clicks from our medicine. I whisper, "Ready up, we're ghosts in thirty seconds, we don't want to be anywhere near here by the time they go checking on their pal that crashed. And we especially don't want to be caught in the middle of their scuffle."

We continue on and hug the buildings as close as possible in the event we need immediate cover... only five more blocks to go now. All of the buildings that have been leveled and destroyed look different from what I remember of the city, but I'm able to pinpoint exactly where we are because of the street layout at this five-way intersection.

The building we're heading towards used to be a large museum before I went under. A bunch of people must have gotten diagnosed for the museum to be converted into a major intake site for CN.

We have a couple of hours until sunrise with only a few more blocks to go. If memory serves me correctly, the museum has the entire lower level dedicated to telling the story of the great fire where part of the city was left abandoned underground. The medical storage should be down there if they followed the same model of other hospitals housing Cerebral Nervorum patients.

Hopefully it's still intact, there's barely any ceiling or flooring in between the ground and lower levels from what I recall. If the building is wiped off the map, we'd have to continue traveling by day to the next location. Daylight is the enemy to our survival; the Ladrones can spot us from a mile away in the sunlight.

This is it. The museum is up ahead, we stay hidden in an alley about a hundred yards away. The problem with this location is the parking lot is completely empty and massive, there's a ton of open terrain between our position and the building.

"Alright, we can stop for a short breather here. See that large building out in the middle over there by the water? That's where we need to get to, there is nothing between here and there to seek shelter, when we go, we need to go without stopping. Let's scope it out for a minute."

The area is eerily serene, no signs of the enemy. Strangely enough, the building is exactly how I remember it, a museum standing all alone near the epicenter of downtown, once hidden by towering buildings until you got close enough. Standing at three stories with a glass dome in the center of the roof, the building itself looks untouched from the invasion, at least from a distance.

"Ready?" Everyone nods.

I lead the way and slowly make the first few steps out of the alley, looking down the road both ways in case we missed something. All clear. If we do this right, we shouldn't be out in the open for more than twenty seconds.

We all start running, shoulder to shoulder as we make the mad dash to the museum. We are making quite the racket with our boots slamming into the dilapidated concrete road with bits of loose gravel all along the way. Despite the dead sprint we're doing, I can't hear anyone gasping for air as if we are all collectively holding our breath for this final push to our next destination. Fifty more yards to go…

A growing unsettling feeling in my body makes its presence known as the hair on my arms, neck, and even the fuzz on my ears all stand straight up during the sprint. The sound we've grown to fear and dread rears its ugly head and the ground begins to rattle… so much so that myself, Brian, and Ellie briefly lose our balance and stumble but continue to move.

I put on the brakes and wave everyone down to seek refuge behind the other side of a three foot high wall of rubble about fifteen yards in front of the entrance. I surmise that it used to be a part of the staircase leading up to the building. We all dive and take cover, we're so close!

As I look back towards the slowest member of our group, Shawn is still a step or two behind before he makes his dive over the wall as the ship flies across the sky, intersecting our former position in the alley. We are all together at the mound outside the entrance and lay as flat to the ground as possible.

I lift my head to look at the ship. The lights come on and shines down in the alley. Were we spotted by an enemy ground unit? The ship is hovering over what looks exactly to be our old position not more than a minute ago.

The ship spots something, a high pitch winding noise emanates from the ship and a bright purple laser beam shoots down to the ground followed by a large explosion near the alley. The awesome power of their weaponry is demonstrated as large chunks of boulders explode from the ground and come crashing down after a couple of seconds in the air. Whatever was there isn't shooting back and is probably vaporized. It's time to take advantage of the situation and not let this opportunity slip away.

I get up into a crouched position, still using the wall as cover, I point my rifle down range and motion the group to enter the clinic with my right hand, still keeping my rifle pointed towards the ship, I feel them frantically running by, using my shoulders for balance as they graze past me. I turn around make a quick look at Charlie as he leads the group in trying to locate a door that isn't locked. Unlike our previous waypoints, the roof and the walls of this building are all completely intact and we actually have to locate a proper entrance.

The alley we were scouting the clinic from is surrounded by the skeletons of a few tall buildings, you can see right through to the other side. This is the diametric opposite of the condition of the museum. It would appear that the Ladrones concentrated their bombing campaign on the buildings that are clustered together, making for easy targets.

The clinic is completely untouched by any fighting or bombing with the exception of the area around it. Any damage caused to the smaller isolated buildings are more than likely a result of their ground units fighting whatever resistance we had left after the bombings.

Lance uses the butt of his pistol to break the glass of one of the doors to gain entry. He scrapes the barrel along the frame of the door to knock down any loose fragments of glass remaining on the door before we can walk through.

I follow the group into the clinic, even the glass doors are all still in one piece with the exception of the one that Lance smashed. If our prayers are answered, the medication is also safe.

We search the first floor for a ramp, stairwell, or an elevator, no luck so far... Charlie starts to throw up and I can hear Ellie crying above us, she must have found a set of stairs.

They found the areas where hospital staff was housing patients on the first and second floors... and so did the Ladrones.

On the first floor, near where Charlie stands on the northern side of the building are piles of decomposing corpses of about ten people in hospital gowns, discarded like trash. The putrid smell of decomposing flesh finally reaches my nose. I pull my t-shirt over my nostrils in an attempt to mask the smell, it doesn't work.

Ellie is upstairs on the second floor concourse, with her hands over her face, whimpering. I run up the stairs and slow down when I near the last few steps. The scene on the second floor area is considerably more disturbing. There are three patients, still in their hospital beds with some sort of black plastic looking tubing going into and out of several of their orifices.

I grab and hug Ellie and turn her away from the sight. These people are clearly dead now and possibly being experimented on. These tubes are connected to all sorts of foreign devices that look to be powered on. There does not appear to be any knobs, buttons, or any type of interface on the black, rubbery cylinder for each patient where all the tubes are feeding into.

There are only a handful of small random yellowish orange lights, blinking at random times on the device. For these poor soul's sake, I hope that they had expired before they felt any pain or suffering from whatever was being done to them.

To take their minds off of what they are seeing, I start barking orders to the group to search downstairs, hoping for a better result in the lower levels. "Shawn, look for the medical storage area on the first floor, everyone else, move downstairs and do the same. I'll check the second floor. We can't relax until we've found those needles."

I figure Shawn, in his former line of work, has more stomach than most to see these kinds of things. And I, I have already seen the worst here. There's no reason to subject anyone else to seeing what they are doing to us if they capture us alive.

Unlike the other clinics, the entire building appears to have only serviced CN patients according to a note on the map. There is no central location to look for our meds which makes the task much more difficult. No luck on the second floor and I hear lots of cabinets opening below me, but no announcements of success.

Shawn and I make our way down to the basement level after sweeping the upper floors for the syrettes to no avail, we rejoin the others.

During my walk down the stairs, it hits me, but I keep my thoughts to myself. There are no signs of damage to the entrance, the elevators, or the stairs. Yet, all of this alien technology is inside.

This can only mean one of three things, when these Ladrones leave their mech suits, they are of similar size of humans or smaller to be able to enter and exit the facility... scary scenario number two... there are human collaborators who are aiding in the extinction of our race OR an even more frightening thought, the sergeant mentioned on the video tablet that these things have the ability to look like us. Are they watching us now? Who in the group can I trust... if any of them at this point, if what the sergeant said was true?

I try my best to act natural amongst the group as paranoia has asserted its grip on my thoughts. It doesn't appear that anyone else in the group thought much about the implications of our current situation. I don't know who I can trust, or if one or all of them are Ladrones themselves. Are they studying us to see how we would react to this kind of stress? I keep this revelation to myself until I'm absolutely sure of who is and isn't human.

As Shawn and I finally reach the lower level, we see everyone gathered around a clear cabinet, the light is on, so that at least means we have power down here. But they don't look all too excited, in fact, they look a little shaken. It also looks like none of the patients were housed down here either, a few hospital beds down here but no bodies. They must have all been moved upstairs.

As I get closer to the cabinet, I see the predicament. There are only five syrettes left… there are six of us. This presents quite the quandary. Basic math tells us someone is not going to be getting their shot for tonight. The air in the room is wrapped in tension, no one is making a dash for the medication, but at the same time, we're all probably thinking about it.

Lance finally breaks the silence in the room, "So… How are we going to do this?"

All is Fair

We ponder Lance's question to ourselves for a moment. None of us has a medical background, there's no way to know if we are able to evenly distribute the pouches of nanomites by six instead of five and if that would even work. There's also no fair way to assess who in the group deserves it and who doesn't. Either way a decision needs to be made before we descend into anarchy, three of us have guns and three of us don't.

The only thing that comes to mind to make this as fair as possible is drawing straws. Lance is already on top of it. He reaches into one of the medical cabinets, grabs six wooden tongue depressors, breaks the tip off one, shuffles them in his hands behind his back, and holds them in one hand so that they all appear equal in length. "Alright, simple old school way to do this, person that draws the short stick doesn't get the med. Everyone, touch a stick and keep your fingers on it, I'll keep the one that no one is touching." He says.

We all look around at each other before we slowly move in unison to huddle around Lance and prepare to pick one. Brian reaches in first and has a hold of one. Ellie goes, followed by Charlie, then Shawn. Two sticks left, one will be mine and the other will be Lance's.

I announce to the group, "Look, no matter what happens, the person that draws the short stick will have to head to the next location... like, right now. Whoever it is, can't stick around and should get on the road ASAP, CN hits hard and fast, we all know this, and we can't have any dead weight that could jeopardize the whole group."

Everyone nods in agreement, hoping to themselves that they aren't the one. The mood is wrought with stress. Everyone looks nervous, taking small breaths with a large exhale, praying to whatever God or Gods in their heads to not be the odd man out.

"OK, now everyone pull." Lance says.

We all pull our sticks away from his hand and hold it out in front of us. Mine is whole, so is Lance's, I look over to Ellie... She has a look of terror in her face as the bottom tip of her stick is broken off. I begin to imagine her traversing the terrain and coming into contact with one of those things, she wouldn't last a minute out there by herself, let alone in the daylight. Her eyes begin to flood with tears as she knows that her fate is essentially sealed.

I don't know why I did what I did. Is it sympathy? A crush? Or perhaps a death wish after learning Eve had left me? I can only make a few guesses, I will never know for certain why. Maybe it's because Ellie reminds me of Eve and my subconscious is attempting to be her knight in shining armor, or simply my own sense of self-preservation.

If any of these people are not who they claim to be, going it alone from here on out is the best course of action. There's also the whole issue of the bodies upstairs… who knows if and when the Ladrones will return to check on their experiments. There isn't a real choice, I snatch the broken piece of wood from her hand and replace it with mine.

In shock, she immediately stops crying and gasps, "But Michael, you can't, they need you… I need to go, it's only fair."

"You guys have been doing great. Keep doing what we've been doing to get to the last waypoint and you'll be fine. Keep your head low and always be close to cover in case you need it, maintain noise and light discipline, and take your time if there's any question about trouble being nearby. I'll meet up with you all there and we'll head to the sanctuary together. Remember, those things could return to check on their experiments upstairs at any time, rotate shifts for guard duty, and pick a spot down here where you can sneak out if you need to."

Ellie knocks the stick from my hand and pulls me in for a kiss, one hand on my cheek and the other on the back of my neck. My eyes are wide open as she kisses me. This feels strange with everyone watching and considering that Eve is the only one I had ever kissed in my life. She stops and apologizes, "Sorry… thank you Michael." She ends the kiss with a hug and her face resting on my chest as she lets out a little sniffle.

It all felt so wrong, but I play back the message in my head where Eve told me that we were no more and that she is now married to another man, a man who she has a child with... She left me, end of story. There is next to no chance of anyone waiting for me at the human encampment. I let my emotions come over me as well. As she pulls away, I close my eyes, pull her back into me and resume kissing, I don't care that the others are watching, this could be it for me.

She steps back and mouths the words, "Thank you," as she starts to cry again.

"Don't worry about me, I'll see you in less than a day, try to keep up."

I smile at her, stroke her cheek to wipe a tear. I walk away and make sure I have everything I need and rest my feet for a minute before I continue the journey. There isn't much time to waste. I use what little time I have wisely to drink some water and eat an MRE for the trip. I choke down the food and water quick to utilize the hour or two of darkness that remain.

Heading upstairs, the sun hasn't risen yet, but the sky is starting to appear and the moon and the stars are slowly fading away. Everything above ground, even with little daylight there is, looks different. The fire bombing campaign has really done a number to the city. The streets and skeletons of buildings are all where they should be, but there's no sign of vegetation, or life for that matter. My city has transformed into a wasteland in a matter of a couple of weeks, no longer filled with the urban greenery in the midst of towering glass structures that makes it unique from the rest of the country.

I begin my journey, guided by the light of dawn. Although I'm no longer shrouded by the cover of darkness, I can see the Ladrones as clearly as they can see me. It means I have to plan my routes a little more carefully, a little more conservative in my approach, and limiting the amount of time spent in the open.

I kneel down by the entrance behind the mounds of debris to scan the open area. Like last night, there is quite a bit of distance between this building and the nearest place of shelter I can hide in. With more light from the sky, it even looks a little further than before.

I look to my left, to my right, and scan the skies… all clear. Ready to pump my legs and sprint… I hear some footsteps approaching behind me from inside the clinic. Whoever it is, they're light on their feet. I turn around when their shoes crunch on the fragmented glass on the ground; Ellie emerges from the shattered door.

"What are you doing here? Get back inside, the sun is about to come out and light us up like a Christmas tree!"

She replies, "I'm not letting you leave without me, you can't stop me." Ellie smiles at me for a millisecond and breaks eye contact and stares out towards our next destination, the buildings in the distance to shield us from the watchful eyes from above.

I can't say I'm not touched by her gesture and that she cares about me enough to assume the risk of traveling by day. I wish I could say I am reluctant to have her tag along, but her presence is very much welcomed.

She obviously likes me, and maybe I like her too... I guess I never saw her that way until hearing Eve's last few messages. Our best chance of survival relies on me directly communicating what I need from her and her compliance. "Fine! You have to do exactly as I say and when I say it... stay on my hip, got it?"

Ellie nods.

We're so close to our new "home," just this leg and the next to go and we'll be there. But it hits me... we're racing for our lives only to be put back to sleep so that we can "live." I doubt finding a cure to CN is anywhere close to the top priority for the survival of our species, let alone there being anyone with the ability to come up with a cure that is left amongst the last of us.

This dangerous operation to travel by day doesn't seem so much like a bad idea anymore when the ultimate goal is really to go back to sleep indefinitely once more. I need to clear my head of these thoughts that may cause me to take unnecessary risks and endanger both our lives, not just mine.

The possibility of Ellie being one of the Ladrones comes to mind, but the alternative of being surrounded by four possible Ladrones calms my paranoia, I just have to remember to keep my guard up.

I scan the area once more as the skies show hints of sunlight still under the horizon, but its rays lighting up the clouds above. All clear, I hold up a "3" with my fingers, a "2," and finally a "1" before making a chopping motion forward to signal Ellie to run. I spring up and start pumping my arms and legs to get to the office buildings across the way as fast as possible.

I make a quick glance behind me and Ellie is keeping up her end of the bargain, she isn't more than a step and a half behind me... impressive.

No signs of trouble... yet. We make it about ten yards shy of an alleyway between two barren buildings and slow down to a jog. Concealed from the sky, we have a moment to reclaim our breaths.

Traveling by day isn't as perilous as I had anticipated despite the sun breaking the horizon. We're engulfed in the shadows of the graveyard of what I remember were once behemoth buildings.

Back when I was in college and living outside the city, it used to be so crowded and busy, I would rarely venture out here. Walking through downtown always made me feel like I was being swallowed whole by the towering skyscrapers, the only way to see the sky was to look straight up. I definitely wasn't a city boy.

Though some of these lofty buildings haven't completely collapsed and still stand close to its original height, the feeling of being claustrophobic is non-existent while walking down the street. The majority of the floors, ceilings, and interior walls on each level of each structure are mostly gone. I can still see parts of the sky right through the middle of most of these high-rises.

What puts my mind at ease for our two-person excursion in the daylight is the buildings that aren't standing are still about three or four stories tall of rubble and debris, still high enough to conceal our movements. Any patrols by air would have a hard time spotting us, even if we remained in the middle of the street. Contrarily, we would be able see exactly where they are.

During the day, there are no craters to look out for, no beams or rebar that we might accidentally run into. Our only concern is an encounter with ground units lurking about, they're loud when they're on the move… we would at least have some kind of advanced warning. These tight corners between each intersection can be used to our advantage as long as we make deliberate movements before any blind turns or street crossings.

The lack of enemy sightings or movements makes us a little too comfortable, especially Ellie; her questions become more prying and more personal in nature. My guard is immediately raised despite the newly unearthed, but gradual, growing fondness for one another.

"I know we've only known each other for a few days, so you don't have to answer if you don't want to. But… what did you hear on those tapes from your wife the other day?"

I continue walking and scanning the area with my rifle up, keeping my body busy while I ponder how to answer her question. I know the answer, but I'm debating with myself as to whether I should tell her.

I continue walking. I muster up a reply, "You ever have someone tell you something so Earth shattering, that it pretty much changes your whole belief system and what you know to be true and set in stone cold fact reality? That's essentially what I heard that night."

"Care to elaborate?"

Before I could answer, the sound of a ship is nearing our location. There is no extra warning from vibrations in the ground, the ship is maintaining high altitude to stay above the skeletal buildings. It's impossible to pinpoint which direction the patrol is coming from.

The obscured view and acoustics of the concrete jungle is making it more difficult than I thought it would be. I don't know where it's coming from. What I do know is that we need to get off the street. There's a partially collapsed mall on the other side of the road, the first couple of levels look intact. I grab Ellie's hand and pull her into a near sprint to get inside.

We make it through the entrance and take refuge at one of the checkout counters. The ship's engine booms somewhere overhead in our vicinity. There's no way they spotted us, we were quick and they couldn't have gotten line of sight on us with all of the buildings concealing our escape. Ellie looks up at the ceiling with a frightened stare and heavy breathing.

To calm her down I start to whisper to her what I heard that night on the audio tape. "Eve… my wife, well, I guess ex-wife now…"

She freezes; her eyes come down from the ceiling and are now focused at mine. She puts her hand on my shoulder, and listens intently, completely forgetting about the ship outside.

"… We met when we were young, back in elementary school. She was the only one that I had ever loved and cared about. The thought of having someone care about me the way she did is a foreign concept that is impossible to fathom. The messages she left for me kept me up to date with things that were happening in her life and her daily struggles.

Eventually, it led up to her meeting someone else and that someone else apparently having a kind enough heart to keep me alive in the hospital while they started a family of their own. Eve divorced me and married him…."

"I'm so sorry Michael…" She closes in for a hug and I welcome her embrace. The sound of the ship grows distant but we hear the sound of concrete breaking with each step, their ground forces are marching nearby. We don't let go of each other as to not make a sound or any sudden movements that could disturb the ground and debris beneath us. We look each other in the eyes as we both hear them stomping around outside of the entrance we came in, there's at least two of them, maybe three.

I use my right hand to put my pointer finger over my lips and slowly let go of her as she does the same. I turn around to peek around the corner of the counter to see what we're dealing with, trying not to make a sound.

I can only see their lower torsos and the weapons on their arms. They appear too tall to enter the structure which is a welcomed relief. But that doesn't mean they won't burst through the walls if they spot or hear something inside. We remain still and quiet as possible, I feel a bead of sweat roll down from the back of my neck all the way down to my hip. One mech is posted outside the entrance and the others continue marching down the street, making their presence known with each crushing step.

"We'll try to wait this one out, if it doesn't move in the next ten minutes, we'll make our way through the mall until we get to a part of the street that's clear. Most of these buildings on this block should be connected." I whisper.

Ellie nods.

Crouched behind the counter, we wait… I look at my watch and realize that twenty minutes have passed, the mech unit outside hasn't moved an inch.

I tap Ellie on the shoulder and nod my head to move inward into the store and towards the center of the mall. We stay low and move deliberately as to not disturb any loose debris. We are now fifty yards away from the exterior entrance where the mech was last seen, out of view but no sounds indicating that it has moved. If we turn left and head to the next department store, it should spit us out on the other side of the street corner, out of view from the mech's side of the street, even if it were to turn around.

The mall is eerily quiet. Ellie and I match the silence as we navigate ourselves through the concourse. Staying low, we approach what looks like a wishing fountain outside of the entrance to the next store. It used to be covered in tile, all that remains are a few pieces that haven't chipped off covering the naked concrete.

I look inside and see all of the shiny coins, the sunlight shimmers into the water creating a reflection of the blue sky outside through a gaping hole in the roof. Seeing the coins in the fountain becomes a bizarre experience.

It reminds me of how money was the obstacle that prevented me from being able to be with Eve and to go about our regular lives after being diagnosed. Going even further back, if my parents could have afforded their own care, I could have graduated with Eve and not be forced to join the Initiative.

Now… all of those shiny metal objects, paper printed with dead presidents, lines of code in a computer program telling everyone how much they are worth had become irrelevant in this world. The only thing that matters now is food, clean water, weapons, and shelter from those things outside. Safety is now the definitive currency that everyone would trade anything for… without it, everything else becomes a moot afterthought.

There's still water in the fountain. The water is calm in this chaotic world full of death and carnage that surrounds us. I hold my rifle by the barrel with one hand and reach in with the other to splash my face and rub my eyes, I need to stay awake.

The water starts to violently ripple and becomes chaotic like its surroundings, however, quickly calms itself within mere seconds. Ellie does the same, except she also soaks her face as well as her hair and rings it out as best she can. She catches me staring and smiles. She flicks her finger at the water and playfully splashes me.

We've been walking for over ten hours straight since last night. There is still a ways to go to get to the trauma center. The near encounter with the mechs outside didn't exactly expedite our journey.

We continue on to the next store, the front end of the interior entrance used to be the shoe section. The tiny plastic shelves on the wall displaying the footwear are partially melted and litter the walls near the entrance.

It's a little darker on this side of the store, but we see some daylight piercing through from the back of the shop towards the street. The fitting room walls in the center of the store are obscuring our direct view of the light and consequently the doors that will lead us to freedom from the immediate threat behind us.

Still no signs of the enemy from inside the mall, but we can't take any chances. We approach the source of light and get down low at one of the cashier stations, "Ellie, stay here, let me check it out first, stay quiet, and watch my back."

"Gotcha."

Three pairs of glass doors are standing between us and the outside.

I approach the doors that are all still intact and gently push one open as it grinds on the uneven sidewalk outside. I try to move slower; it only prolongs the assault to the senses, but it keeps the decibel level to a minimum. Once I get it open wide enough for me to squeeze through with my rifle, I set my backpack on the ground on the inside until I can pull the door open a little further, so it won't get caught in the door.

Some hydraulic steps reverberate around me, I can't pin point its location so I dive towards the line of cars parallel parked on the street and lay flat on the ground... it's a mech! The noise is coming from the intersection to my left, moving closer and closer until it finally stops in the middle of the street.

The mech is facing the building on the other side of the street, more than likely trying to locate the source of the noise of glass grinding against the pavement. With the car between me and the mech, I look inside the store and I don't see Ellie near the checkout counter where I told her to stay put until my return. I wait a few minutes for the mech to move only to hear it rotating its turret back and forth scanning the area.

Turning my attention from the building back to the mech, I look inside the car and devise a plan to crawl into the backseat and curl up into a ball in the event another mech makes its way here, I'm a sitting duck.

Impatient, I place my backpack beside the car, have another look at the mech, it's still motionless, facing the building across the street. I crouch back up with my rifle and make my way back, quietly through the glass doors that are still propped open.

Bad thoughts start entering my head upon re-entry into the store when I confirm that Ellie isn't by the counter. She is nowhere to be found, I whisper her name twice, no response. A few seconds later, she emerges from the interior entrance of the store staying lower than all of the product displays, panting and crawling her way to me.

"You're okay… I told you to sit tight, what happened!?"

"Trust me…"

"What!?"

"That thing is going to be running down the other way through the street in a few minutes. We'll have a clear shot to get back on track... in theory…"

"How do you know this? What did you do?"

"A little thinking outside the box, trust me... watch them go."

A few minutes later, the mech makes a mad dash down the street from where we came, two loud crashes of walls being knocked down and crumbling, follow in its wake. The mech's primary weapons are heard firing off with the sound of debris and concrete getting penetrated or ricocheted from their rounds not far behind us.

"Okay, let's go." She says.

Confused, I follow her lead. We run to the door, I look to my left and my right down the street, all clear. I pull the door open further to give her enough room to comfortably get through with her pack. We're back on the road with no enemies in sight.

After getting a comfortable distance away from the mechs after a few minutes of light jogging, my curiosity and paranoia gets the best of me and I can't accept good fortune without an explanation. I inquire again, "How did you do that?"

I must have spoken with an interrogative tone as she gives me a funny look, like I've accused her of something rather than congratulating her for coming up with an escape plan. I really wanted to know why, it was my intent in the question, but I didn't think I was showing my cards... or Ellie is just that perceptive.

"Did you notice the electronics store by the water fountain?"

"No, and I don't see where you're going with this."

She gives me a grin before she continues, "I grabbed one of those portable solar radios in the store. It was dark in there so I knew it probably hasn't had any juice for a while. I jammed some paper in the trigger that activates the transmission and left it near the water fountain, out of reach of the sunlight. It was only a matter of time until it activated on its own while we were away."

"How did you know that would work?"

"I didn't... we didn't exactly have a lot of options, but I did remember they told us not to use radios to communicate since those things could track us. I saw you pinned at the car, so I had to do something quick."

I am amazed of her bravery and quick thinking. I remind myself that the feelings of attraction I'm experiencing towards Ellie aren't immoral and that I don't have any obligation to anyone anymore. I pull her in for a kiss.

The untested stunt she pulled quite possibly could have saved our lives back there. She's surprised at first but reciprocates and puts her hands around the back of my neck. The kiss that started as initial shock ends with a satisfied smile from the both of us.

We continue marching through the downtown sidewalks with no sight of patrols on the ground or the air. In plain view, in broad daylight, we see some soldiers and some people dressed in civilian clothing a block ahead of us facing away from us down the street. They look like they're in a fortified, defensive position behind a couple of cars, but we don't hear any gunfire from them nor the enemy.

An incredible sight, they are the first new survivors that we will have encountered in all of this since Bill. Ellie and I jog up to them to get there a little faster, trying to create some ruckus as to not spook them since we're approaching them from their flanks. "Pssst… Hey!" I whisper loudly.

No response.

Ellie gets ahead of me and taps a woman on the shoulder and nudges her, no response. Their backs are still turned to us. Upon the second attempt at contact as Ellie gently tugs on her shirt, the woman spins one hundred and eighty degrees as she collapses. As she falls to the ground I briefly see her eyes rolled to the back of her head and some dried blood stains on her mouth, neck, and chest.

Ellie gasps and covers her face as she lets out an audible squeal when she realizes that everyone here is dead; five soldiers, two women in scrubs, and two men wearing business attire. Whatever hit them, it caught them by surprise for them to still be frozen in a defensive position like this. Maybe it came from above?

"Go ahead and hang tight over there on the sidewalk, you don't have to look. I'm going to check them for food and ammo."

I try to spare Ellie from view of the gruesome scene; she's just a teacher, there's no way she could have ever imagined being put in this position to witness these grisly scenes of lifeless bodies here and back at the museum. As I grab some ammo from a soldier's belt to place in my backpack, I recognize the soldier's face and the chevrons on his arms... I look at one of the nurses and recognize her haunting eyes as they are still open, pupils staring back at me...

It's the nurse and the sergeant from the video back at the hospital! The delay in the medication taking effect to wake us up may very well have saved our lives. We didn't get up in time to evacuate with this group, but here we are, finally caught up to them. They probably reached this point on the first night since they didn't have to zig zag from hospital to hospital like we did. It's unfortunate that they didn't make it; they're only a night's trek away from reaching the base camp.

"Alright Ellie, let's move, there's nothing we can do for them."

We only have a few more blocks to go as we start to lose daylight, not because the sun is setting, but the skeletons of tall buildings obscuring the last couple of hours of sunlight.

We finally make it, after marching several hours into the night and day. Eve is a trooper. The entrance to the building reads, "Neighborhood Health Primary Care." Traveling by day wasn't as hairy as I thought it was going to be, I suppose it is better to be overly prepared and cautious than getting caught with your pants down against a merciless enemy that outclasses you in every category.

We have under an hour to spare to find and use the meds before our last injection wears off. There's no time to waste, we enter the building to look for the basement entrance. A giant blue and white sign hanging from the ceiling reads, "Stairs" near the center of the first floor. I pull open the brown metal door, no dice for this route. The stairwell is completely collapsed, there's no way to get through all of the rubble. It's all in large pieces and far too heavy to move and there's no way to squeeze through.

"Let's look for the elevators. We can use the shafts to shimmy our way down."

We split off searching. The ambient light outside is making the search a bit easier than previous locations.

"Over here!" She says.

I join her at the elevators near the back of the building. I set my pack down and rummage through in the hopes of finding a tool I can use to pry the doors open. A crowbar would be ideal. I dig through and there's nothing that big or heavy that could possibly be a crowbar inside.

"Ah-ha!"

The next best thing... a hammer! I flip it around to use the claw side to spread the doors open. I line the claw up with where the elevator doors meet and firmly press the claw in with both hands, there is now a half inch gap between the doors. I let go of the hammer and it remains suspended in between the doors about five feet off the ground. I put all of my fingers in between the door to pull it open from the right side.

"Ellie, get over there, jam your fingers in here like me. When I say pull, we both pull as hard as we can, got it?"

She gets her fingers into place, nods, and we both inhale...

"One... two... three... Pull!"

We pull with all our might as it slowly moves an inch at a time, the hammer crashes to the ground and both sides of the door slide open as far as possible and remain open on their own. The light from the outside isn't enough to see up or down the elevator shaft. Cracking and tossing a couple of chem lights down solves the problem, they hit the top of the elevator car about five feet below us.

Waiting until the light gets bright enough or until my eyes adjust to the dark seems to take an eternity. I should have shaken the chemicals to speed up the process, but alas, we wait for what is probably only twenty seconds in reality.

Finally bright enough, I lower our bags down the shaft on top of the elevator. "Give me your hand, I'll lower your down."

Ellie grabs my hands, smiles, and replies, "Yes mister boss-man."

I get a chuckle out of it and raise a single eyebrow as we grab each other's wrists to lower her down. She probably didn't even notice my expression. I pick up the hammer from the ground and tuck it into the side of my waistband.

Instead of climbing down, I hop down, big mistake… Not only did my impact create a loud crash and commotion, the top of the elevator car is an uneven surface, part of my foot must have landed on one of the ridges, I hear and feel my ankle pop as I land and let out an "Oww!" The acoustics of the elevator shaft echoes my yelp and the impact of my landing.

"What's wrong Michael!?"

"I think I rolled my ankle… but we have to keep going, we probably have less than a half hour left until we need our shot."

Ellie picks up the chem stick to look for a service hatch release so that we can get inside the car from the top.

"Bingo!"

She pulls the latch and a panel in the ceiling of the elevator swings down on a hinge, I lower our packs into the car. Ellie leads the way by cracking another chem stick and tossing it into the car and slowly lowers herself as far as she can before she lets go and lands inside the car.

Her display of athleticism and upper body strength is impressive and a little attractive. I follow her lead and land on my good foot and nearly fall over until I use my bad ankle to catch myself. There is some pain in my ankle, but not too much, my good foot took most of the fall.

"It looks like we have to pry this door open again, you still have that hammer?"

"I sure do… miss boss-woman." I reply as I can see a smile in the faint green light.

Prying it from the inside will be a little more difficult, we don't have as much room for leverage on the inside and we'll have to pry open the car's doors as well as the basement level doors if it's not already jammed shut. I press the hammer into the first set of doors.

"One…. Two… three… Pull!"

The doors were a little easier than the first time. Once we get it going a few inches, the door nearly opens on its own. We're a few feet below the basement level, the elevator car must have bottomed out. I wedge the claw of the hammer as high on the door as I can from down here to get an optimal fulcrum point for leverage when we have to pull.

"Ready again? One more time… on three… one… two… THREE!"

We get this one going for about a foot and the doors slide open. She raises her leg to take the step up into the basement level, I hand her our gear and roll onto the basement floor. Ellie grabs me by the hand and helps me up on my feet as I try to keep my weight off of the bad ankle.

This clinic is quite a bit smaller than the others, there are only two empty beds here and the room can't be much bigger than my childhood living room. We can't locate a light switch so we crack a few more chem sticks and toss them to each side of the room to find our way around. I begin to worry if there aren't that many beds here, there might not be enough syrettes for our group that's inbound.

"Hey hey! Look what I found! Oh good, there's a bunch left, enough for the group when they get here." Ellie opens the clear medical cabinet still with cold air rushing to her face. The light from the cabinet shines on her cheekbones and highlights a sign of relief in her flawless smile, keeping the disease at bay if not for one more night.

I limp my way over to her as she removes two syrettes from the container. She plunges one into her neck and gives me the other and I smoothly dose myself with the nanomite cocktail. The clock resets for another twenty four hours until the next one. The others should be leaving by now and arriving in several hours.

"Have a seat over there on that bed, let me wrap up your ankle, we can't have you hobbling around like that, next stop is home!"

I sit on the bed as she raids all of the cabinets and drawers for some wrap and tape. My boots come off and I remove my socks to assess the damage. It's not swelling, at least not in this lighting… hopefully it's a minor tweak and something I can shake off.

Ellie pulls up next to me on the bed with some medical wraps. She gently taps her thigh three times to get me to put my foot there, I oblige.

"Don't worry Michael, I know what I'm doing, they gave us basic first-aid training for our students, let's see if I can remember."

She scoots in closer and holds me by the calf to examine my ankle.

Ellie grabs my foot and lowers it onto the bed, she slides out from under my leg, tosses the medical wraps to the ground and crawls on top of me to kiss. She straddles me by the stomach with both of her hands on my shoulders and puts her face as close as she possibly can without touching. I can barely see anything but I can sense her face nearly up against mine.

She exhales through her nose, I feel the gentle warm air on my face. We kiss once, pause, and caress each other's cheeks. This time, there is no one around to interrupt us, I can feel my body tensing up.

My natural instinct is to push her away, but Eve should be a distant memory. My heart is still unable to grasp that concept, so I let go to fulfill my natural inclinations, whether it's purely carnal or if it's my body's attempt telling me to get over Eve.

I pull Ellie in for a second kiss, except this time, I hold her there longer; run my hand down her back as we continue kissing. She feels different, not better, not worse, but different… we lay there on the hospital bed.

She stops, rests her head on my chest and says, "Thank you for today."

Someone Familiar

I wake up to Ellie still in my arms as we cuddle underneath the Mylar blanket. I rub my eyes and notice some light originating from the elevator shaft.

In a state of panic, I look around to see if any of the others have made it yet, no signs of them… the light coming from the elevator shaft would indicate that it's morning. Ellie awakens with her body tense and a look of surprise that transforms into a smile.

She holds me tighter and kisses me on the cheek. We only went as far as kissing last night, but I get the feeling this could be the start of something great once I get past some feelings of undeserved guilt.

"Hey, they aren't here and it's morning..."

She sits up and looks around. "What do we do?"

"I don't know, I'll go check out what's going on up above."

I sit myself up on the bed and wiggle my ankle around, no pain… so far so good. I grab my rifle and sling it around my back. I set my feet to the ground and gradually put some more weight on it… feels fine now, must have been a weird landing.

"Ellie, stay here, I'll be right back."

I make my way to the elevator, but before I could make it to the door, Ellie runs up behind me, grabs me by the bicep to spin me around to kiss me. I grab her by the small of her back, we continue kissing until I let go.

She holds up two MRE pouches and says, "Hurry up! I'll have some French toast, bacon, sausage, syrup, coffee, and some fruit ready when you get back."

I give her a short but audible laugh as I climb into the elevator car. Once I get inside, I line myself up with the open flap at the ceiling of the car, squat down and jump. My hands get a firm grip on the roof of the elevator and I do a pull-up to get my head out... I'm not as strong as I used to be, there is definitely a little bit of atrophy that the shock therapy didn't quite get to.

For the next part, I'll have to get a little creative. As my legs are dangling from the elevator ceiling, I swing my feet to find the inner walls of the elevator to use it as leverage to push the rest of my body up and out of the car... success!

I didn't have to look at my watch to notice that it wasn't the morning and more than likely the early afternoon. It was incredibly bright, even for being in the center of downtown.

No sign of the guys. I do a sweep of the entire floor, no gear, no chatter, nothing. I get to a pillar about ten feet from the entrance and kneel beside it to see if I can make visual contact with anything outside... nada. I stay as still as possible for any sounds that may carry through the wind... still nothing.

Downtown had become a ghost town, once a place where you could only walk as fast as the person in front of you, shoulder to shoulder like ants in a colony, only we are fallible humans so we would constantly be bumping into people walking in the opposite direction. Now it's a ghost down, fifty thousand people used to live and work here on these five blocks alone.

We haven't seen a ton of bodies lying around the city, hopefully it's because everyone got to shelter on the outskirts of town or they all made it to the human sanctuary, a sanctuary that will gain six new members if we can find the stragglers.

I notice that the front check-in counter provides good concealment aboveground; perhaps we should relocate to this position to keep an eye out for the guys or anyone for that matter that might make their way down this street on their way to the encampment.

The survival of our species depends on numbers, numbers we can't afford to lose, even if it's one person. A cloud of guilt looms over me for abandoning my fellow patients and leaving them without someone trained to keep them out of trouble, or to get them out of it. They're about a half of a day late to this rendezvous point. I make my way back down the elevator shaft and stick my head down the roof of the car.

"Psssst… Ellie, bring our gear up here. We're going to wait up top during the day to keep a lookout. How many syrettes are left in the cabinet? We'll stay here as long as we have enough food and meds for the six of us before we absolutely have to leave."

"Um…. Let me see….. We have seven, which means we have enough for…"

I cut her off, "I know what it means… we have to leave tonight, with or without them."

I don't hear a response, only the sounds of lethargic footsteps as she brings the backpacks to the elevator. She sets her bag down and looks up as she lifts up mine. I see the look of sadness and dread in her frown as we both know that the rest of the crew probably won't be joining us if they haven't arrived by now. After I set our bags outside the elevator doors, I reach down and grab her by the wrists to pull her up.

I don't know what to say, so I reiterate my rationale for staying above ground instead of below. "This place will give us ample cover and great line of sight on the street, we'll be able to see and hear them or any other friendlies that might wander through the area. If the enemy sets up nearby, we'll know their position before they get too close to warn the others."

Ellie maintains a blank stare to the outside while I speak for the sake of speaking. I don't blame her, not only have we not made contact with anyone that we knew before the invasion, but also our new friends, Bill, and now perhaps Shawn, Brian, Lance, and Charlie may have all suffered the same fate or worse.

An hour passes and there is still no sign of them or of the enemy, not even in the skies. To break the silence, I ask Ellie, "Back in your teaching days, what games did you play with your students to have them break the ice at the start of the school year?"

Her face lights up from her previous look of despair, she replies, "I would ask the students to turn to their neighbors and tell them what their favorite memory from summer break was."

"You got them to talk about something that made them happy instead of being focused on being nervous about introducing themselves to new classmates... nice. So... What was Miss Ellie's favorite memory from her summers back in grade school?"

"So slick Michael, are we doing the 'get to know each other date' right now? Let's see, my favorite memory was this one time when my dad took me to the county fair. I was too afraid to go on one of the roller coasters until one day he told me that he paid the guy running the ride to slow it down, just for me! Of course he didn't, but it gave me enough courage to try it out. I had so much fun, he told me when we got off the ride how proud of me he was for conquering my fears and that the ride actually went faster than normal. Okay, there's mine... what's yours?"

"Wow, that is pretty awesome and specific… let me think, I doubt I'll be able to top that. Mine is kind of stupid in comparison to yours, I don't want to say it now. But here goes… I really loved fireworks growing up. My parents would always drive me to the stand outside the grocery store every year to buy some. Well, one year, they were too busy the day before the fourth and we hadn't gotten any fireworks yet, so they asked my uncle to drive me instead. Suffice it to say, he didn't take me to the one outside the grocery store… he took me to a Reservation where he bought a lot of stuff that had louder and bigger explosions. I remember being so excited."

"That's cute, so you were a little pyromaniac, are the explosions and what not what led you to join the military?"

"The reason was actually a lot more serious unfortunately. I was about to start my senior year of college, but my parents grew ill and didn't have insurance. To make sure they would get the medicine and treatment they needed, I had to drop out before I could finish and join the A.N.I. so they could hop onto my insurance plan. This of course was before all of those budget cuts. The whole irony of the situation is the Initiative wouldn't cover the expenses of CN since it was newly discovered and incredibly expensive to treat, at least that's what they told me."

"Oh… I'm sorry so about that, I didn't mean to bring that…"

"Nah, it's okay, I'm starving now, let's eat! Did you bring that French toast and bacon up here like you promised???"

"Sure did." Ellie grabs two small MRE pouches full of protein powder from my bag and wiggles them by her cheeks as she smiles.

A few hours go by and the sun is starting to set, still no sign of our friends we left at the museum. We do hear a couple of patrols, but they sound way off in the distance, nothing in the immediate vicinity.

I wonder to myself why they're not patrolling more of the interior of the downtown area. I suppose I shouldn't complain about our good fortune. But perhaps they've had to reallocate their resources to fight off another faction of their own race that we saw a couple of days ago? Or they didn't have much luck in snuffing us out of these tight spaces with their large vehicles?

"Stay here, I'm going to go downstairs to grab our meds, be ready to go in about twenty minutes."

I climb down the shaft, remembering not to land on the uneven part of the car and make my way down. I grab one for me, inject it, and grab another for Ellie. I hold it by the cap of the needle to keep it as cold as possible by the time she injects herself. I set it on the floor as I climb out of the shaft.

"Got it right here for you, nice and cool…"

No response.

I check behind the counter where we were sitting a moment ago, she's not there. Maybe a bathroom break?

I whisper, "Ellie! Where are you!?"

A quick sweep of the first floor, I come up empty, where did she go? To get a better view outside, I walk up to one of the pillars near the front entrance. There she is… standing in the middle of the street. What on Earth is she doing?

"Ellie! What are you doing!? Get back here!"

It looks like she is talking to someone on the other side of the street, I can't make out who it is, and it's getting dark out. Is it Lance? Did the guys finally make it?

I didn't seem to notice until it was too late, the intense growl of a ship's exhaust looms overhead, it doesn't sound like any of the other ships, perhaps smaller as the ground or structures around us aren't shaking.

This time I yell as loud as I can, the sound of the ship is hard enough to shout over, "Get in here, there's a ship right over us, get the hell inside! What are you doing!?"

Night turns to day, the ship's light illuminates any alleys or cover the buildings once provided over the street, the shadows that once concealed the mysterious person that Ellie is talking to immediately vanishes, I can see his face.

My stomach drops and heart stops beating for a second or two, impossible... Even though I had only known him for a day, I remember his face. It will forever be etched in my brain. I will never forget the look of sheer terror in his eyes, his body frozen while I took aim and was prepared to put him down. I saw him get sucked up into the ship with my own eyes… it exploded into smithereens… Bill!

Gray hair, beard and all, it's definitely him. He nonchalantly walks over to Ellie and they both hold each other tight as she rests her head on his shoulders during their embrace, completely ignoring the ship that is directly above them as they stand under the lights. I put my body tight to the pillar as I possibly can to hide from the ship's lights. Bill and I make eye contact through the door and he has a grimacing smirk as he stares back at me while holding Ellie.

A second later they are launched into the air towards the ship. For a fraction of a second, I could hear Ellie's screams until it is drowned out by the ship's exhaust. The light outside is so bright that it freezes me in my tracks and I can't gather the courage to see their fate for fear of being spotted. The ship hovers away as the light that once engulfed this entire block returns to complete darkness.

I fall to my knees and realize that all of my companions that I started this journey with are now dead or missing. If rumors of the sanctuary prove to be false, I am completely alone in this world. I realize that I still have Ellie's syrette in my hand and promptly return it to the medical cabinet. I can't give up hope for the others; they could still be out there, making their way here.

I decide to wait one more day in case they show up, every survivor counts as Ellie won't need hers now. I've suffered too much loss to be sad or crying, my feelings become dull like I'm just going through the motions now.

Two hours pass, the moon illuminates the sky once more, still no sign of them. Even if they show up in the next few minutes, they would already be an hour past the twenty four hour mark for taking their shots. I tell myself that I'm staying above ground all day to watch out for them and not give up hope that they are still making their way here.

If I'm being honest though, I hadn't realized how lonely it is in this world when no one is around, that loneliness would only be amplified downstairs.

Being alone and still shaken with my thoughts, my mind wanders to strange places as I grapple with the events of the last few days. How is Bill still alive? Why would Ellie go to him and stand out in the middle of the street when there was a ship right overhead? Was that in fact Bill? What did they do to him that he would take her? Does this alien lifeform have the ability to imitate us, enough to convince Ellie that it was him and compel her not to move through some form of telepathy? Why didn't he get me?

He knew I was hiding behind the pillar. These are serious questions that may go unanswered and are integral to the survival of our race if we are to evade them for the remainder of our existence.

Several hours pass, nothing comes through the street in front of me. Footsteps approach from the only blind spot of the clinic. I don't hear the sound of any voices, they're doing a superb job of maintaining noise discipline if that's them, they should be coming into view soon.

The steps get louder and louder until they get so loud that those steps don't belong to humans. An enemy ground patrol is waltzing through on the other side of these walls. Some of them must be out of their mech suits.

Not only are they walking down the streets, they are searching the buildings… I can see smaller figures walking around the mechs but I can't make out if they're human or alien. I sit there frozen on the first floor, if I stay here, they'll find me, if I shoot them, there's no telling what will happen. Bill's intel is no longer reliable, I can't trust anything he told us.

I need to slowly and quietly make my way back into the abyss that is the basement level of this structure. I leave my rucksack behind the counter to stay agile as I make deliberate movements, crouch, and sidestep my way back to the elevator shaft.

I can see the mechs hunched over in the building across the street, bashing out the walls that are obstructing their path, creating all sorts of banging and shaking as parts of buildings collapse. The next time they run into a wall and make a ruckus, I'll make my move down the elevator to mask the sound of my escape.

"Boom, crash." The mechs bulldoze another wall.

I make a move and hop down the elevator, hoping they didn't hear me, and that their own commotion concealed my retreat. Once in the elevator car, I realize the likelihood that they can or would come down here is minimal, it would be a tight fit for them to search down the shaft that is reinforced with steel beams.

However, fear and paranoia flood my thoughts... if they create enough debris to prevent my escape; this basement could be my final resting place if I get sealed off and trapped down here.

I hear them getting closer through the trembling of the ground above me. Dirt and dust sprinkle my face with each step, and it becomes quiet, quiet enough for me to hear the mechanical rotation of their torsos like a tank's turret. The whining noise of the twisting mechanical beast halts. I try my best to remain calm and silent while the dust, falling from the ceiling settles on my face.

Enough gets on me that it tickles my nose. A sneeze in my sinuses is starting to develop. I have got to hold it in; it's a matter of life and death. In a panic, I plug my nose, close my eyes, and cover my face with my forearms. I brace for the sneeze as a nervous sweat starts dripping from my forehead... a sneeze that never happens passes.

A minute later, the mechs are finally on the move again, away from my position as their steps and smashing fades away.

The shaft is still intact, there is some ambient light coming from the elevator car… I'm still alive and I'm not trapped alone in this sarcophagus of a musty basement.

Just Beyond the Horizon

I have an extra dose to spare, I should stay here for one more day if by some miracle, Shawn, Lance, Brian, and Charlie show up. If they don't by then, they would be far too gone to even function once Cerebral Nervorum takes hold of them anyway.

Out of fear from yesterday, I wait for my friends downstairs, away from any chance of getting killed or captured by those things, I am too close to reaching my new home to start being careless now.

Alone with my thoughts for hours upon hours into the night and into the morning, my mind plays tricks on me. I catch myself nearly falling asleep and being half awake when I hear Eve's voice. "Michael, I forgive you... and I still love you."

What have I done to need her forgiveness? She's the one who ended things not more than a few years into our marriage. These feelings of guilt are rooted in some form of truth in my subconscious.

I can't shake the feeling that I betrayed Eve for having feelings for and kissing Ellie. My mind and body gears up to defend my actions to Eve until I snap back to reality, the reality of sitting all alone in this basement. Ellie is gone now anyway.

To keep my mind occupied, I head back up to the surface for some natural daylight and pull out the map to plot the remainder of my route to the camp. I make sure the course I have set has plenty of places to hide along the way in the event any patrols decide to go on a hunting party. This route will take longer, but there's no need to rush and there's no one else to slow me down.

Hope for the men to reach this rendezvous point is quickly fading like the daylight. I am waiting, waiting for the sun to go down at this point so the blanket of night will cloak the remainder of my journey. I gather my things, make my injection and kiss this basement goodbye as I make my way out the elevator shaft.

The air is still as I approach the threshold of where once stood a door. Staying low, I scan both ways down the street for any of the mechs that might be nearby, zilch, not a single peep, an unsettling silence. I remain low, on one knee, sweeping the street again with my rifle, expecting something new, something to jump out, still nothing.

As I am about stand up and begin the march, a woman's loud shriek pierces the night air, originating somewhere nearby, but I can't even tell from which direction due to the acoustics of the buildings. I can't discern how high or how far away the screams are coming from... there it is again, I can make out the words!

"MICHAEL!!! MICHAEL!!! THEY'RE WATCHING YOU!"

I couldn't believe my ears, it was Ellie's voice! How in the world did she escape? Where are they keeping her? How did she find her way back here? I wanted so badly to shout back to her and have her tell me where she is, but I fear giving away my position to the Ladrones that might still be lurking about.

The enemy not knowing where I am is the only thing keeping me alive. But if they're watching me, does this mean they already know where I'm at? Is this another trick they are deploying to capture me like they did to get Ellie? Is my mind playing tricks on me again?

These questions quickly become irrelevant.

A short burst from a mech's main cannon rings out and a quick flash of light flares up on some nearby buildings. Even if that was in fact Ellie calling to me, she's gone now. The screaming had ceased. A couple of things are certain. A rescue mission would be futile going up against those things alone, besides the fact that the evidence and logic pointing to with a high level of certainty, Ellie is dead now.

Ellie came into my life and was taken away twice from me now... If the Ladrones are in fact watching me, I need to get a move on, there's no time to grieve. I'm not sure how the mechs got so close to me without the presence of any ships all day, I'm not going to stick around to find out.

I shed my rucksack and carry only a bottle of water, some chem sticks, and an MRE pouch. The rest of the way

I'll be more mobile for any run-ins with the enemy. The roads are clear and there doesn't appear to be any movement up top. All I know is that they're within earshot so I have to be careful. As long as I remain in the shadows, it should be impossible for them to track one man.

I make it about a quarter mile down the road before I can hear the large steps faintly behind me. I turn around to see the commotion, the mech units searching my old position... I'm not sure if the lack of sleep, time alone, dehydration, the disease taking over, are all causing my to lose focus, but our fight against the Ladrones is even more hopeless.

Next to the towering mechs is a smaller shadowy figure, moving in stride with the Ladrones. It's walking upright like a human, we were warned about this. I can't tell if the human is under duress, collaborating with the enemy, or if it's the enemy themselves that can look like us... None of that matters, there's nothing I can do about it now other than to be cautious around other humans I may encounter and to warn the others when I get to the sanctuary.

I remain disciplined for the first quarter mile of the journey by staying low, making each movement deliberate to navigate out of the downtown area.

As I make my way out of the city, I don't know what is coming over me, I'm not sure if it's complacency or a desire to be caught or killed growing within me since everyone that I've ever known in this life and the previous, are all gone.

I continue the march walking upright with my rifle slung over my shoulder in the middle of the street without a care in the world. The route that I charted earlier to make for a safer journey is completely disregarded, I'm taking a straight line to the sanctuary, if they catch me, I'll go down fighting. I only knew Ellie for a few days and she's been gone for less, but I already miss her.

No longer having to shoulder the responsibility of others, I don't care anymore, I want this to be over and to get to my new home.

I see an enemy ship flying behind me about a mile away. It hovers over the downtown area, probably searching for me as it shines its light down on the dilapidated city skyline. All they would have to do is look for me in the middle of the street towards the freeway to find me.

Today is my lucky day I guess, the ship banks hard left in the opposite direction of my path as I continue walking. Am I really this fearless? Or am I utterly hopeless and have come to terms with the futility of my situation? This carefree attitude is making the last leg of the journey much easier and immensely less stressful.

A few hours into the march and I'm almost there. Not a single mech patrol or any enemy ships present in the sky.

Perhaps the survivors picked this location for a reason and it's hidden from enemy detection.

There it is. A couple of hundred yards away stands a dark mountain of debris, about three stories high going as far back and wide as I can see in the dark. There is enough ambient light from the half-moon tonight that I can make out two silhouettes that are posted at the entrance as I get closer.

Two armed men in military fatigues are posted at the gate. Every step I take is a step towards the rest of my life, whatever that may look like on the other side of these walls.

I approach the two guards with my hands held high in the air and sling my weapon behind my back until they can clearly see that I am a human approaching them. They don't bother raising their weapons at me. Not really expecting any good news, I ask them as a formality, "Did my friends come through here within the last couple of days? There were four of them, four men."

Both guards' shake their heads to say no. One of the guards puts his left wrist up to his face and speaks into his cuff, "He's here."

A few seconds later, both of the guards step out of the way and point me towards the metal fence, the gate slides open at a turtle's pace.

I fall to my knees for a moment, thinking about my fellow "patients" I had lost along the way. We all shared the common experience of being put to sleep and waking up to this hellish nightmare... I failed them, Lance, Charlie, Brian, Shawn, and of course, Ellie. The woman I was growing fond of over the course of this week. Other than Eve, she is the only other woman I had ever kissed. In one horrific week in my mind, I experienced the loss of two companions that were in my life.

I'm not even sure if I even want to be in this world, a world where we are hiding only to survive annihilation, a world where the doctors will put me to sleep again, only to exist in a mere shell of my body with no one waiting for me this time around as soon as I set foot into the sanctuary. I get up off my knees and compose myself as I enter the darkened corridor that will lead to a new home to seek shelter in and new faces to learn only to forget in an eternal dreamless sleep.

Homecoming

I head through a long corridor with a metal hand railing lit by lamps on skinny poles, alternating sides every ten yards. The corridor begins to angle upward into a slight incline and my inner ear balance tells me I'm gaining elevation instead of going further underground, contrary to what the video I woke up to led me to believe.

There's a door about thirty yards away, lit by a single tube of fluorescent light over the top of the door, illuminating both the door and the ground in front of it.

I hear murmurs of several people in the distance on the other side. I can feel the pulse from my jugular, jumping out of my neck, and heart pounding at a slow thunderous drum beat. My feelings of despair turn into excitement at the sounds and prospects of several survivors. Who knows, there could be many others worldwide.

The door doesn't have a handle or a knob, but I notice a security camera next to the light and a small red light under the lens indicating that it is on and recording. I give it a wave and the electronic door slowly slides open. At least we have some semblance of technology left.

I walk through and I'm greeted by a short brunette woman with wavy hair, crossing her arms with a clipboard covering her chest. She is wearing a wired headset over one of her ears, the kind with a microphone that can bend around and hold its place. She points down to the floor.

"Michael, if you could please step on that 'X' down there, thanks... Oh, okay, I got him right here; I'll send him over when you're ready. Alright, I'll be right there... Michael, hang out here for a minute, stay on that piece of tape, the host will be with you shortly."

"How do you know my name!? Host?"

She turns away without acknowledging my question. On her way out, the woman removes a black drape from the wall, revealing a video monitor about five yards in front of me in the dark room. Ellie, Bill, and Lance are on the screen, each sitting on their own chairs next to one another smiling with a dark blue curtain in the background, Bill and Lance are wearing collared dress shirts as Ellie is wearing the same outfit she was in when I last saw her.

A voice off-camera asks a question, "What were your first impressions of meeting Michael?"

I watch in disbelief that shocks me to my core, the hairs on my arms and the back of my neck stand on end as my skin feels like it's vibrating at high frequency. My hands start to tremble, I keep them close to my sides.

The camera pans to Ellie.

"He was really nice and sweet, I can see how his wife fell for him. Michael is an all-around swell human being who would do his best to get us all to safety through the city."

The camera focuses in on Bill.

"Being a veteran myself, I feel safe knowing that he represents the generation of warriors that signed up to defend our people. Michael demonstrated skill, courage, leadership, and coolness under pressure. He believed that he was in a life and death situation and handled himself quite well."

The camera zooms in on Lance.

"They told me to antagonize him to create some conflict within the group, to drive him to lead the group. But I was afraid that if I pushed too hard, he might have caved and the whole narrative wouldn't have been driven by his character which was kind of the point for all this… he held his own. Michael is a sharp and assertive kid who did pretty well being tossed into this situation."

"Ellie, this question is directed at you, what is going through your mind right now… we just 'abducted' you from the show, what was going through your head when he volunteered to give you his last syrette and what are you thinking now as we watch him wait for you and the other survivors before he makes his way here to the survivor's camp?"

Ellie nervously looks down and smiles before she replies, "It caught me off guard really. I felt that we were getting a little closer and felt a connection when he learned his wife had left him years before all this had happened, but never did I think that he would make that kind of sacrifice for me. I honestly thought that he might simply go with me to the next clinic, but never did I think he would give up his medication and risk the disease messing with his mind and body and eventually killing him.

I know none of this is real, but the moment he did that, Michael had me believing that I was right there in that world with him, where we could die at any moment, where he cared about me, and where I started to develop real feelings for him when he made the gesture. I guess you could say that scene made this whole thing authentic for me too. Once my emotions came into play, it was pretty easy to act."

The camera pans to the host, a tall man in his thirties, short brunette hair, and wearing a business silver business suit with a pink tie. "For those of you tuning in that don't already know, Ellie is our only actress that has had absolutely zero acting experience before joining us on the show."

The monitor switches over to a live feed of a heavyset woman in her mid-forties sitting in the studio audience with the spotlight on her, the host holds a microphone up to her face. "What's going through your mind after seeing the finale of the show? You got a front row seat to all of the action here at Echo Studios and had the opportunity to witness the behind the scenes work done on set."

The woman replies, "Oh my, I just can't believe how convincing everything was. It was such a touching moment when Michael gave up his medication for Ellie. I wonder if they'll get together when all of this is over. It was amazing to see the story unfold from Michael's point of view, if I were in his position… I think I would have believed this whole thing too! The whole time, I was hoping that Michael and the group would make it out alive, the supporting cast and the special effects team did a fantastic job."

A voice off-camera asks another question, a man with glasses in a white polo shirt appears on the screen, the subtitle beneath him reads, "Ryan – Writer / Producer."

"Did you have plans to include other real patients in this show? Or was the original focus always going to be on one, only Michael? Also, did you have any concerns that the story might not advance the way that you had envisioned it with your writers?"

"We thought about having multiple patients partake in this show, but we loved the backstory that Michael and his wife Eve provided, so much so that we wanted to have the focus just on Michael. Additionally, it would have been a logistical nightmare to keep everyone together and make sure certain targets weren't shot at since none of the guns were actually loaded with real ammunition. We only had to direct the movement of one individual that was gently nudged by our actors, special effects, and production teams.

If there would have been multiple 'contestants' on this show, there would have been too many variables to keep track of, it might be something we can experiment with next season? I see our budget getting much larger for next time through some big investors and advertising after how successful this season was, there's a good chance of that happening.

I'm not trying to brag or anything, but I only really had one concern in the whole narrative, where Michael wouldn't advance the story that we drew up for him. We were afraid that he wasn't going to listen to the audio journals fast enough to create the love interest story arc with Ellie. We didn't anticipate that he would parse them out the way he did, we thought he'd listen to them all at once to hear his wife's voice. We had to tell Ellie to keep her distance until the file where Eve divorces him was played. We didn't have a backup plan to that story arc concerning the love interest; it had the potential to be completely scrapped.

The clinic where we rigged the group to draw straws on who would be left without the medication would have taken a strange turn. I guess it still would have worked, but the story wouldn't have been as compelling as it was for Michael and the audience.

I also want to add that all of the actors did a wonderful job to keep the story going as well as the behind the scenes teams… Logistically, we weren't able to get into total detail with each building in the interiors, they were able to steer him clear of those."

"There have been numerous protests against this show and how you have taken advantage of Michael and his condition, and above all, invaded his privacy without his personal consent… how would you like to respond to that?"

"Firstly, we received permission to do all of this from his wife, who has power of attorney over Michael and she agreed to everything we threw at him. Secondly, we didn't take advantage of the couple; we offered them a solution to a tough bind they were in. They have any and all of their medical expenses paid for and made a cool million dollars in the process that will change their lives forever… for the better. All parties benefited from the transaction. Additionally, I want to point out that our show became the most watched television show in a very long time, those protesters are the vocal minority."

"You've set the bar pretty high now for the future of reality TV shows, how will other studios compete with this?"

"I believe we are pioneers in a new wave that is coming to reality TV. The question you have to ask yourself is, can love be manufactured? There were so many instances of sacrifices that would only come from people that truly loved each other, whether it was Michael giving up his meds to Ellie, or how she tried to sneak back onto the set to tell him that this whole thing was all a ruse.

You can call reality TV fake, but what we all witnessed here seemed pretty real to me. The actors actually had no idea how long this season was going to go, of course we told them the major plot points we wanted, but a lot of things happened with our actors thinking on their feet and influenced by Michael's leadership. Of course there will be other studios that will try to imitate our success, but we are the trendsetters and hopefully we'll stay ahead of the game in upcoming shows. I'm excited for the future."

The camera switches over to a young man with a beard wearing cargo pants and a flannel shirt, the bottom of the screen reads, "Gene – Special Effects." A voice off-camera asks, "Where would we have seen some of your magic? It all looked so real from Michael's perspective, were there any parts that made you worry that he'd figure it out if any of the special effects failed?" It had to have been at least in the back of your mind since the last two seasons of this show didn't exactly work out the way you had planned it."

"The funny thing is, there was a lot you didn't see, simply because they weren't triggered by the storyline that Michael followed. What I mean by that is all of the guns the survivors were armed with were loaded with blanks and equipped with invisible lasers. If they ever fired at any potential targets such as the mechs, ships, other humans… it would have triggered the reactive targets to explode, spark, or in the case of humans, have the blood packets spatter.

The fact that we had the nurse and the soldier in the video set the stage for Michael and the group, that they needed to travel by night. This made our job disguising the five square mile set much easier. The only time we had to go into heavy detail was the area around each of the clinics.

However, to give the second to last episode more zing, we made the point between the museum and the next waypoint as close to realistic as possible to give Michael and the audience an idea of what the terrain looked like during the day. We had to do at least one daytime shooting.

We were a bit concerned that Michael would figure out early on in the scene with Bill. Michael is military trained… he more than likely knows where his bullets are going to land when he fires his weapon.

We were worried that he wouldn't see Bill was planning on suicide bombing that ship if he were captured. If Michael shot Bill instead of letting him infiltrate that ship to destroy it, we would have had to rely on Michael believing that he shot Bill wherever the blood packet splattered, rather than where his rifle was actually aimed at. "

"Several members of the studio audience are wondering how your team pulled off the abduction scenes. From our point of view, it looked incredibly realistic, what kind of effects did you use for that?"

"Actually, that part was pretty easy and low tech. All we needed were the ships on guide wires nearby, shining a bright light down to Michael's position to limit his sight. We would have our actors ready and rigged with a camouflaged bungee cord, from there, the actor would be anchored to the ground by their feet until the special effects team flipped a switch to launch them into the air, giving the appearance that they were disappearing into the night and sucked into a ship. When in reality, our actors were suspended in the air between two poles or tall structures until our production team would retrieve them. It wouldn't have been wise to stick around after a ship flying in his area, we kinda relied on him wanting to avoid the aftermath of these encounters."

The camera switches over to an African American man with a mustache, smoking a cigar named, "Gordon – Tech Consultant."

"Our producers inform me that there was some hot new technology put on display here in this show that made the experience more immersive for the viewers around the world. You're the man to thank for that?"

"Not exactly, someone else created it, I just know how it works. First thing's first, the actor was never put in any real danger, even from the disease. The injections we were having him use were in fact nano-technology, however, not to combat the disease though. These injections allowed the viewers to literally see and experience the emotions that Michael and the other actors went through while meeting everyone, fighting to survive, running for their lives, experiencing sadness, joy, and falling in love.

Those nanomites tapped into their spines and brains are programmed to interpret the images that their eyes were seeing for us to see what their perception of the image was. It's not necessarily a camera per se, but it taps into your brain and interprets the signals of what you see.

Additionally, these nanomites measured their adrenaline, endorphin, hormone levels and other chemicals present in their bodies. Obviously, it can't detect emotion, but it can read their chemical levels. Our algorithms would then interpret those levels and show the audience what emotion Michael and the other actors experienced based on these levels, fascinating technology that I'm oversimplifying... For the purposes of this show, it seemed almost completely accurate given each situation they were thrusted into.

This technology is another way our show has revolutionized reality TV, to show the characters' true emotions despite whatever they were displaying on the surface. These daily injections also helped us to keep our star on a desired path throughout our studios. We were limited in this technology in that it had to be injected every day before it lost power and made its way out of their bloodstream. The low temperature for the injection actually wasn't required; it was another way to dictate Michael's movements.

We also introduced some breakthroughs in audio engineering technology that were more behind the scenes. This one I can claim credit for since the software used was from one of my patents! We were able to create those entries that "came from Eve" which were convincing enough for him to believe it. We took several audio samples from her voice and were able to generate realistic sounding speech patterns with all of her inflections and what not, it is pretty groundbreaking."

Eve comes up on the screen in tears with a handkerchief in hand as she wipes her eyes. The voice off-camera asks her, "What emotions did you go through when watching your husband traverse what he thought was his destroyed hometown fighting an alien force for survival and the relationships he built with his fellow survivors?"

Still whimpering, Eve answers in angry tone, "You're not going to get your sound bite from me, no comment."

The screen goes dark for a moment and the monitor shows a live feed of me on the screen. The host in the silver suit and pink tie enters the room, wearing a mic on his collar. He walks up to me, puts his arm around me and points towards a camera that rolls in from the shadows, the room slowly becomes more illuminated.

"Michael, your wife, she made this all possible, there she is... wave to her."

"What's going on here? What did you call her?"

"Your wife… Eve… Right, I should probably fill you in. We approached several families of patients that are caring for their loved ones who have been diagnosed with Cerebral Nervorum to scout for ripe candidates to apply to be on our show. The best applicants were the ones that were reluctant to do so.

Your wife didn't want to enter you, but medical expenses became impossible once she lost her job. My bosses stepped in and offered to pay for your medical expenses, and all future gene therapy sessions I might add… so you two could be together and become millionaires overnight.

This all started with the idea that reality TV has lost its way over the last few decades. People say that it's all fake, scripted, and the emotions aren't sincere. Well, here at Echo Studios, we wanted to change that tone and return reality TV back to its glory. The best way to make the experience more candid and the interactions more genuine would only be if the actor didn't know they were on the show at all.

Your wife actually visited you almost every week to record a message, we had to omit most of them and engineer a few to construct a narrative that you played out wonderfully. This season is the best yet because of the audio journals she recorded for you that made it possible. In previous seasons which were never aired, the story and the set weren't as compelling; the participants would figure it out two thirds of the way through and knew that something was off, but you, not you. You went along for the full ride!

We made a few improvements to the set and special effects, but that was only the icing to the cake. Your wife's voice is what sold this story to you, to our studio audience, and to audiences around the world! Although we wanted it to be as realistic as possible, your safety was priority number one, you were never in harm's way with the explosions or structures collapsing. Before we woke you up, we actually put you into the latest CRISPR gene editing treatment, you would already be set for not needing any treatments for another few weeks.

The stuff you heard about regarding you and Eve's divorce was all manufactured, she loves you very much. We used the audio sampling from all of her entries to engineer sentences that would make you more inclined to create a love interest narrative with Ellie."

Eve appears from behind the curtain still crying a combination of tears of happiness and disappointment. Upon seeing her, my stomach churns and I start to recall every one of the terrible thoughts I had about her when listening to the final three entries.

A vortex of emotions swirls inside of me as my perception of the world has been flipped around once more. My brain and my heart don't know whether to feel happy and excited to see her or shame and anger for everything that has happened. She keeps a stoic face as she walks in, attempting to hide her tears, resentment, sadness, and perhaps maybe even elatedness of seeing me. Eve didn't want to give them any more than they had already taken from us for the sake of everyone else's entertainment.

I couldn't look her in the eyes as she joined me at my side holding my hand. Knowing everything that I had done was caught on camera for the world to see, where my true love who stayed faithful to me throughout these years had witnessed it all… I don't feel worthy of her affection. The host asks, "Michael… is there anything you'd like to say to your fans or audiences around the world?"

He extends his hand holding out the check for a million dollars and a promissory note for all future medical expenses, Eve snatches it from his hand. We turn, walk toward the exit of the room, not saying a single word to one another.

Despite interlocking our fingers as we hold hands making our way out of the studio, she applied no pressure to her grip but still giving the appearance that the events that had taken place on the show did not damage the foundation of our relationship.

I'm still trying to wrap my mind around the fact that Eve is still alive and that she did not leave me when I needed her the most. I fear the worst for our marriage as I think back to the day I was diagnosed, when I made a promise to myself to cherish every moment I have with her if I ever found out I was in the clear from the disease. I pray to whatever God that will listen that she will understand and that we can work this out.

-Redacted Files-

Eve's Audio Journal

February 17, 2040 – Time 1605hrs
-Begin Message-

Babe, this could be one of my last entries should I choose to go through with this, I wish you were here to help me decide on what to do…

I got laid off a few weeks ago and no one is hiring. I'm going to run out of money soon and your folks already loaned me some. At the end of my last visit with you on my way back to the car, I was approached by a man from some studio company. Apparently, they would stake outside of hospitals for visitors of CN facilities and would present them with an opportunity.

He offered to pay us one million dollars AND would pay for all of your medical treatments so that you could be up and awake… like the rich people… if I sign over your life to a reality show. I don't know which one, but he said that the first two seasons weren't successful so they were never aired but the contestants were still paid.

I'm trying to put myself in your shoes and think about what you would want me to do. I know you'd want to live given the chance to get out of here, but I also know that you would refuse to be put in a cage like an animal under a spotlight for the whole world to see. We could do a lot with a million dollars and all of your expenses paid for, the best part is, we'd get to be together again.

All I have to do is sign something and sit and watch. But I wouldn't be able to make you any more of these messages or try to interfere with the programming no matter what happens after I sign. They guaranteed your safety though. The show would start in a month or two. Our lives would never be private again, but at least we'd be together. They're giving me a few days to think about it, I'm going to go visit your folks to see what they think I should do. Love you.

-End Message-

March 9, 2040 – Time 1213hrs
-Begin Message-

Michael, it looks like the studio is going through with putting you on the show. They loved that you have a military background and that I've been recording these audio diaries for you. I have no idea what they're going to do with them or what kind of show you're going to be entered in, but regardless of what happens, they've offered to pay for all of your future treatments and we'll be overnight millionaires. Whatever the competition is, I know you'll kick some butt!

This will be my last recording for you, if you can hear me in there right now, I'll see you soon… I can't wait! I love you! I hope this is what you would have done if you were in my place.

-End Message-

-Redacted Files 2-

Ellie's Deposition

October 10, 2040 – Time 1400hrs
-Begin Message-

"Please let the record show today's date is October 10th, 2040, the time is 2pm Pacific Standard Time. I am Eric Martin, General Counsel for Echo Studios. Please state your name for the record."

"Ellie Harris."

"Thank you. Please let the record show that Ms. Harris is providing her testimony under oath in arbitration with Echo Studios for her breach of contract for her work on season three of the reality show, 'The Invasion.' We are conducting this fact finding interview simply to discover the motivation behind her actions, actions that had the potential to inflict major financial and intellectual property damage to the studio and the production of the show. Ms. Harris, what were your initial thoughts on Michael when you first met him, the sole contestant in the show?"

"Is this relevant?"

"Please answer the question."

"…He was a very sweet man, he made it his mission to lead us safely to the sanctuary despite all of us being complete strangers. Michael was a confident and assertive leader for our group. Despite learning that the majority of human life on this planet was wiped out in the invasion, he had unwavering love and hope that his wife Eve was still alive and out there waiting for him… up until he listened to that fake audio file you all produced."

"How did that make you feel? Knowing that the studio had led him to believe that his wife had left him for the sake of creating a love interest narrative with you on the show?"

"I didn't really have any qualms about it at first… it was my job and what I was paid to do when you pulled me out of the accounting department. It would have been much easier to do if he were a jerk, but that wasn't the case, he was sweet, caring, and lovable, even audiences around the world thought so."

"What do you mean at first?"

"The more time I spent with him, the more he started to care about me… and I him."

"The answer to my next question is pretty obvious, but I need it for the record. What would you say was the turning point for you, which led you to have enough feelings for Michael to breach your contract?"

"First off, I didn't breach my contract… But if I were to pick a specific moment where I started to really care about him, it's when we drew sticks and I drew the short one. It was me that was supposed to not have the meds and it was me that was supposed to go on that leg of the journey alone, but he made the sacrifice for me. I thought he would join me in the trek to the next clinic at best, and that he would use the meds for himself."

"Who?"

"Michael."

"What were you thinking or hoping to accomplish when you snuck back onto the set, calling out his name after you were written off the show."

"I don't know, I wasn't thinking honestly. I'll admit that me and the other cast members went out drinking the night I got 'abducted' in the show to celebrate the last appearance of any of us before the show wrapped up. I drunkenly came back on set and I guess subconsciously, I felt bad that we were taking advantage of him and his family's situation. I played a role in all of this and maybe I thought it would be my act of contrition to right the wrong and let him know that he was the subject of a show and deceived him about the fidelity of his loving wife."

"So you would have sabotaged the whole show if security didn't stop you?"

"Is this the part where I HAVE to say yes for the agreement?

"You don't HAVE to say anything, no one is forcing you to be here."

"Under threat of being sued and having my name blacklisted everywhere though right?"

"……"

"Yes, if security wasn't there, I may have told him everything."

"Alright. Would you be willing to do another season with Echo Studios in future seasons of similar shows using Cerebral Nervorum patients as our contestants?"

"Absolutely not."

"For purposes of our arbitration agreement, do you consent to the release of your testimony here today to Echo Studios for use in how they see fit, examples being trailers for the show, bonus material, end credits etcetera?

"I do."

-End Message-

Second Act

One month before the finale of "The Invasion…"

By no stretch is this Agent Pearson's first undercover assignment in the field, but it will be one that she is not prepared for.

"Pearson, you're up on a new assignment, short notice with some serious implications. A judge has approved our warrant on the investigation of Brier-Burton Pharmaceuticals and its ties to Echo Studios. We have received some intel and substantial evidence from our informants and field agents that both companies have violated local, state, federal, and international laws. We want you to go in without any prejudices; you're going to go in blind into this assignment. Your job is to investigate the financials of Echo Studios, the warrant is nearly limitless, do what you see fit to investigate and gather more information on this company."

"A movie studio is criminally related to a pharmaceutical company sir?"

"Precisely, your cover will be a new hire accountant. You will infiltrate and investigate Echo Studios' side of the operation. We have prepped your background with the appropriate credentials so that anyone looking you up or your references will find a work history peppered in accounting and finance, it matches your educational background, your cover is the easy part. We tapped a head hunting firm and they have given you a high recommendation to join the studio to help them with a backlog in their work.

Your objective is to dig into their financials to see if you can locate any missing funds, anything out of the ordinary, or any ties to Brier-Burton that may be hidden from plain view. We don't know how long you'll be in there, assume you're staying out in the field until your handler is satisfied with your findings and we can clear them or charge them. You start tomorrow, any questions?"

"No sir."

"Excellent Ellie, be safe out there, and happy hunting."

Agent Pearson spends the remainder of the day going over the dossier with her cover story and brushes up on accounting in preparation for her upcoming assignment. To keep things simple, undercover agents are often given the same first name as cover so they react the same way they naturally would when hearing their names. Agent Ellie Pearson's new persona will be, Ellie Harris.

Ellie Harris attended Wichita State and graduated Magna cum laude in Business and Accounting. She has worked as an accountant in a large tech company and is looking to move locations and signed onto a staffing agency to look for quick work until a more permanent one is found.

Most of Agent Pearson's field work has involved being a large quantity buyer for narcotics operations or running some of the FBI's informants. Never has she been put into the field of work she actually studied in as her cover, nor has any operation lasted longer than two weeks. The upcoming assignment would change all of that.

There isn't an obvious connection between the studio and the pharma company, but enough confidential informants have convinced the higher echelon and a judge to sign off on a search warrant to send in an undercover agent to investigate.

It's time for bed and a good night's sleep, Ellie has a busy day ahead of her tomorrow, putting on a face to meet new people, starting a new job, all the while investigating a large corporation undetected.

…..

Ellie pulls into the parking lot of Echo Studios, an up and coming movie studio in the city. This location is the studio's corporate office, it is gorgeous and decadent, the majority of the exterior of the building is covered with excessively large windows. No movies or TV shows are filmed at this site but their logos are everywhere on the building and signs into the parking lot highlighting their latest releases.

Before she enters the building, she forces herself to remember to smile, getting in good with these people will better her chances to access valuable information unnoticed. Ellie approaches the information desk, and makes eye contact with the security guard manning the post.

"Hi there, my name is Ellie Harris, I'm new here and I'm looking for the Accounting Department, would you be able to point me in the right direction?" She says with a smile.

The older heavyset gentleman with gray hairs answers, "Sure thing miss, the elevators are right around the corner over there, the Accounting Department is on the second floor, turn left when you hop off the elevators and follow the signs and you should see it."

Ellie glances at his nametag and replies, "Thanks Marvin!"

Everyone else in the office building goes about their morning routines walking right past Marvin without acknowledging his presence. Getting in his good graces may be of use later, Ellie thinks to herself.

On her way to the elevators, Ellie notices more artwork, props, encased costumes, and wax figures on display than there is time to appreciate them. They are for the several projects that Echo Studios has been involved with and perhaps some future projects. There's so much to see.

Fearful of being late on her first day, Ellie does not waste any more time admiring any of the decorations in the main concourse and continues on to the elevator.

She gets off of the elevator and finds the entrance to the accounting department; upon grabbing the door handle it appears to be locked and doesn't budge when she pulls on it. A keycard swipe pad is required to get in. Next to the pad is a doorbell, she presses the button.

A soft ring like one you'd hear on one of the middle keys of a piano, rings from the inside, "ding dong." Through the window, a woman wearing a black blouse approaches. She smiles at Ellie as she opens the door.

"Hello there! You must be Ellie, come on in, we've been expecting you! My name is Anne, pleased to meet you."

The two shake hands and Anne leads Ellie to her workstation.

"You guys kinda take your security around here pretty seriously don't you?"

"I guess so, all of the departments are under lock and key here. The main building is open to the public to promote the current projects coming through the studio, beyond that, you need an ID badge to get anywhere else."

"Gotcha."

"Here's your workstation, coffee and the water cooler are around the corner, past these set of cubicles. Your login ID is your first initial, last name, all lowercase, and your password is 'Password10' with a capital 'P.' Once you login, you'll create a new one, from there you will see on the shared 'F' drive the financial reports that need to be processed. When you work on a file, transfer it over to the 'G' drive, files saved in there are currently being worked on. You've come to us highly recommended, these quarterlies should be a breeze to you. Any questions?"

"Nope, thank you Anne! I think I got it from here."

"I don't want to add any pressure, but we are dealing with a significant backlog, our manager, Dean expects results, even if you're new here. I'll be at the front desk if you need anything."

"Got it."

"Oh! Before I forget, at noon during your lunch break, we'll need you to head down to the first floor at the security desk, and ask Marvin to take your picture and create your ID badge so you can have access to our department."

Ellie nods and begins her work. She picks a file from the first quarter of 2035, they weren't joking about a backlog. As to not raise any suspicion early on, Ellie works diligently at her station for the first couple of hours. A quick look around, she doesn't notice anyone near her workstation or any security cameras that might catch her looking where she shouldn't be looking. She begins to dig.

Clicking through the network folders yields no results. Ellie looks for anything that she may not have permission to access, everything so far appears to be on the up and up as far as locked files are concerned, perhaps her supervisor Dean has access to network folders that no one else does.

Thinking outside of the box, Ellie remembers an idea of how she used to hide files back in school when playing pranks on her friends or hiding personal files that she didn't want others to see that happened to be on her computer. She clicks through to search hidden files… It worked! A hidden 'P' drive appears, as expected, it is encrypted with two-factor authentication. A roadblock.

Ellie looks at her watch and panics, it's already a quarter past noon, she was supposed to be downstairs getting her photo taken for her ID fifteen minutes ago. She rushes down the stairs instead of taking the elevator and finds Marvin.

"I'm so sorry Marvin! I got caught up in my work. I'm here to pick up my badge?"

He smiles at her, "It's okay sweetheart. Let's calm you down before we take your picture though."

Frazzled, but reassured by Marvin's demeanor, Ellie recomposes herself and smiles for the camera.

"Say cheese quesadilla!"

She can't help but laugh.

"Awesome, wait right here and I'll go pick up that badge for you, I'll be right back."

"Actually Marvin, is it OK if I go to my car and pick it up from you later? I was going to go grab a quick bite before going back to work."

"Sure thing darling, I'll be right here."

Except, Ellie isn't going back to her car to get food, she heads to her car to transmit an update to her handler and to find equipment to hack into the secure files and folders on the network.

================================
Secure Connection Established. Begin Transmission:

Report:

Handler, I'm in. I've established my cover as an accountant at corporate. Upon inspection of their network drives, I have located a hidden drive that has a two-step verification guard. I will be placing a thumb drive on my workstation to allow our team remote access to the terminal to break into the secure files. Does the warrant cover this type of operation and intrusion? There will be countless confidential financial files within the network drives that they are trying to keep secure for legitimate reasons.

End of Report:

Handler: Proceed. Be sure to place the thumb drive on a different workstation in the event they are able to trace the data intrusion, we need you to maintain your cover and the integrity of our investigation.

End of Transmission: Connection lost.

=====================

Before she opens her trunk, she looks around to make sure there are no prying eyes about, she opens it only enough for her to see inside. Ellie's trunk is filled with several espionage tools and a small lockbox with a sidearm. She locates the thumb drive in the black, hard plastic case filled with various counter intelligence equipment.

She goes through the motions of picking up her ID card from Marvin and returns to the office back at her workstation. Knowing that she is going to have to burn someone and potentially end their career. She hasn't officially met anyone else in the office but poor old Anne, the receptionist. But it must be done.

She heads over to Anne's desk, leans up against the cubicle wall nearest to her computer tower and asks, "Hey there Anne, I meant to ask you, where are the bathrooms on this floor? I may or may not have gone down to the first floor to find one."

As Anne is telling her the locations of each restroom and turns her back to point out their approximate locations through the walls, Ellie quickly seizes the opportunity and places the thumb drive in one of the USB sockets on the back of Anne's computer, no one would ever notice it buried under the wires. However, a small dialog box appears on Anne's screen, indicating the device is being installed… it vanishes as Anne turns back around and catches Ellie staring at her screen.

"You caught me new girl!"

Ellie is caught off guard and fears that she has been made by a middle aged woman with no criminal history or counter intelligence experience. Ellie's heart starts to pound, but remains cool on the surface. She recalls that this assignment is much different from the rest as it is nowhere near as dangerous as her previous undercover stints where she was dealing with drug dealers, gun-runners, murderers, human traffickers etc. But her cover had never been blown either.

"You caught me looking at wedding dresses and venues, my boyfriend proposed to me last week! I know I know, I'm using company time to look this up. Can you keep my little secret?"

"Of course!" Ellie says with nervous laughter.

Relieved, Ellie heads back to her workstation, she hears a man's voice call out from behind her, "Ellie Harris?"

She continues a few extra steps before she turns around, "Yes sir, that's me."

"Hi there, I'm Dean, the accounting manager, can you please follow me to my office?"

"Sure thing."

The man in the suit and tie leads her through the maze of cubicles to his office in the corner. Ellie follows as her mind is racing a mile a minute, wondering if she has already been burned and if she was too careless during her communication with her handler or if she was caught planting the device on Anne's workstation.

She pays close attention to where each turn is made through the cubicles in the event for a need of a hasty escape. For this assignment, carrying a firearm is more of a liability than it is an asset, the only weapon she has on her person is a small knife strapped to the side of her upper thigh.

Dean escorts her into his office, shuts the blinds and closes the door behind them.

"Please, have a seat."

They both sit. Dean's desk separates the two of them. Ellie feels the knife through her skirt and makes sure it is there, her heart races. She remains calm and steady, constantly reevaluating the situation, and thinking of possible exits to the building if things turn violent. If he were to try anything, he would have to close the distance by going over or around the desk to get to her, not before she could pull out her knife to defend herself.

"Ellie, I know today is only your first day and we think you're doing a fantastic job for a couple of the reports you've already submitted, but something has come up."

She remains steady on the surface, but underneath, her mind frantically paddles like a duck's feet underwater as it is seemingly moves effortlessly gliding across a pond on the surface. Ellie's hand is now on the grip of the knife, Dean's view of anything below her waist is obscured by his desk, she is ready to counter attack if the situation calls for it.

"Are you the type of person that is good at pretending to be someone you're not... or lying?

Before she opens her mouth, Ellie clears her throat and relaxes as best she can so that her voice doesn't tremble when she speaks.

"Um... that's an odd question. I guess I'm a pretty good poker player when I play with my guy friends, mainly because no one really expects it from a female."

She feels herself perspiring and her voice trembling as she uttered the last few words despite her best effort. Even a highly skilled and trained field agent can't control the body's natural physiological reactions and functions under stress. But she remains still and ready to go for the jugular if need be.

In hand-to-hand combat, Dean would be able to overpower her, to gain the initiative, Ellie would have to strike fast and hard.

"Interesting... I'm sorry, I know this all sounds weird, and I don't mean to alarm you, but it comes all the way from the top. Our HR department noticed something when your photo ID went through for processing. Nothing bad, I assure you, but the higher ups would like to use you for something else other than accounting. You actually have no say in the matter, you can either leave or agree to be put on this other project."

Confused, Ellie replies. "Um…. okay…. What would I be agreeing or disagreeing to?"

"The people upstairs want you to star in one of our reality shows that we're launching in less than a month. The pay is three times as much as you're making now and it will get you some exposure in front of the camera for a career in film or TV if that interests you. I can't say what show it is or what the project is because it's even above my paygrade. But what they did tell me was that you have the look they want for the co-star.

It pains me to say this, again, it's not my choice, but if you say no, I can't keep you on for our accounting needs despite your stellar job thus far."

"Wow, this is crazy, I don't even know what to say." She couldn't conceal her bewilderment on this revelation. Being a on a reality show isn't exactly ideal for an FBI agent that is on the clandestine side of the agency.

"They would like an answer as soon as possible."

"Can I at least sleep on it?"

"You have until 7pm tonight, call the number on this card when you make your decision either way. I guess this is where we part ways and I bid you farewell."

Before she stands, Ellie releases the knife and smooths out the creases on her skirt she created by the death grip she put on the weapon through her clothing. The two stand up and shake hands.

"I guess I don't need this anymore." Ellie hands Dean her ID badge as she exits.

She drives back to her apartment to make contact with her handler.

=============================

Secure Connection Established. Begin Transmission:

Report:

Handler. The device has been planted on a workstation, but I was removed from my position. They've asked me to be on one of their TV shows because of my appearance, they will not allow me back into a corporate position or on their premises and I have to notify them of my decision by 1900 hours local, how should I proceed?

End of Report:

Handler: We were able to crack the files on the network and it yielded no results. Stay with it, this opportunity may get you access to their senior leadership once all is said and done. We understand that this may prevent any future possibilities of you going undercover, but you're the only one we have on the inside of Echo Studios for this investigation, follow the trail and see where it leads, the order to follow all leads no matter what. This comes from the top.

End of Transmission: Connection lost.
=====================

Briefing

"Hi there, this is Ellie Harris, I was given a card to call this number to let you know of my decision regarding a show with Echo Studios?"

"Hello Ellie, this is Warren, VP of Reality TV Operations with Echo, we've been expecting your call... have you come to a decision?"

"I'm in so far, but I'm going to need more details before I agree to anything further."

"Fair enough, that's good to hear you're on board at this juncture, but for me to divulge any additional information, you'll have to come into our offices to sign a non-disclosure agreement. What we're doing is going to be revolutionary; we can't let any of our secrets out. Can you come on in tomorrow morning around 7am? Immediately after you sign the paperwork, we'll loop you in with everything and you can make your final decision at that time."

"That works... Can I at least ask one question though? Why me? I don't have any acting experience nor do I care to be on TV. If I'm being honest, if I do it, I would only be doing it for the paycheck."

"The fact that you aren't a wannabe actress who is trying to get her big shot in the industry, trying to get some camera time, entices us even more to select you. I can answer your question, but you're probably going to think what I have to say is extremely vague, but it will all make sense once we speak to you in person… You look like the person we want as the co-star to our main character."

"Okayyy…"

"We'll see you tomorrow morning with more details."

Tossing and turning all night, Ellie is unable to fall asleep while thinking about what would be in store for her near future in the spotlight. The question that Dean asked reminds her that she IS good at pretending to be someone that she's not. It is essentially her job every time she assumes an identity for an undercover role.

This time however, her every move would be scrutinized by a national audience, her face would be known, and any future clandestine assignments would be off the table for the remainder of her career.

Ellie taps her watch, it now reads "0400," in a few hours she will learn exactly what she will be getting herself into for her country. She has no choice in the matter, only her cover to preserve, and a company to investigate is all that her superiors are concerned with.

Still tense and wide awake, the bright rays of the sun begin to pierce through her bedroom curtains. This isn't an unusual occurrence for Ellie, the night before a major operation is usually sleepless.

This assignment will require her to remember and compartmentalize her lives as an FBI agent, an accountant, and an actress. Any slip ups can compromise the investigation into Echo Studios and Brier-Burton Pharmaceuticals.

In an attempt to relax while being productive before her meeting since she is already awake, Ellie goes for a run in the early summer morning while the weather is still cool and the sun is partially over the horizon.

The fresh crisp air and the quiet early morning, all help to clear her mind. The streets are a little damp from the morning dew as the sun's rays make the wet asphalt shimmer. Five miles down and she turns around to head back to her apartment complex.

Outside of the apartment, she stands straight up with both of her fingers interlocked behind her head, her heart and lungs worked hard, she is awake, focused, and alert… Ellie is ready to tackle whatever is thrown at her in this assignment.

After a quick shower and a short drive, she arrives to the studios to sign the documents to learn more about what is in store for her. Ellie is greeted by a familiar face, Marvin, the security guard, who remains seated at his desk. A man in a business suit holding a briefcase accompanied by another man in cargo shorts, flip flops, and a T-shirt standing next to Marvin's desk are watching Ellie as she approaches them.

"Hi there, you must be Ellie, my name is Ryan, I'm a producer for a show here at the studio and this is Eric, he is general counsel for our company."

The three exchange awkward handshakes as she is indecisive in whose hand to shake first.

"It is a pleasure to meet you both."

"Right this way to the elevators, we'll be meeting on the fifth floor conference room. Are you excited to potentially be working with us and to be a TV star?"

"Not exactly, I've never done anything like this before, so I'd say more nervous. You do realize that I was originally hired as an accountant here to help you with your quarterly reports right?"

"And that right there is part of the reason why we like you."

'Ding…. Ding.' The elevator comes to a stop and the doors slide open. They exit and proceed to the conference room with only completely transparent windows and no walls. The centerpiece of the room is a large glass table lined with several black leather chairs. Ryan casually walks in first, his sandals make several 'clopping' noises until he stops to hold the door open as he gestures the other two in with his hand.

Eric, with a stern look, gently sets his briefcase down on the table and pulls out a small stack of papers and aligns the pages by bouncing the sheets on their edges and hands them over to Ellie. Ryan reaches into his pocket, presses some sort of remote device which causes all of the windows to immediately turn white as if all of the windows simultaneously fogged up within a couple of seconds.

"Here is the non-disclosure agreement that we need you to sign before we can tell you anything more about the show. Take all the time you need to go over the document, the short of it is that you are not able to communicate what you are about to see and hear to anyone, this includes any friends or family, posting it online, anything of the sort that would reveal our intellectual property to others. Initial each of the pages and sign and date the last one."

"Got it."

Ellie skims through the document, makes the appropriate initials, and signs and dates the last page.

The attorney picks up the document, licks his finger before he flips through the pages to examine her signature and finally gives Ryan a thumbs-up.

"Excellent. Ellie, we're going to be shooting the next evolutionary step in reality TV here at Echo Studios. We've had the narrative and the set ready for quite some time now, we've been waiting for the right people to star in it to maximize the chances of this show being a major success.

We have learned from the first two attempts not to rush this process. We have the perfect candidate for this idea, he is our third Cerebral Nervorum patient we're thinking of trying out. He has been in a deep, medically induced coma for about six or seven years now. We are going to wake him up in the middle of our five square mile studio, and lead him to believe that an alien invasion has occurred."

"Oh my God, that sounds awful."

"CN patients are the perfect, unadulterated candidates for this show. His wife has left him some audio diaries that we are going to utilize to our advantage and make the story more believable for him. She wanted no part in it at first, but we offered to pay for their medical bills which will allow this patient to stay awake and be present with his wife in addition to offering them a cool million dollars.

He's military, so he'll display some actual tactics in fighting and evading the aliens that we have created for him and his fellow survivors. The narrative will also be more believable for the audience in that a trained military man would be capable of surviving such a harsh environment."

"If I agree to this, how do I fit in?"

"We're asking you to play the role of one of his fellow survivors in this post-apocalyptic landscape… who also happens to be female. We know you don't have any acting experience which is perfect, we don't want you to act. We want you to be yourself and react the way you would if this kind of nightmare actually happened.

The writing and special effects will be pretty convincing, even after the fact that you know this is all manufactured. We'll engineer some situations that will create a love interest arc with your character and his; all we ask is that you follow it to wherever he leads it. Part of the reason we have selected you is that you look very similar to his wife, someone he might be physically attracted to."

"So what you're telling me is that if he has the inclination to cheat on his wife, let it happen???"

"Maybe… if it comes to that."

"I don't think I can do that. That will interfere with his real life!"

"Look Ellie, I know they might have told you that the offer for this gig would be three or four times the wage that you were making in accounting… but I'll be blunt. I am authorized to offer you ten times as much. We know you're new in town and we know you could use this. We would compensate you at this hourly rate every time you're here learning the background to this story, training, stunt coordination, and the whole time the show is live."

Torn, not between money and morality of what is asked of her. But rather, torn between morality and seeking truth and justice. In her head, Ellie is committing to the idea of not causing any further emotional damage to the poor soul than she has to. The man will unknowingly be placed in this terrifying, make-believe world for the entertainment of others. Under the altruistic belief that she is putting the country before herself, she agrees.

"I'll do it."

"Excellent, you'll start next week. Get rested, you'll be putting in a lot of hours getting your backstory straight, workout drills, and some special effects training that we'll put you through in the event the storyline requires to do so."

Ellie begins to wonder about the actual actors and actresses that audition for roles such as these, simply for an opportunity to get in front of the camera and foregoing any sense of morality to be famous. A man's life will be put on display for the world to see without his consent. He'll be put under all sorts of psychological stress for the sake of entertainment. At this point in time, there is nothing illegal about what they are doing, awful but not illegal, her investigation continues.

===============================

Secure Connection Established. Begin Transmission:

Report:

Handler. I met with one of the target's producers and their general counsel. The only strand of a link I could find between the studio and the pharma company is that the star of the show they will be shooting is a Cerebral Nervorum patient. I start working for them next week.

End of Report:

Handler: Carry on and pursue any leads. You have a new objective. If and when you are able to get in the same room as an executive or their general counsel again, plant a transmitter on them. We have built a strong enough case for a judge to OK this part of the operation. Finances show that the two companies are loosely linked, place the transmitter or find a deeper link.

End of Transmission: Connection lost.
=====================

Smile

A month passes as Ellie prepares for her upcoming role with no leads or evidence showing any wrongdoing on Echo Studio's part or their connection to Brier-Burton Pharmaceuticals. 'The Invasion' is one day away from premiering. The director has all of the actors in a classroom setting to review the events that need to happen, the rest can be spontaneous and done on the fly to the natural progression of the narrative.

"Here are the things that absolutely must happen, pay attention, the rest can be ad-libbed and improvised. You all need to take the syrette shots filled with the nanomites throughout the show, not only does it have to be done to keep the façade that all of you are sick and need it to survive, but it also has the nano technology that will allow us to see what you see and the bodily chemical readings to show the emotions you are experiencing in each scene.

It is also integral to the success of the show that you guide Michael from hospital to hospital where we have setup some alien encounters and where you will be sleeping each day and taking your 'medication.' Traveling by night is also vital to hide the guide wires and lack of detail in most of our set, the only exception is when you reach the Central District where we have put in a lot of work for the finale.

Limit your communications with staff to emergencies only, you never know if Michael can see or hear you. Don't worry though, you'll be able to hear us if we need to get a hold of you through the earpieces we will be implanting in your ear canal tomorrow morning.

After we break from here, we will be having you do some stunt training we haven't had you practice before. We worked on your character, your fitness, improv, and acting natural around Michael, but there's something our special effects and stunt team needs to go over with you all... you'll need to get this part right, good luck."

The actors have no idea what's in store for them or even what kind of stunts that would need to be rehearsed.

A few hours into stunt training....

"Okay, from the top Ellie. Screaming is absolutely fine, in fact, we want you to at launch. But remember, you need to be completely silent after about one second. We want to simulate that you've been sucked into a spaceship to make it more believable for our contestant. The faster we can get you to do this in practice, the faster we're done here and we can all go home."

Contestant? Laughable. Such an interesting term and spin on the label, he's more of an unwitting and unwilling participant at best. Ellie is unable to control her blood curdling screams as the bungie cord strapped to the harness under her shirt, launches her into the sky tethered to two high rise poles to simulate an alien abduction.

This next try will be the fourth attempt for her, the other actors only needed two attempts at most to get it right for rehearsal.

"Don't tense up, you don't know what the ship is going to do to you, you have to relax and just let it happen. We'll keep doing this until you get it right." Gene, the special effects manager tells Ellie through the megaphone.

"Places everyone. Safety checks complete. Ready…. steady….. launch!!!"

Ellie imagines being asleep on her plush memory foam mattress back at her apartment. Her mind is in a state of tranquil ease until she is violently launched into the air as she screams and immediately goes silent as she is bouncing up and down, suspended between the two poles that are about one hundred yards apart and thirty stories high.

Ryan, the producer, reviews the footage on film from the perspective of the camera crew on the ground. It looks and sounds perfect, like she is screaming for her life while getting sucked into an alien spacecraft.

As Ellie is being lowered to the ground, she is still visibly shaken from the experience. Despite being a hardened veteran field agent, events such as these are completely beyond her control. No matter how alert, skilled, or trained she is, her fate rests in the hands of the people in charge of her safety and the machines that manufactured these set pieces for the stunt.

It's finally over… for now, a feeling of weightlessness and not being in control remains until her boots finally touch the ground as she is slowly lowered to the ground.

"Awesome work everybody, we're done here. Go home and get some rest, I'll see everyone tomorrow around noon for medical prep, we go live tomorrow evening. We don't know when our star will wake up, but we'll be hitting him with the medication tomorrow morning, he could be awake any time from tomorrow night until the early dawn. Again, good job today. Actors that will be playing as a patient tomorrow, remember, no eating tomorrow, we'll be hitting you with some sedatives around noon."

The actor that will be playing Lance says, "Hey Ellie, the four of us are grabbing dinner and drinks tonight before we start tomorrow, you interested?"

"Oh, thanks for the invitation, but I'm exhausted, I think I'm going to head home. I'm sooo not looking forward to the abduction scene."

"Don't worry about that, you did great! That's cool though, we'll see you tomorrow, later."

The first thing Ellie does when she gets home is draws a warm bath with plain water. She rests her eyes and quickly falls asleep using a rolled up towel as a pillow as her hands rest on the sides of the tub.

Intrusive thoughts of being forced to become a homewrecker as part of Ellie's job as an actress whilst maintaining cover for the investigation interrupts her from this deep state of rest. She has never met nor seen pictures of the man, but she imagines a sad woman watching her husband being seduced by her during this out of body experience.

In a panic, her hands flail about, causing water from the tub to splash on the floor as she startles back to consciousness. Still panting, Ellie reassures herself that nothing will happen between them. As she dries herself off to put her pajamas, Ellie thinks to herself that she will act warm enough around him to please the producers, but not enough for him to develop any real feelings for her.

Despite all of the stress she had endured throughout the day and concerns about the lack of progress in the investigation, she sleeps like a baby from sheer exhaustion the second she pulls her blankets up to her neck in her air conditioned room.

In the morning, there are no updates from her handler regarding new orders or objectives, the plan remains the same. A transmitter will have to be planted on one of the executive members. She won't be able to accomplish this feat during the show, it will have to happen after wrap.

The day finally arrives. The actors are instructed not to cleanse themselves nor brush their teeth this morning to give the illusion that they have been abandoned for days at a time in the hospital. Three all-terrain jeeps transport the production crew and the actors through the studio's five square mile set, showing a completely decimated wasteland of a city post an alien invasion and bombardment campaign. The entire ride is bumpy and jarring as the driver attempts to find the flattest possible path through the crater filled roads.

Ellie and the actors stare in awe at the realistic setting that surrounds them, several buildings in the distance that appear to be severely damaged, rubble and debris in every direction, and hundreds of shells of cars that look exploded or burnt to a crisp. The crew thought it best for the actors not to rehearse or practice their stunts on set to make the experience that will be caught on camera untainted.

The jeeps slide a few inches until they come to a complete stop outside of a hospital where the walls and portions of the roof appear to be barely standing. Ryan, the writer and producer, is the first one to step out. "Okay, actors and my nurse, please head to the ventilation shaft over there, there's a ladder inside to help you down into the basement. Your hospital beds where our actor Michael is already down there.

Once the nurse administers the sedative to knock you out, the crew will be about two blocks away in the event of any emergencies. Alright everybody, it's go time, this show goes live the minute Michael wakes up, good luck everybody, let's do this!"

Ellie and the actors known as, Shawn, Lance, Charlie, and Brian, make their way down the vent followed by a nurse in plain street clothing with a red satchel filled with medical supplies. Once in the basement, the actors hover around Michael, the star of the show as he is peacefully lying there unconscious with a heart monitor, beeping at his side.

He isn't very tall, a clean cut brunette man with lush hair. His defining facial features would have to be his large nostrils and chiseled jaw. The electro shock therapy has allowed him to retain his muscle definition despite being in a coma for over seven years.

"Alright, everyone, get into your beds, I will be hooking you all up to an IV line that will knock you out cold within fifteen minutes. When you wake up, it'll be dark in here, those sticks you see on the ground and puddles of water are glow sticks, you'll be able to make your way around once your eyes adjust to the dark. Good luck."

The nurse makes it look so easy and routine as she walks around, attaching all of the heart monitors and inserting IV lines into the actors. It looks as if she has done this procedure at least a thousand times as she quickly glides from each patient performing the procedure five times in a row.

Wipe the injection site, insert the needle, attach the electrodes, and push the medication into their lines. The actors watch her exit the room until it goes completely pitch black until their eyes re-acclimate to the low levels of light in the room.

The clicking from the nurse's steps on the ladder fade, a loud rumble reverberates through the ventilation shaft as the feet of the ladder bang on the walls of the vent as the crews pulls it up and out of the shaft.

Lance breaks the silence while the medication kicks in. "Cheers everybody, see you all on the other side."

Their eyes become heavier, until one by one they all go unconscious. The only noises remaining in the room are the leaky pipes sending droplets of water onto the puddle filled ground and the constant beeping of the heart monitors attached to each and every actor... and Michael, the contestant.

In a few hours, Michael will awaken, the world he left as he remembered it is completely gone and destroyed... in its place is a playground full of lies and deceit for him to explore to the world's amusement.

Rise and Hide

Ellie's vision is hazy as she comes to; the dark room is not making it any easier for anything to come into focus. The sedative is a bit stronger than she had anticipated. She awakens in a panic, screams, and starts to run in place while lying down. A hand appearing from nowhere covers her mouth within seconds to muffle her screaming.

A man's voice comes out from the darkness, "Shhhhh… calm down, calm down, you're safe, no one is going to hurt you. But me and the others need you to stay quiet so those things don't hear us. Nod if you understand me."

Ellie nods knowing the man probably can't see her but can certainly feel her head movements. She is legitimately disoriented for the first few minutes until she remembers that her every move is being filmed and watched. Michael removes his hand from her mouth. The look of her panicked disorientation is genuine as she has no idea how long she has been incapacitated.

Ellie feels a muscle ache in her neck from the syrette filled with the nano technology that Michael presumably injected into her. She catches eyes with Michael in the darkness, the nanomites in her bloodstream are coursing through her veins and indicating readings that show her elevated hormone levels.

Despite the minimal lighting in the room, Michael appears more attractive than she remembers walking by his lifeless body. The studio audience and the folks at home can see the signs that she is at least physically attracted to him, despite hiding any visual cues on the surface. You can wear your emotions under your sleeve, but you can't change your body's physiological reactions.

Michael explains the current situation to the group, talking about a video that has shed light on what has happened to the planet. Brian hands Ellie a tablet that contains the video. It is something that no one has seen before; her reactions to it are completely authentic. Her adrenaline readings shoot up for all the audience to see as she watches the story unfold like watching a gripping movie.

Despite knowing that everything around her is engineered, the fear and excitement turn real when immersed in such a world so perfectly crafted, the element of acting becomes natural. The director barks orders to the camera technicians, "Alright, keep the night vision one and zoom in on Ellie's face, I want to capture her shock, she looks great, the audience will eat this up, yes, keep that frame around her."

The limited sight in the room and the ominous noises outside would convince anyone that something is not right in this world outside of these walls.

The consensus amongst the actors prior to the live shoot is the most difficult part in all of this is not constantly looking at the main character, Michael, as he is supposed to be the focus of attention.

All of the cameras are well hidden with the exception of the eyes of the fellow actors, however, this is easy to forget. A month of preparation and getting scolded each time one of the actors looked at him had become ingrained and became enough of a deterrent that it is second nature to everyone, especially Ellie who was chastised the most during rehearsals using a stand-in.

To no surprise, Michael takes charge of the situation as he takes a mental inventory of the supplies and gives his fellow survivors a background of what's going on outside the walls of the hospital, and gives instructions on the tasks that need to be completed. The irony of the situation is that it is he who is the one with a naïve understanding of the world. Still, that doesn't stop him from assuming the role of leading the group.

As the other patients begin questioning his authority and where he gets his information of the situation outside, Michael attempts to break the heightened tension by explaining himself and making light of the situation by cracking a joke, "… my job before all of this was a fortune teller."

Ellie couldn't help but smile and admire his quick wit, and humor.

Per their instructions in the ever evolving script, the group continues to question his authority, but remembering not to push so hard that Michael relinquishes his command. The story must be guided by him to keep the story's natural flow as to maintain the illusion that the audience is following the journey that Michael creates and not what the writers or inserted actors create for him.

Michael makes it a point that due to his military experience, he is the best candidate for leading the group in survival and evasion tactics. Everyone here is an actor besides Ellie, the "Accountant." She finds it a little humorous when the other cast members who are actors by trade, talk about their occupations prior to Earth's invasion, specifically Shawn. His claim that he is capable of handling a firearm due to the fact that he used to be in law enforcement is a dangerous backstory, dangerous in the sense that members of law enforcement and military can smell each other a mile away.

In the producers' infinite wisdom, they decide to give Ellie the role of a teacher in her past life, to instill a passive but nurturing character for Michael to confide in, to protect, and eventually fall for.

During introductions, Michael speaks of his past life passionately, especially about his wife and his strong belief that she is still alive in this post-apocalyptic world, waiting for him at the human sanctuary. Ellie's bodily chemical readings indicate that she is nervous, nervous from thinking about what the director and producers expect of her role in potentially breaking up this happily married couple. Her heart rate shoots up as it becomes her turn to introduce herself to the group.

In a trembling voice, "My name is Ellie and I was a third grade teacher. I'm not sure if I'm more scared now or the day I found out I was diagnosed which seems like yesterday."

The group breaks off to scavenge the hospital for supplies and to walk around and stretch to give Michael the impression that they are all using muscles that they haven't used in several years. As they are exploring their immediate surroundings, even the actors are shocked at the level of detail in the collapsed walls and the leaky ceilings. Anyone who walks in on this set with no context would have to believe that something catastrophic had happened.

Michael and Brian return from their excursion through the basement of the hospital to let the group know that an exit has been located through the ventilation shaft. To kill time, Michael begins listening to the audio journals that his wife Eve had left him. Ellie's heart rate races once more, thinking that he will finish the journal to kick off the next phase of the love story arc, however, he stops short only after a few entries.

"Can we get some audio on what parts of the journal Michael is listening to? Broadcast it to the audience please, thank you."

A few air patrols throughout the day pass by overhead that sound like jumbo jets, slowly hovering at low altitudes over the hospital. The ground shakes and the cast looks around at each other, wondering how the special effects team is creating this auditory deception and making the ground beneath them vibrate. Through an earpiece placed deep within each of the actors' ear canals, the producers direct Ellie.

"He's not listening to the journal anymore. Make your way to him and engage him in conversation. You can't wait until he's done with the journal to make your move, put in some face time Ellie."

She makes her way towards Michael as each step she takes creates a little splash from the puddles on the ground, also with each step she takes, her heart rate rises. Agent Harris is not one to be flirtatious, in fact, she doesn't even know how to flirt at all. She had always been focused on school and went straight into the academy at Quantico and made work her life. Every move she makes towards him feels awkward and foreign to her. She gestures with her hand at the far side of the spot on Michael's bed and asks.

"May I sit here?"

"Sure."

"What are you up to? What are you listening to?"

"It's a bunch of recordings my wife made for me while I was under. The hospital staff supposedly played them for me so I could hear her voice from time to time. If I'm being honest, I still miss her even though it feels like she and I were talking yesterday… I wanted to hear her voice. I was thinking about playing another entry, but maybe I'll save it for later."

Ellie can tell why his wife Eve fell for him. Michael's demeanor is charming and his face is easy on the eyes, the dark brown hair in conjunction with his sharp green eyes make for a great combination. His five o'clock shadow in tandem with his slightly muscular build gives him a tough and rugged look.

"Awwww… that's so sweet! The only man that was in my life was my pup-pup. I left him with my sister before I went under a couple of years ago. It kind of hit me this morning when I was trying to sleep that they more than likely didn't make it."

To make her story easier to remember and more believable, Ellie pulls information from her actual life, such as having a sister and a dog, a dog that brought her sixteen years of companionship until she had to put him down due to his frail and aging body.

Bringing back the memory of her lost pup accesses a part of her emotions that can be useful on-screen when the need to elicit these feelings becomes necessary. The production crew could see that talking about her dog brought back some tearful memories, her lowered levels of serotonin indicates that she has some buried feelings of sadness.

Through her earpiece, Ellie hears, "Great job Ellie! The studio audience is loving this, keep it going!"

"We can't think like that, if there's the tiniest of chances that your sister, your pup, and my wife made it out alive, there is still a chance! So... you became a 'sleeper' pretty recently. Were there any notable events in the five years leading up to your hibernation?"

Ellie starts swinging her crossed feet, dangling from the bed, and her eyes look up into the darkness of the room to dig through her memories.

"Um... let's see, the United States converting completely to clean energy was a big deal. I know it was probably mostly already noticeable here in our city, but everywhere else in the country has been converted and upgraded, with the exception of you people... the military. Uh, the last game of professional football was played a few years ago until it was ultimately banned after more research was published about brain injuries related to the sport. Oddly enough, boxing still existed."

"I actually remember that... they banned tackle football for kids, up until they entered high school anyway.

The two continue getting to know each other until Shawn and Brian return from another trip to scavenge supplies from other accessible parts of the hospital that weren't completely destroyed or visible from the outside. Not only did they locate supplies, but also some bags and backpacks to carry them in for the upcoming journey.

The scarcity of supplies is irrelevant should the group consume them too fast. To Michael's obliviousness, the production crew is able to stock each location with additional food and water if it becomes necessary. Still, he congratulates the two men on their finds.

The sun begins to set and the group runs through their checklist of preparations before their journey begins, which includes taking their next round of shots to Michael's chagrin. The entire group quickly jabs the sides of their necks with the syrettes to inject the "medication," except for Michael, Michael remains hesitant. Ellie notices this pause as well as the production crew. A voice chimes into Ellie's earpiece.

"Here's another opportunity for you to get closer to him and gain his trust... do it."

As Michael is soliciting help with administering his shot, Ellie quickly snatches the syrette from his fingers and plunges it into his neck without any regard for gentleness and squeezes the nano tech into his system.

Michael stands there, frozen in his tracks. "Wait, I thought you were a teacher."

"I am, but I have experience working with frightened children." She winks and the whole group chuckles.

Ellie thought her actions were a calculated, cold, and an impersonal act, however, her natural sarcastic instincts in response to Michael's request somehow charmed him enough to crack a smile at her to her surprise.

None of the actors had seen the set at night, only in the daytime during their arrival to the hospital. They are in for quite a treat as they make their way up the ventilation shaft that leads to the outside. The only required plot action at this stage of the narrative is that Ellie must be one of the last ones to exit the hospital. The first or second person will have to play the role of an emotionally distraught individual when they have their first up close and personal encounter with the alien ground force known as 'mechs'.

A mentally troubled paramour would be an even tougher sell to Michael, even if he discovers that his wife had left him years ago, Ellie needs to remain at the rear.

Michael kicks the grate out that is obstructing his exit from the vent, the first to ascend with some supplies is Lance. Lance will be the one to flex his acting muscles as a PTSD stricken individual throughout the remainder of the narrative.

As Michael and Lance are gathering supplies at the rally point established near the hospital's entrance and prepare to help pull up the next person, an enemy ship approaches fast overhead.

Lance stares in astonishment of how believable the ship appears from a distance in the dark as the blinding light shines down on their position, both of their hearts race at an alarming rate. Michael shouts orders to the group still inside the hospital to get back down into the basement and to remain silent.

He hides in the above ground portion of the ventilation shaft while Lance is stuck at the rally point, under the sheet of metal over a low wall.

Even though Lance knows the ships and the aliens are manufactured, the viewers can clearly see that he is genuinely frightened as his adrenaline and heart rate rise to unsustainable levels. The camera focuses in on his face. This plays perfectly from Michael's perspective, as he is watching Lance through the vent, terrified of what's to come.

Lance instinctively draws his pistol from his waistband as a form of security and protection and points it in the sky toward the ship from his cover, all the while Michael is frantically waving at Lance to get his attention not to fire.

The only background the actors received on what they would encounter was very limited during rehearsals, only that they would be evading an alien force that has ground and air capabilities. Any intelligence they would gather on the enemy would be found on the set and all captured on film. They have no idea what they look like or even if they would ever encounter the Ladrones.

Three successive crashing noises slam into the ground away from the hospital but within view of Lance. The ground force that the production crew told the actors to expect is making their first grand appearance. The ground forces being referred to as mechs, crash to the ground, each standing around ten feet tall, a hydraulic mechanism in their bent legs creates a walking motion, crushing the earth beneath them with each step.

Each step sounds mechanical as well as the motion they make when they rotate their upper torsos like a tank turret, a turret with two arms bent at the elbows and 20mm cannons where the hands should be... a terrifying adversary for any survivors to face off against.

Lance's horrified gaze with his eyes and mouth wide open highlights the genius foresight on the part of the producers. It didn't matter what fancy acting or film school they went to if the fear that they would portray is genuine.

The mechs meander pass the hospital as Lance watches from his cover where everyone else can only listen. Michael only catches a glimpse of their mechanical legs as they walk by until the sound of their monstrous steps fade away into the distance after several ground crushing steps.

Lance does his part and remains in a state of shock and horror after what he had just witnessed and won't leave his cover to instill additional fear and mystery of the opposing force into Michael.

Ellie and the rest of the group, unsure of what had transpired above ground, finally make it out of the ventilation shaft to make their way to their first destination. The first few blocks are tense after the near encounter as the group inches their way from cover to cover, not taking any chances of getting spotted by the mysterious enemy.

In those first few blocks, Michael appears to get winded and tries to catch his breath. Despite his military background and training, it becomes apparent that he has not pushed his lungs at all since being confined to a hospital bed for several years. The electro muscular stimulation the hospital had provided could only bring his body so far.

"Remember, you all are supposed to have been lying in a hospital bed for the last few years, act tired and out of breath, don't give him any breadcrumbs into thinking this isn't real!"

The group acknowledges the commands of their overlords and nearly in unison begin to pant and hunch over to give the illusion that they too are pushing their bodies to the limit.

The city landscape post invasion and bombardment is breathtaking as the shadows cast in the moonlight show an ominous, catastrophic event had taken place. Everything looks burned, charred, and some buildings are left partially standing. Most walls and windows are nearly non-existent.

Anyone who has been to this city would believe that this is what it would look like if a nuclear bomb went off. Even the studio audience is quietly pointing and gasping at the famous landmarks and buildings as the camera pans out to drone footage of the landscape that is put on display to the big screen for the audience.

…

The group approaches a stryker armored personnel carrier on the street, presumably sent in by the All Nations Initiative to aid in the retake of the city in the narrative. This is Ellie's cue to act, it signifies the impending introduction of a new character to the group of patients, Bill.

The two had spent a fair amount of time together in rehearsal to develop the special type of bond and chemistry that is only seen in a father and daughter, a bond that is hopefully gripping enough to fool Michael and the audience.

As the group gets closer and closer to get a better view of the stryker, Ellie lets out a startled noise and feigns some whimpering for the cameras. In a few of her investigations as an agent, she has seen dead bodies before. At first glance, the bodies of the three dead soldiers appear hyper realistic, the group looks in amazement. They can't tell if those are actual cadavers, actors, or realistic looking molds. In this case, they are clay molds produced by the make-up and special effects artists.

Upon closer examination, Michael determines that the armored division these soldiers belonged-to are based out of his own; the insignia on their patches tell the tale. The producers could easily have left the bodies inside the stryker unit, however, every detail and decision has a purpose.

To demonstrate the awesome firepower of the invading force, the production crew cut a perfect cylindrical hole through the stryker, showing they were forced to exit in a hurry for fear of being burned alive from the alien weaponry which is able to pierce armor like a hot knife through butter.

Every scene has a story, and within each story, a mystery is sprinkled in as the fourth member of the stryker vehicle is missing. A trail of blood is discovered moving away from the area. Out of the shadows beyond the burning vehicle, a voice rings out, "NO! NO! NO! Don't! Don't touch it!"

Michael, Lance, and Shawn draw their weapons and point them towards the inbound voice. With Ellie's FBI background, it is clear as day which of the three men has handled firearms before. Michael and Lance both have their index fingers off down the slide of their weapons while Shawn, the supposed former cop, has his finger resting inside the trigger guard and ready to shoot.

Ellie catches Michael's quick glance at Shawn's posture for a split second. To the layperson who hasn't been around firearms, this doesn't mean much. But to anyone familiar with handling guns, this is one of the blatant signs of lack of experience with firearms and goes against several rules of gun safety.

Michael isn't a layperson, he is former A.N.I. The best the cast and crew can hope for is that Shawn's cover isn't blown over this microscopic detail and that it would be forgotten in the heat of a tense moment.

Bill, the older gentleman makes his appearance. He informs the group that there is a trap set inside the stryker vehicle meant for the "Ladrones," a word that neither Ellie nor the rest of the group had heard before until now. He leads them to his shelter, the basement of a nearby house less than a block away from the armored personnel carrier.

The group's general understanding of what happened in this post-apocalyptic world is further enlightened by Bill. He discusses the events leading up to the invasion and the bombing campaign that ensued which has caused all of the destruction around them while in the comfort of his shelter. Exactly like the obliviousness of the group to the details of the invasion, Bill too is unaware of the time constraints that the group is on due to their so-called medical conditions to illicit a genuine reaction.

"… We're actually on kind of a schedule here. You see, we're all traveling together because we all came from Harbor Point Medical a little ways back… we all have CN and need to get to the next clinic to take our injections before the disease does its thing. We're ultimately on our way to the underground survivor's encampment, you should join us. We've been told it's all about survival now and not fighting these… Ladrones."

"Oh my…. I'm sorry to hear that. How much further do you have to go to get to the next clinic and when do you have to get there by?

Michael's attempt to recruit Bill for the expedition to the sanctuary falls flat; Bill's desire to put his guerrilla warfare skills and tactics to use and his thirst for revenge consumes him. After gathering some supplies from Bill's hideout, the group departs and continues their journey.

The bonding of Ellie and Bill is saved for their next encounter. Bill only shoots a few glances at her, enough for Michael to notice and spark suspicion of his intentions. The group exits the basement and reenters the harsh realm of Earth's new landscape of a nightmarish reality.

"I want an exterior shot of the groups exit, pan out and keep the building out of the frame, I only want the basement entrance and our people leaving."

The group continues their march toward the next clinic and ignores protocols of noise discipline. They begin talking about what their lives were like before their diagnoses. This directive by the producers is whispered into the ears of the actors in the hopes of getting Michael to open up on telling the group and consequently, the world what life was like from his eyes prior to the invasion.

Michael begins telling his tale, but in a much more quiet tone than the rest have been, "You know, besides a few hiccups in college that lead me to dropout my senior year, I had my life planned out pretty well. Finish my six year commitment with the Initiative, marry the girl of my dreams that I've known since I was twelve, and live happily ever after. I guess I did get to marry that girl, but it wasn't the way I had planned it."

Ellie chimes in. "How so?"

"Me and Eve were engaged and were in the planning phases of our wedding and wanted to have all of our friends and family to celebrate with us, but that didn't happen once I got the diagnosis. We were married back there at that hospital by the in-house chaplain. It wasn't ideal, but we finally did it, she's my best friend."

The group continues exchanging stories of their actual lives for the ease of remembrance, something that they could backup with facts in the event Michael inquires further. A few blocks away from their first destination, they notice several charred cars with no interior, only the metal frames and engine blocks are all that remain. Not even the rubber from the tires endured the supposed scorching fire that rained down from the heavens.

They are fast approaching the clinic. The cars aren't the only thing that are near the entrance, the entire group sees for the first time with their own eyes; a single mech unit standing in their way to safety. Here, Michael, the star of the show, the leader of the group, has one of three choices to make.

One, engage the enemy and storm the site and immediately seek refuge in the lower levels of the clinic if available, two, wait out the mech and simply hope that it moves on before sun up, or three, try to sneak by the alien war machine and use the cover of night to get into the facility.

"Alright, let's try to steer his next move and see if he'll stand firm on his choice or if he'll bend to the group. Charlie, try to get him to attack the mech."

Whichever route Michael chooses, the production crew and his co-stars must be ready to evolve with the situation.

To rationalize the choice, Charlie reminds him of what Bill, who has been fighting these things told them about their weak spot.

"Michael, what are you waiting for? We got the drop on him, shoot him! Remember what that old man told us, shoot it in the dome! That's the weak spot!"

Michael retorts by reminding him of the other little detail that Bill mentioned, "The man also told us that a world of hurt will come down on us if any of those things are attacked. We have plenty of time until dawn, we'll wait him out unless we absolutely have to engage. We don't need patrols buzzing around in the air and the ground forces marching around the area when we're trying to move in undetected. Everyone hold and seek whatever cover you can."

Michael decides on the passive approach. Remain in cover and wait it out, however, he adds, "If an aerial patrol is inbound, we might have no choice but to rush the mech, secure the building, and find the basement entrance right after I put a few rounds into that thing."

Michael raises his rifle and takes aim in the event the shot needs to be taken. The group is tense but at the ready, awaiting Michael's orders. At this point in the narrative that the writers have concocted, no one in the group is to break from protocol and must follow everything he says.

As the studio in the audience and audiences around the world are watching this intense moment unfold, they can see that every member of the group's heart rate is elevated as they await Michael's next command... except for Ellie. She is as cold as ice, calm and ready to await and execute instructions.

She has been on numerous raid operations where the suspects were armed and hostile. Awaiting the order of the agent in charge is routine. In fact, through training and experience, her adrenaline levels remain low and heart rate remains at rest as she constantly re-evaluates and reassesses the evolving situation with a cool head on her shoulders.

Something or someone is creeping up on them from the rear. A voice whispers out from the dark, "Michael... is that you?"

Alarmed, their guns are drawn and pointed into the shadows. The group recognizes the voice and realizes that it's Bill, rejoining the group. A much needed presence for their current predicament. Bill joins Michael up front and center a few yards ahead of the group to assess their situation. In private, he explains to Michael what brought him back is Ellie; she reminds him of his daughter who had passed away years before.

"That gal back there, Ellie. She reminds me too much of my daughter. My little one died of cancer years before any of this happened. I imagine that's what she would have looked like if she had a chance to grow up. It didn't feel right not getting you all to where you need to go without my help."

Michael's vitals indicate sadness and sympathy. The reason for Bill's return is irrelevant, Michael is relieved to have an experienced fighter join the team to increase their chances of survival.

"What do you think we should do? That thing is what's standing in the way of where we need to go. We probably have two more hours until the sun rises; we haven't heard any patrols since we left your place either, so we might be due."

"Well, if you bring that thing down, there will definitely be a patrol right on top of us in no time, so I would highly advise against taking that course of action."

To the benefit of the group, a decision does not have to be made. Automatic gunfire from human weapons start rattling off in the distance. A large spotlight activates from the mech and it begins sprinting away towards the sounds of the violent crackling. The survivors not only saw the immense power of the enemy's arsenal from the disabled stryker back near Bill's hideout, but now, with their own eyes, they can see how quickly their ground units are able to move through uneven roads and patches of debris and rubble.

The brief moment of sympathy Michael expressed from Bill's story about his daughter quickly transforms into fear. This is the precise moment Michael realizes the human race is outclassed in every way possible in a tactical engagement against these beings. Evasion is the only answer for their survival.

"Let's go everybody, on your feet! Now's our chance! Move it!" Michael blurts out.

They don't waste any time seizing the opportunity to reach the clinic, they make a bee-line for it, taking advantage of the distraction that other humans are providing somewhere far away who will soon suffer a terrible fate.

The group reaches their first destination unscathed, no casualties, and no injuries, a success. A wave of relief washes over the group as they make their way through the dilapidated clinic. Stress levels decrease across the board as the structure provides them plenty of cover from the demons in the sky. The next step is to locate the basement and the medication that will keep them alive.

"Brian, you're up for more air time, if Michael can't find the entrance to the stairwell within the next couple of minutes, it's in the back corner to your left over there. The door to the stairwell is actually knocked over and covering up the entrance."

A few minutes pass and Michael is unable to find the entrance on his own, Brian shouts, "I think I got something."

Sure enough, the entrance to the stairwell leading to the basement and medication is underneath the door as the producers had promised. Heading down the stairs, it reminds the patients of their prior underground residence, except different in every other way. More lighting, no puddles on the ground, and a structure that is more intact... at least in the lower level.

The lights work and so does the refrigerated medicine cabinet where their syrettes filled with nano-tech are stored. They don't need them for several more hours, but knowing it is there puts Michael at ease.

"Alright, rest up, we gotta do this all over again tomorrow night and we have to go a little bit further."

Everyone nods, but no one is making any motion to pick a spot on the floor to lie down and sleep. Their first day out in the world was far too exhilarating and frightening. Bill makes his way over to Ellie to officially introduce himself. From Michael's perspective, the chemistry between the two appear natural, the handshake and smiles are a major selling point.

Bill and Ellie are out of earshot of everyone else but still stick to the script for the cameras while they talk about the past lives of their characters that mirror their present day ones in the real world. However, in Ellie's case, she leaves out her experience in the FBI.

It's hard for everyone to focus on their small talk as Michael continues his role as leader by checking in on his fellow survivor's, specifically Lance. Lance plays a very convincing individual that is emotionally distraught after witnessing something traumatic. His acting is amplified by his large frame and the persona he chose as tough guy from the outset of the show.

"I'm just going to ask you straight up man, when I retreated back into the vent when those three mechs fell from the sky, and you were up against the wall under the metal sheet, you had the closest view of them… what did you see that has you so spooked?"

"I saw them... their eyes, their faces…"

"Oh man… the Ladrones? What did they look like?"

"No… I saw the eyes and faces of people… their heads were piked onto the shoulders of those mechs… like a trophy. I can still see the look of fear and terror in their eyes that are frozen on their faces at the moment they were killed! Michael, you owe it to us… if they're about to take any of us, you need to promise us… promise that you will gun us down and put one right between our eyes if it comes to it. Promise me!"

Some horrific imagery that would surely shake anyone to their core had they actually witnessed something of that nature. To add a little pizazz, with one hand, Lance pulls Michael in closer by the collar of his shirt when he makes the request to put a bullet in the head of any member of the group if they are about to be captured.

"Great job Lance, you got Michael rattled, exactly what we wanted."

The rest of the group stops their conversations mid speech to stare at the commotion the two are causing until Michael breaks free and returns to the side of the room where everyone else has gathered.

The morning sunshine makes its arrival as it peeks through the stairwell, signifying to the survivors that it is time to get some rest. The lights in the room are shut off, the only light originating from the basement is coming from a thin sliver of sunlight, faintly lighting the stairwell and a chem stick on the ground near Michael.

Pretending to sleep, Ellie watches him as he puts in his earphones to listen to his wife's messages. The light from the chem stick, lights up his face, enough to see the whites in his eyes and highlighting his cheekbones that are glistening from sweat that his skin is reabsorbing.

She wonders if this will be the point at which his wife leaves him in the journal, where Ellie will be expected to if not ordered to get closer to Michael. She watches him with intense curiosity that the audience mistakes for attraction.

She weighs her options for when the time comes for her to take action and attempt to become an item with Michael. There will be a delicate balance to strike between maintaining her cover for the investigation and her professionalism throughout this show as her actions will be reviewed with extreme scrutiny at the conclusion of the investigation when all is brought to light.

"Ellie, it looks like Michael has gone through all of the audio journal entries this morning, but we can't confirm if he was actually conscious for it or not. Our camera feed from his view was impossible to see in the dark and his heart rate was at rest the whole time, nothing concrete. You'll have to play off of his reactions when he wakes up. Remember though, tonight is the perfect opportunity for you to get close to him when we abduct Bill, you're going to be completely distraught, looking for comfort, make sure you're near Michael after it happens."

Snatched

1730 hours, the cast sits around wide-eyed looking at one other, waiting for the moment Michael awakens from his slumber. The camera dials in on Michael's tablet and slowly traces the cords back to his ears… he fell asleep listening to the recordings, but at what point did he lose consciousness?

The cast makes idle conversation as they begin gathering their belongings to prepare for the journey ahead of them. Subjects such as the distance of the march, inventory and supply checks dominate the conversations until Michael would awaken to guide the story.

As Ellie is gearing up and loading her supplies, she nervously glances at Michael every ten seconds as she is counting down the minutes when the love story arc is expected to begin.

"Ellie, you can't do that, stop looking at him so many times, keep your focus on one thing at a time, this looks really weird for our viewers. You're supposed to give the impression that you like him, not this intense panic you're projecting."

Her conscience can't help it. Today or tomorrow, she's expected to become close with him after his heart is shattered into little bits from actions years ago that didn't actually occur. All the while his wife is back at home or in the audience watching everything unfold, from the moment of introduction, to subtle flirtation, and ultimately… seduction. Ellie doesn't want to be the bad guy, even in this fake life she is currently living.

In the midst of all of the shuffling and commotion, Michael stirs awake. He rubs his eyes for a few seconds, gathers his thoughts and reaches for his map to plot a course to the next medical facility marked on the map, a course that would obscure their travel for anything looking for them from the air. However, Bill interjects. "We won't be able to start here, or it will leave us exposed for too long that is. A skyscraper went down there and it's blocking the street for at least two blocks, that's roughly where I was when all of this started when I came into town to visit. We'll need to head at least two blocks that way to get around it."

Bill's updated information on the new landscape of their route is only partially true; the route Michael had originally plotted did not coincide with the special effects team's plans for Bill's abduction and suicide mission. The patients would have to exit their current location from the east, not the west.

Nearing the time for departure, Ellie takes the initiative when injecting their shots, she grabs one for Michael and sticks him in the neck before he even has time to react.

"You're welcome" she says.

The producers and the audience can see from Michael's eyes, a hint of attraction emerging and some sparks starting to kindle for Ellie.

"Nice work Ellie, we're getting positive feedback from him, but we're still not sure if he's listened to the whole tape yet, ease up a little."

Inside, she feels sick with herself, playing a part in messing with his emotions. She was sent here to investigate the company, something she has yet to make any progress on. The only way that she can carry on with the mission is to compartmentalize her guilt for the greater good when toying with this poor man's emotions.

The lights are shut off before the group opens the door to head up the stairwell, the room turns pitch black as their eyes readjust to the darkness, the cameras switch back to night vision. Michael heads to the front to lead the group and makes his way up the stairs to get above ground. It is still completely dark in the stairwell, everyone's breathing is amplified due to their heightened sense of sound until Michael pushes the door up over his head to look at the surrounding area on the surface.

The ambient light outside is enough to make their faces visible as each member of the cast makes their way out of the stairwell. No enemies in sight, the group makes their way into the street to head east.

Within a few steps into their trek to the next clinic, Bill runs up to the front in a near sprint to scout on ahead, he's on a mission to create some distance between himself and the group. Michael stops to wave everyone else forward and performs a mental head count to make sure everyone has made it out as he holds up the rear.

Bill gets up about a block and a half ahead of everyone else. He waits for the rest of the survivors to catch up. His heart rate intensifies and sweat dribbles down his forehead and neck, not from the physical exertion but for what is to come. Like a child confronting his fear of a scary amusement park ride, Bill mentally prepares himself to be flung into the sky at a high rate of speed into the empty darkness.

Out of nowhere, two men wearing all black nylon suits come out from the shadows and startle Bill enough to cause an internal jump within his body. They quickly rig a harness on him and clip the bungee cords to prepare the launch. All of this is accomplished within a few seconds.

As quickly as they appeared, the two men are gone, giving no chance for Michael, or anyone making their way to Bill, to spot them. The bungee cords begin to stretch at high tension at his waist. His foot is anchored and clipped into a cement post buried deep within the ground, a metal ring is barely noticeable amongst the gravel and debris.

The special effects team is in charge of triggering the release when the time comes, the only thing keeping him grounded to the Earth is a carabiner with a remote release. To keep the illusion of the fourth wall alive in the show, the camera feed into Bill's perspective is cut off and remains with members of the group and cameras near their location.

"Alright, we have him anchored in, give us the signal when you want us to launch."

"Wait, hold steady, let Michael and the group get a little closer… perfect"

"Bill, wave your arm once you're ready, we'll send out the ship and prepare to launch."

After a deep breath, Bill waves towards the group, this puts into motion the vibration of the ground and the sound of a ship vertically lifting off on the other side of a high mound of dirt and debris at Bill's position. The area becomes lit up, night becomes day. Everyone immediately dives to the ground, trying not to be spotted and blending with the ground, there's nowhere to run.

The ship is now hovering fifty yards over Bill. While the entire area within a few blocks turns into a bright white haze, a dark blue spotlight pierces down with Bill at its focal point. He drops to both knees and is frozen as he prepares for the bungee cord to fling him in the air.

"Alright Bill if you can hear me… show your suicide vest and trigger to the cast, Michael is getting ready to make a kill shot on you… alright, he can see the vest and the trigger, get ready, we're about to send you."

Bill continues to feign his struggle to move but makes it obvious that he is wearing a suicide vest rigged with plastic explosives. Even through the blinding light and the chaos caused by the loud ship, Michael recognizes what is happening and lowers his weapon and gives the order for everyone to retreat. "BACK TO THE CLINIC, NOW! NOW! NOW!"

Bill laughs maniacally as everyone follows Michael's command to run away. Bill's laughter turns into screams as his body shoots towards the light until he disappears into the light and his screams cease. The sound of the ship's exhaust drowns him out. The ship continues to ascend and makes its way towards the group's general direction until a small explosion appears at the rear of the ship.

The guidewires for the ship are angled downward to simulate a crash in the distance. The ship's momentum carries it a hundred yards beyond the clinic until it crashes in a fiery blaze some ways away and skids on the ground creating more flames. The scene created by the crash is a magnificent sight that cannot be denied, even from the most skeptical eyes.

Back at the abduction site, in complete darkness, the tension on the bungee cords attached to Bill loosen until his feet reach the ground and the men in black nylon suits reappear, undo the harness, and quietly remove him from the set during the confusion. The remainder of the group gathers back at the clinic seeking shelter from the retaliation the invaders will unleash.

The group plays ignorant to the events that had occurred and await Michael's explanation in his own unscripted words as to what happened tonight, however, he remains silent, waiting for the sounds of enemy reinforcements, standing alone at the top of the stairwell. He lifts the door to visually scan for any signs of them, nothing. Only some faint light, projected by the fire coming from the general direction the ship had crash landed.

After fifteen minutes, Charlie breaks the silence, "What did you see? What happened? Did something shoot that down?" Additional voices chime in, "Yeah, what's going on?"

Still, Michael doesn't budge. He remains quiet and hand gestures the group to do the same while trying to get a view of the happenings outside. The producers queue the ships to nudge him back down into the basement. Once more, the ground violently shakes and lights from multiple ships swarm the area above ground.

Michael quietly and carefully lowers the door back down to seal off the stairwell. They all make their way down the stairs into the basement and gather around Michael. He begins to speak in a somber tone.

"Bill is a hero. I'm guessing he didn't plan on getting captured by those things, and if he did, he was prepared to bring them down with him. He rigged himself with explosives, he saved our lives back there."

Putting herself in the mindset of someone who had lost a friend due to someone else's negligence, Ellie takes the route of displaying anger and placing blame on someone, that someone being Michael. "Why didn't you save him? You could have pulled him out of there! It wasn't too late."

Real tears roll out from her eyes as she buries her face into Michael's chest. Those real tears come with real emotion as the monitor for the audience displays her experiencing sadness. The studio audience applauds in awe, they are well aware of the fact that other than Michael, she is the only other cast member that is not an actor by trade.

Ellie channels her experience of actual loss of one of her team members in the field with the FBI years back during a botched raid. This memory not only helps with her acting that night, but also reminds her of the task at hand, the reason she was sent to the studios. Everything she does here is in furtherance of the greater good… at least that is what she tries to tell herself to prepare her for what may need to happen.

Cue to Go

A few hours pass and Ellie's head remains rested on Michael's shoulders and the others keep their chatter to a minimum as if their lives depended on it to avoid the monsters above. They look up at the ceiling after each ship zooms passed or mechs stomping on the ground in their vicinity. They don't dare turn on the lights, the only thing illuminating the room at the moment are a few chem sticks.

Resigned to the fact if the enemy finds them, the game of survival would be over and there is nothing he could do about it. Michael is the only one that is able to relax, relaxed enough to listen to more of his wife's audio journal.

The juxtaposition of the cast's reaction to the situation is undeniably ironic. On one hand, you have an individual who believes the alien invasion is real and his life could end at any moment's notice is the only one at peace compared to the rest of the group that knows they aren't in any real danger. They don't know what to expect next on this terrifying ride that is being labeled as a TV show.

Ellie awakens from the sound and vibration of Michael sniffles and feeble attempts to fight back his tears. Keeping her eyes closed and pretending to be fast asleep, she contemplates how to react when confronting him. From here on out, she must play the part of the love interest in the narrative.

Ellie takes a deep breath, opens her eyes and can see the green light gently reflecting from his face where the tears had rolled. They don't make eye contact, but Ellie can see the shine in his eyes and tear droplets forming and ready to fall from his eyelashes. She watches him a little longer before coming up with the right words to say, perhaps no words at all might be most comforting. Ellie squeezes his arm a little tighter and nestles her head in closer to his chest.

Michael finishes the last two audio files and keeps his earphones plugged in, staring at the wall. Despite the constant tremors the patrols are creating and the near deafening noises around their location from the mechs, Michael is able to fall asleep out of pure emotional fatigue.

The pressure and responsibility to lead the group falling back onto his shoulders will have to wait until tomorrow. In his dreams, he hopes to wake up from this terrible nightmare of Earth's annihilation and the love of his life leaving him and falling for another man.

Awake the entire time, Ellie has nothing to do but remain in his arms, staring into the faintly lit room. Early in the morning, Michael starts to mumble in his sleep, "Eve…. Why??? No… our story can't end here…. I still love you… Come back…"

"Ellie, don't look so weird, he might wake up and see you like that." She doesn't know how to respond.

Michael slowly comes to as he rubs his eyes into focus. Ellie has been awake for some time, still lying in his arms. Whether she likes it or not, her readings are showing an attraction to him despite his saddened state. While the others are asleep, she whispers, "Is everything OK? I saw your earphones in and guessed that you were listening to those recordings again? It's OK to be sad you know?"

"I don't really want to talk about it. The things I heard on there are from years ago and are inconsequential to what we're trying to do here. Thinking or talking about it doesn't help our current situation. How about you? Are you OK? I didn't realize that you and Bill had gotten so close in that short amount of time."

"Yeah, I think I'm fine now... I'm sorry for the way I acted last night, there's nothing you could have done. I guess I've been lucky all my life, up until all this has happened, no one in my life had passed away. I know it's silly to still think that now, since the chances of the ones we knew and loved before all this are still alive."

"You know Ellie... I'm starting to come around to thinking that now myself, the six of us have to stick together if we're going to get through this. There's no guarantee that anyone else is out there but us, even if we make it to the encampment."

"Oh God... I'm so sorry, I totally forgot about your wife. I mean... she's probably still out there, that's why we need to keep on trucking to get to her, she's probably waiting for you at the underground camp!"

"You better knock it off with your verbal judo skills! No, it's OK, I have to accept that she's more than likely gone. All we can do right here and now is work together and survive.

Michael wasn't ready to tell anyone what had happened in those tapes. An awkward silence seizes the room. "OK everyone, Ellie is struggling a little bit with Michael, help her out!"

The actors are quickly discovering the difficulty in acting natural in the process of waking up. This is especially true when someone is telling you when to do so. Nobody knows what they should look like when they wake up. However, the only person they need to convince is Michael, the people they want to convince is the world.

Ellie flinches at the sounds of the others waking and moves away from Michael, the idea of being in the arms of a married man isn't immediately clear to her as being a faux pas, at least not until she is caught in the act with others in the room. She completely forgets everyone is watching her every move from various camera angles and even from her own eyes. For a brief moment, she actually thought the setting was real.

The group makes their departure from the clinic, this time down one person. An air of silent panic comes over Michael and the group as they walk through the area where

Bill was abducted and paid the ultimate price. Michael is visibly disturbed. It's difficult to tell if it is the result of losing a member of their team, finding out his wife had left him, or a combination of the two.

This moment of despair is precisely what the producers wanted in order to make "good TV", but a medical team is standing by in the event his depression rises to a concerning level and he attempts self-harm on live television.

"Michael's readings are at an acceptable level, continue on, there is no need to intervene, our ratings are peaking."

The only item planned on the itinerary for this leg of their journey is an air to air battle between spaceships for the cast to witness. "Once you get near the diner, make sure you get Michael to seek shelter there for a moment. It's the perfect vantage point we've created; you'll be in for a treat."

As the group approaches the diner, Shawn and Charlie grab some water bottles from their bags and stop to drink, in between each sip they place their hands on their knees gasping for air, signifying a need for a break.

Michael takes the bait and spots the diner as planned and instructs the group to make their way in… right on cue, the ships make their presence known by the thunderous roar of their engines until eventually they can be seen through the window frames of the diner with the backdrop of the blackened night with the city's skyline in the foreground.

The ship to ship battle becomes a light spectacle that is even more convincing to the unsuspecting mind when put in conjunction with the roaring of ships and the vibrations caused by the explosions. The pursuing ship fires two laser beams at the lead ship and causes two loud explosions until it catches fire.

Even the cast is amazed as they watch the awesome display of effects of primitive remote controlled aircraft on guidewires with the alien ship's cheaply made exterior. It only needs to look good from far away. The painted look of astonishment on the group makes the experience real, real even for the viewers, especially Michael. The ship streaks across their view with a trail of fire, it crashes into what remains of a few buildings knocking them down on its way to the ground causing more deep tremors felt and heard from afar.

To plant the idea that they might have an ally in this war for survival, Brian asks, "Did you guys see that!? You think one of those things is on our side?"

There is no time to digest the statement; reinforcements of the downed ship may be on the way. They hastily cease their break and continue on course to the hospital, a hospital the crew has built to scale to resemble a large museum in the middle of the city that was once a popular landmark in the downtown area. This will give Michael and the audience an idea of where they are in this transformed landscape.

A couple of hours until sunrise, the group finally makes it to an alley downtown with a direct line of sight on the museum converted into a large intake facility. The parking lot is empty and the entrance is wide open with no cars or other potential forms of cover. To make matters worse, the moon appears to be even brighter tonight, it will highlight their position to the enemy above.

After catching their collective breaths and preparing for the sprint, the group is ready... set... and off to the races. From a bird's eye view, they are seen running side by side with not much separation between each member. They are nearly to the entrance until a ship makes an appearance, unexpected to Michael as well as the cast.

Not knowing what is to come and how Michael will react, they all look to Michael mid stride, awaiting his orders as if he is actually leading them to their best chance to survive the situation. Without saying a word, he waves his arm and points at the ground and dives. Everyone follows suit and immediately hits the deck in front of what appears to be remnants of battered small concrete steps leading up to the entrance of the museum. They scramble to get on the other side to put the mound between them and the ship.

The cast doesn't know if one of them would be removed from the show through another "abduction" or "kill." The fear is genuine for everyone but Ellie, she is the only one slated for required interactions with Michael later in the story. Getting removed from a show means less camera time, less camera time means less exposure for their acting careers. Something all new actors fear most… getting prematurely written off.

To their relief, the ship continues passed the group and closes in on their old position near the alley. They get into the entrance of the museum to locate the medication. Michael recalls the layout of this medical facility from what it used to be, a museum of history and industry. The lower level used to house the exhibit of the great fire beneath the city, the most likely area where the medication would be stored.

For some unexplained reason, this is the only building completely intact the group has seen throughout their journey. This fact doesn't deter them nor call into question their desire to stay there for the day and search for the suppressant at this station. Inside the museum awaits a horrific sight. Michael follows the group into the clinic to seek shelter from any spacecraft that are still lurking in the skies.

The mystery of why this building still stands in one piece is answered. Upon walking through the main concourse, the putrid smell of piles of decomposing bodies on the first floor assaults their senses of smell, Charlie is the only actor in the vicinity to witness the heinous scene up close. It causes a gag reflex until he hunches over with his hands on each of his knees and vomits onto the ground.

The others turn away in search of the stairs to the lower levels.

Ellie on the other hand lays witness to something even more uniquely disturbing on the second floor. This hospital that was once a museum before the rise of CN has now transformed into a site where the invaders are conducting experiments on the native population. Tubes and alien instruments are running through a few lifelike cadavers to add to the realism of the scene. Michael embraces Ellie in order to shield her from the grotesquery of the first and second floor terrors. He motions her to go downstairs into the lower levels to join the others.

The emotional readouts of everyone on scene are that of shock and horror. They frequently have to remind themselves that none of this is real to get through this museum without losing their minds. Everything around them was created and molded from the minds and hands of writers and artists hired to make this as realistic, immersive, and frightening as possible, they earned their paychecks.

Michael doesn't believe anyone else can handle the scene, so he sends everyone downstairs as a group in search of the meds, with the exception of Shawn, the ex-cop. "Shawn, look for the medical storage area on the first floor, everyone else, move downstairs and do the same. I'll check the second floor. We can't relax until we know we're set with the syrettes."

Michael is unaware of what the others have discovered downstairs, but it cannot be worse than the first and second floors. He knows through the video at the onset of their journey, this entire facility was dedicated to CN patients, there may not be a central location where the suppressant syrettes are stored, he and Shawn continue searching the upper two levels while the others search down below.

Per the narrative, Ellie and the group discover the location of the meds and await Michael to make his descent into the lower level to make yet another terrible discovery. There are no bodies or patients downstairs, but there is a monumental problem they face.

Depending on Michael's actions and decisions in the next few moments, there are several different paths for the narrative to travel. Ellie counts that there are only five syrettes remaining for the six of them, for dramatic effect, the four of them wait for Michael and Shawn to make their way down the stairs to see their discovery. The cameras center their focus around Michael and Shawn.

Michael's heart rate increases as he slowly walks down the stairs noticing everyone is motionless and gathered around the cabinet.

Lance asks, "How are we going to do this?"

Wasteland of Forking Paths

"Lance, when you break the stick, hold the broken one second from the end on your left hand. Everyone pick one other than that one, Ellie, that one is reserved for you."

The writers and producers anticipate two possible outcomes in this scenario; either Michael chooses to go with Ellie and they head to the final clinic together or Michael decides to stay with the group and Ellie must traverse the wasteland alone. If the latter happens, the mechs will be sent in to destroy the building and chase Michael out to the next waypoint with an undetermined amount of casualties. The writers could not have possibly anticipated what would happen next.

Lance breaks the tongue depressors, "Alright, simple old school way to do this, person that draws the short stick doesn't get the med. Everyone, touch a stick and keep your fingers on it, I'll keep the one that no one is touching."

One by one, the group reaches in to grab a stick before Michael to ensure that Ellie draws the short one. The group pulls away and Ellie walks away devastated and scared after having drawn the short one. Out of nowhere, Michael snatches the broken stick from her and replaces it with his own whole one.

"But Michael, you can't, they need you… I need to go, it's only fair."

"You guys have been doing great. Keep doing what we've been doing to get to the last waypoint and you'll be fine. Keep your head low and always be close to cover in case you need it, maintain noise and light discipline, and take your time if there's any question about trouble being nearby. I'll meet up with you all there and we'll head to the sanctuary together. Remember, those things could return to check on their experiments upstairs at any time, rotate shifts for guard duty, and pick a spot down here where you can sneak out if you need to."

The entire cast is shocked in addition to audiences streaming the video. The chat rooms light in disbelief, even some members in the studio audience are audibly crying, crying from this act of selflessness, bravery, or perhaps even love.

Ellie, the undercover agent, is overcome with emotions and loses her composure in the moment. She knocks the stick from Michael's hand and grabs him by the collar of his shirt and presses her lips on his and kisses him. The other cast members are in shock as they witness this display of affection. She backs away and says. "Sorry… thank you Michael."

Despite Michael's eyes being open with his hands up, both he and Ellie's readings indicate strong feelings of passion as their hormone levels rise, rise enough to where Michael's emotions overcome him as well. He reciprocates her kiss by pulling her back in for another one. The producers are speechless as they watch from their monitors, unsure of what direction to give their actors. They could not have written or staged anything better than what had transpired.

The director is stunned and does not know the shot he wants for this scene, he pauses for a brief moment then begins barking orders. "Um… I want an overhead view of this, start out zoomed in and pan out on the two, this is priceless!"

Michael turns his back to the group and walks toward his backpack, "Don't worry about me, I'll see you in less than a day, try to keep up." After gathering his supplies and eating a quick meal, he heads for the exit to take advantage of the remaining minutes of darkness in the early dawn.

"Ellie, what are you waiting for? Go after him! You two are supposed to go the rest of the way together!"

Not more than a few steps outside the museum, Ellie catches up to Michael.

"What are you doing here? Get back inside, the sun is about to come out and light us up like a Christmas tree!"

Ellie replies, "I'm not letting you leave without me, you can't stop me."

"Fine! You have to do exactly as I say and stay on my hip, you got it?" he replies.

Ellie nods.

The majority of their journey together is uneventful; there are no enemy sightings or movement to report on.

Ellie uses this opportunity to get Michael to open up about himself, not only for the viewers, but subconsciously for her as well.

"I know we've only known each other for a few days, so you don't have to answer if you don't want to. But… what did you hear on those tapes from your wife the other day?"

"You ever have someone tell you something so Earth shattering, that it pretty much changes your whole belief system and what you know to be true and set in stone cold fact reality? That's essentially what I heard that night."

"Care to elaborate?"

Before Michael can answer, the relentless patrols that have been hounding the group since the beginning of their journey reappear and stalk their movements once more. The ship is higher up than usual, Michael and Ellie get no warning signs other than the sound. Though nearly impossible for the ships to find them from the air in the thick of the downtown district, Michael and Ellie find it prudent to get off the street and make a mad dash for the remains a shopping mall.

The two seek refuge at a checkout counter near the entrance, far enough inside so that anything flying over the buildings would not be able to spot them.

"Alright Ellie, you are looking way too calm out there, this is the first time you have traveled by day, you don't know what to expect. Make the audience believe that you're in a situation where at any moment those things can spot you two and kill you. You're not in control. Act frightened enough to where Michael might grab you and hold you to comfort you... Good..."

Ellie feigns trembling in her hands and stares intently at the ceiling. She could see in her peripheral vision that Michael takes notice, he starts to whisper to her. Eve... my wife, well, I guess ex-wife now..."

She ceases the heavy breathing and begins to listen intently.

"... we met when we were young, back in elementary school. She was the only one that I had ever loved and cared about. The thought of having someone care about me the way she did was a foreign concept that was impossible to fathom. The messages she left for me kept me up to date with things that were happening in her life and the daily struggles.

Eventually, it led up to her meeting someone else and that other man having a kind enough heart to keep me alive in the hospital while they started a family of their own. Eve divorced me and married him... the audio journals stop after that... except for a couple more days leading up to the invasion."

"I'm so sorry Michael..."

Still hunkered down behind the checkout register, the two hug as the sound of the ship grows distant. However, they are not quite out of the woods yet. The sound of multiple mech units are making their presence known with each step somewhere on the street. These are the only enemy units that are put on display during the day as the ship's appearance of mostly plastic molding would not look so convincing in the daylight. They would never be seen, only heard.

There are at least three mech units in their area with at least one outside of the mall entrance that the two had entered. "We'll try to wait this one out, if it doesn't move in the next ten minutes, we'll make our way through the mall until we get to a part of the street that's clear. These buildings are mostly connected until we get to the next street."

The strategy to remain still and hope that the enemy moves on proves fruitless. Twenty minutes pass and the mech is still holding its post. Michael and Ellie decide to go deeper into the mall, hoping to make an exit at a department store that will spit them out on a different part of the street.

The two make their way to a wishing fountain in the mall, there is still water in the fountain. "We're gonna need more flirting from you Ellie. He's washing his face, splash him with the water, do something to get his attention."

In her mind, splashing Michael with water would create unnecessary noise when the enemy is skulking about on the other side of these walls and it would seem unnatural. The two are obviously physically attracted to one another, so she does what she would do given the situation of not having had a warm shower in years. She dunks her face in the water to rinse her face and hair.

While rubbing her eyes to scatter the droplets from her face and ringing out the water from her hair, Ellie catches Michael staring and shoots him a flirtatious smile. Michael can't help but blush as his temperature rises. She begrudgingly obliges the wishes of the producers and gently splashes Michael.

The two continue their trek through the mall creating a damp trail to the store that will put them on the street, away from the mech they had nearly encountered head on. Refuge is sought behind another cashier stand. Michael moves on towards the exit of the store where daylight is entering through the large glass doors. He scouts the situation on this side of the street to determine if it is safe to move out.

"Ellie, stay here, let me check it out first, stay quiet, and watch my back."

"Ellie, when his back is turned, you're going to walk back towards the fountain as quiet as you can so he doesn't notice you missing, there's an electronics store nearby, wait there until we tell you to go back to Michael. We're going to send the mechs running away once you meet back up with him at the cashier stand."

She raises her eyebrows and her hands out of Michael's view. She is confused at the orders the producers are giving her. She whispers. "Why?"

"Trust me… when he asks you where you were, tell him you devised a plan for a solar powered radio to activate away from your position. This will give you both a clear shot to the hospital and a reason for the mechs to leave your area."

Ellie patiently waits for the signal…

"Now go!"

As Michael is trapped outside under the nose of the mech, Ellie is given the order to return after being away for a few minutes.

"Alright, go back. He's pinned down by a mech outside but got away, meet back up with him and remember what I told you."

Ellie reconvenes with Michael after his scouting mission is cut short by a mech outside of the exit.

"You're OK… I told you to sit tight, what happened!?"

"Trust me…"

"What!?"

"That thing is going to be running down the other way through the street in a few minutes. We'll have a clear shot to get back on track… in theory…"

"How do you know this? What did you do?"

"A little thinking outside the box, trust me... watch them go."

The two watch the machine standing outside, guarding their path to freedom. A few minutes pass and the mech turns and runs down the street as they can hear it stomping with each step at high speed. Multiple mechs in the distance behind them are also heard crashing through walls inside the mall. Shots from the mech's cannons ring out as well.

"OK, let's go."

The two run for the door and make their hasty exit and are on their way to the last waypoint until they reach the human sanctuary.

After several minutes of walking, Michael begins to interrogate Ellie as to how she accomplished the feat of luring the mechs away from their position. He remains suspicious of how they were able to make a clean get away. "How did you do that?"

"Did you notice the electronics store by the water fountain?"

"No, and I don't see where you're going with this."

"I grabbed one of those portable solar radios in the store. It was dark in there so I knew it probably hasn't had any juice for a while. I jammed some paper in the trigger that activates the transmission and left it near the water fountain, barely out of reach of the sunlight. It was only a matter of time until it activated on its own while we were away."

"How did you know that would work?"

"I didn't… we didn't exactly have a lot of options, but I did remember that guy told us not to use radios to communicate since those things could track us. I saw you pinned at the car, so I had to do something quick."

Michael's suspicion quickly turns into a continual and gradual growing attraction to Ellie for her intelligence and quick thinking. The two kiss, for a brief second, Ellie forgets that she is on a show and is filled with elation and mutual feelings for Michael as she enjoys the moment and pulls him in tighter by the shoulders during their kiss… until reality hits her, though she remains calm as the two separate from the kiss.

The disgusting truth of reality television becomes crystal clear to Ellie, people are actually watching them for their own entertainment, hoping for conflict, hoping to see a relationship develop, hoping to live vicariously through these characters in a different world. Her colleagues and superiors are also watching, she refocuses on the mission.

They continue their march down the street, only a few blocks away from their destination. The producers tell Ellie that there wouldn't be any more patrols in the air or on ground for them to worry about the rest of this leg, however, they didn't make any promises of any human encounters…

A fortified position is spotted up ahead. A few soldiers looking down the street with some civilians huddled behind two cars are hunkered down taking cover from whatever they see down range. There isn't any enemy movement down the street and their position is also widely exposed in the daylight which makes the situation all the more peculiar.

Michael and Ellie jog up to the survivors in exaggerated, large, and loud steps as to not startle them on their flank. Ellie gets ahead of Michael, gets low and taps a woman on the shoulder and nudges her, no response, their backs remain turned toward them.

"Psssst… Hey…"

Ellie tries tugging on her shirt, the woman spins one hundred eighty degrees as she collapses. As she falls to the ground, Michael briefly saw her eyes rolled to the back of her head and some dried blood stains on her nose, neck, and chest.

None of them are alive. They've been dead and in this position for at least a day upon closer inspection. There are dried blood stains in the front of their uniforms, some of the individuals with their eyes still open. The three civilians include some women in hospital scrubs and two men in business attire. Michael tells Ellie to step away to shield her from the scene as he scavenges the bodies for ammo and supplies.

Upon doing so, Michael happens to recognize one of the nurses and eventually the sergeant of the fire team. They are the same two people that appeared in the video when they first woke up. The writers thought putting these corpses would instill fear; fear that he too may suffer their same fate as they were only a day or two ahead of Michael's group and less than a day away from the sanctuary.

"Ellie, if he doesn't recognize those people from the video, it is your job to point it out."

It's clear as day that Michael recognizes the two bodies as he spends extra time around them while scavenging and reads aloud the names of the soldier and the nurse. Those corpses are real people with some serious costume and makeup work done. To add to the effect, the "actors" have been sedated with a cocktail that also keeps their breathing and heart rate low. Michael fills up his backpack with ammo and water, "Alright Ellie, let's move, there's nothing we can do for them."

They finally make it to "Neighborhood Primary Care," the penultimate leg of their journey has been completed, they are only one day away from reaching the underground camp. First things first, they must locate the medication for their next shot as it has been nearly been twenty-four hours since their last injection. The stairwell to the basement is completely obstructed by immovable boulders of concrete.

The only other viable route to the basement would be the elevators that can't possibly be functional as the top few floors are completely missing from this building. Michael comes up with a plan to use the elevator shaft to shimmy down to the lower level. Making his way down, he nearly rolls his ankle as he jumps down on top of a broken elevator car that appears to have bottomed out.

"What's wrong Michael!?"

"I think I rolled my ankle... but we have to keep going, we probably have a half hour left until we need our shot."

The two make their way through the elevator car to the basement level, but Ellie is now tasked with searching for the medication as Michael hobbles around. This care center is the smallest of the CN patient facilities that they have come across as there are only two hospital beds in the room which presents a quandary in itself... if this location doesn't house that many CN patients, there may be a limited supply of syrettes.

"Hey hey! Look what I found!" Ellie opens the medical cabinet and feels the cold air rush to her face.

After a sigh of relief, they inject their syrettes. Ellie offers to look at Michael's ankle and wrap it up to prevent any further injury.

"Have a seat over there on that bed, let me wrap up your ankle, we can't have you hobbling around like that, next stop is home!"

This is Ellie's moment, she must fulfill the producers' wishes to maintain her cover in the studios, she promises to herself that she would not go any further than kissing. As Michael is lying on the hospital bed, Ellie swoops under the bad ankle and says, "Don't worry Michael, I know what I'm doing, they gave us basic first-aid training for my students, let's see if I can remember."

Holding up his foot for no more than one or two seconds, she gently sets it down and moves in to seduce him. She straddles him by the stomach with both of her hands on his shoulders and presses her forehead against his as they engage in a kiss. Both of their hormone and adrenaline readings are off the charts, but she remembers the promise she made to herself and remembers that Michael is married to a loving wife that is possibly watching the entire scene unfold.

They kiss for a few minutes and caress one another's cheeks until Ellie, still completely clothed, moves into a cuddling position. She places her head on Michael's chest and simply says, "Thank you."

With her face so close to Michael, the producers dare not contact her, Ellie's positioning in this entire scene is purely intentional and methodical. She does enough to keep her cover and keeping the audience and producers intrigued with the love story, without compromising Michael's real life outside of "The Invasion," or the judging eyes of her superiors and coworkers, examining each detail of her undercover assignment.

After spending the last sixteen hours running for their lives, the two immediately fall asleep into each other's arms.

Re-Entry

Immediately after Ellie's abduction and removal from the show, the producers pull her aside and reunite her with fellow cast members for interviews and ask them several questions about the show and specifically, her feelings about Michael. She submits, but after a few too many prodding questions directed at only her, she answers, "Alright guys, I think that's enough, I want to get out of these clothes, head to medical and get all of these devices out of me, and take a nice, long shower."

Ellie is still visibly shaken and disoriented from the abduction stunt, her internal organs feel like they have all shifted out of place and are slowly settling back into place. She heads to medical for a brief examination and to remove her ear implant then immediately heads straight to the locker room for a long overdue shower.

In these brief moments alone, she no longer shoulders the responsibility of being Ellie Pearson, uncovering the missing link in a major investigation, or Ellie Harris, rising actress who tried to swoon a happily married man, in this new form of bread and circus.

This blissful existence in limbo would only last as long as she remained in the confines of the locker room. For this reason alone she bides her time drying her hair, shaving her legs, and gathering her things from her locker.

Upon powering up her phone, there are numerous text messages waiting to be read. Most are from family and friends who saw her on television, but there is one that stands out from the rest. It's from an unknown sender and is time stamped as being sent an hour ago.

Ellie touches the envelope with a question mark to open the message. "This dispatch is urgent and is NOT over a secure line, time is of the essence. We have strong human intel reports that indicate Entity 1 is engineering and producing a weapon of mass destruction on-site at your location. It will be in the basement of a brown warehouse missing two of four of its walls near the northern edge of Entity 1's set. Gather the evidence. - Handler"

A look of shock comes over Ellie's face. It begins to make sense as to why the Bureau has sent in a veteran agent to investigate something as heavy as WMD production on U.S. soil. They must not have been sure as they sent her in with no prejudices as to what she is investigating, something solid must have come up. Just like that, Ellie is thrown back into the lion's den before she even exits the room.

After a deep breath, she grabs the door handle, exhales, and twists the locker room door. Beyond the doors are her fellow cast members, Lance, Shawn, Brian, Charlie, and Bill, all greeting her with smiles with their hands out, reaching for a high-five. Caught completely off guard and startled, her look of seriousness quickly transforms into a bug-eyed smile.

Lance is the first one to speak, "Great job out there Ellie, we all know that you're a newbie, but you did an amazing job! You should have seen the audience's reactions to your performance, we were there sitting with them watching you, they loved it! We're getting drinks in the dining area, you're coming with us and we aren't taking no for an answer. No cameras, just us, no stupid post-wrap interviews, let's go."

Without saying a word, she shrugs her shoulders and smiles while she puts her arms around Brian and Charlie's shoulders as they walk as a group to the studio set's dining hall. Not sure when she will be able to break away from them to investigate, she plays along and has a few drinks with the guys which keep her on the studio's grounds while the show is still filming.

They get to the buffet style cafeteria to get some food and reconvene at a table with a booth. Bill has a large grin on his face, looks around, and pulls out a bottle of rum from a brown paper bag. "We pretty much have to celebrate right?"

He pours out a healthy shot for everyone and they all raise their glasses. "It's been fun working with all of you over the last month or so, and I truly mean it when I say I wish you all the best in your future endeavors. I see a great future in film for all of you."

"Hear hear!" a few of the men shout.

One drink becomes five. Ellie is intoxicated but is still cognizant of her assignment. She has enough awareness to know that her state of inebriation would make a great pretext in the event that she is discovered in restricted areas of the studio.

"Alright guys, it's been great hanging out with you and getting to know you all, but I have to call a taxi and head home." Ellie gives each and every one of the guys a hug, she walks away, looks back, and is able to see that all of the men remain at the table to continue their drinking to celebrate the impending finale and wrap of the show.

She checks one more time to see if anyone is watching her head back into the locker room to access the staging area to get back on the set; no security cameras or figures of authority in sight. Ellie manages to get back to the locker room and back to the staging area undetected. The next part is the difficult one. The only entrance she is aware of back onto the set is only a few feet away but is locked by a card reader, something none of the cast members were granted.

Ellie spots a production assistant talking on his phone in the hallway, preoccupied in conversation. The column he is leaning on conceals her approach as she swoops in and unclamps his ID card near his side pocket without his knowledge. She swipes the card, the reader flashes green, beeps and the door unlocks. Ellie is back on the set, she slides the card back into the hallway before she gently shuts the door behind her.

The text message did not include any coordinates and it is now late in the evening, nearly impossible to see the colors of buildings in the vast studio. Her only clue is to head north, her point of exit from the show was near the northern most point of the set, like the show she must march on with only the moonlight to guide her way.

After thirty minutes of wandering, she realizes how aimless her search is as there are several buildings meeting the description that was given to her in the text message. She pauses for a moment before deciding to break protocol and calling the field office on her phone to receive further guidance. She pulls out her phone to make the call, it starts to vibrate before she dials, an incoming text from 'Unknown' once again.

"Head five blocks due northwest. It should be the largest structure in the area. - Handler"

Unaware of how she is being tracked, she moves along as instructed, slightly stumbling every few steps from the drinks she had earlier. Her experience this time on the set is much more peaceful, no one around her is armed, she doesn't have to feign terror from an enemy that is out to kill or her capture her that doesn't exist… but her surroundings are hauntingly silent without the chatter of her co-stars or the companionship of Michael.

Ellie approaches the warehouse matching the description provided in the text. Two missing walls, largest structure, she moves in to investigate and pulls out her phone, deletes the texts from her handler, and turns off the flash function to take photographic evidence for her investigation.

A few steps into the structure and there is absolutely nothing aboveground. She must locate the basement entrance like her character did several times in the show. Near the center of the interior of the structure, sits a twenty by twenty foot metal cube that doesn't look like any of the other set pieces in the studio, it's crisp, clean, and not charred at all.

She carefully walks up to a corner of the box, trying to make every step quiet as her shoes cause the gravel beneath her to crunch ever so slightly. Before she makes it around the next corner of the box to find the entrance, the gravel behind her crunches wildly and gets closer and closer until a couple of flashlights are shining in her face and a man's voice yells, "What are you doing here!? This is a restricted area, you're not supposed to be here!"

Despite her hand-to-hand combat training, Ellie is defenseless, she cannot even see her assailants due to the blinding lights in her face and is unable to determine how many of them there are, or if they have weapons. Plus, they probably already caught her skulking around on a security feed. Her cover and the integrity of the investigation would be blown open for sure if she fights back. Thinking on her feet, she screams as loud as she possibly can, "MICHAEL!!! MICHAEL!!! THEY'RE WATCHING YOU!"

A few seconds later, gun shots from a "Mechs primary cannon," rings out into the calm night sky. Ellie and the two security guards instinctually duck their heads down into their shoulders for a fraction of a second, the two men immediately grab her by the arms and cover her mouth, she does not resist.

Yelling out for Michael is the only thing that Ellie could think of to maintain her cover. The studio would simply close up shop and change production sites if there is even a hint of suspicion that someone is onto them. They escort her to their jeep.

"Are you done? We don't wanna have to put you in restraints."

Ellie nods, but they still tie some cloth over her mouth but keep her hands and feet free from any restraints as one of the guards sits next to her in the backseat of the jeep.

The jeep doesn't make a sound when the driver pushes the button to start the vehicle, the only noise that is made is the loose gravel on the ground when the vehicle gently accelerates. As they drive away, she looks back at the metal cube until it fades into the obscurity of the night. That had to be the entrance, her handler's intel was good but not her ability to remain undetected.

"Control. We have the subject. Female, brunette, about 5'4", smells like she has been drinking, we'll be back in a few minutes."

Ellie's time spent at corporate headquarters and on the show had yielded no results for the investigation. The window of opportunity is closing, whatever the studio and pharmaceutical company were doing, they will probably get away with it.

-Redacted Files 3-

Search Warrant

Three months before the premier of The Invasion…

In the matter of the search of all properties and premises of Echo Studios Corporation, filed May 4, 2040 in United States District Court:

I Casey Wickstrom being duly sworn, depose, and say:

I am a Special Agent in Charge at the Federal Bureau of Investigations for over twenty years and have reason to believe that Brier-Burton Pharmaceuticals and Echo Studios Corporation are engaged in global and domestic terrorism, money laundering, insider trading, and mail fraud.

Through an informant within Brier-Burton Pharmaceuticals, sufficient physical and electronic evidence has been gathered against Brier-Burton Pharmaceuticals on charges of said crimes. However, evidence has also uncovered that Echo Studios also played a major role in the commission of these crimes.

Background:

The Federal Bureau of Investigations was tipped off by a whistleblower within Brier-Burton Pharmaceuticals' organization that his company is engaged in global and domestic terrorism, money laundering, and mail fraud. The informant is the company's IT Network Systems Administrator who has access to all of the organization's e-mails and electronic files stored on the network drive as well as three hard drives of three separate workstations. He noticed these files and e-mails during a routine cybersecurity checkup on the system's networks and vulnerabilities to cyber-attacks.

The informant provided the agency evidence that Brier-Burton Pharmaceuticals knowingly engineered, produced, and spread the disease most commonly known as Cerebral Nervorum (CN). It has been determined that this disease is not in fact a disease, but rather an engineered nerve agent designed to mimic a neurological disorder.

This nerve agent is not contagious. The company was able to limit the exposure and outbreak by placing single particles into fine powder through physical mail to random addresses (some instances of targeted attacks) around the world. Methods include using fictitious sweepstakes contests, coupon mailers, urgent billing information etc.; essentially any way to convince the recipient/victim to open the envelope and become infected.

There were several schemes on ways to profit from this manufactured disease. Methods include but are not limited to; CRISPR gene editing therapy treatments, contracts to retrofit medical facilities to handle the influx of patients with CN, suppression medication, and eventually a cure that would be released to the market once enough individuals had become infected. A demand would be created for who would get access to the first batch of medication.

Evidence includes:

(1) E-mail correspondences discussing the progress of the creation of Cerebral Nervorum. (2) E-mail correspondences discussing the methods of spreading the disease. (3) E-mail correspondences discussing the various ways the company could profit from the disease. (4) Several suspicious wire transfers to numerous shell companies. (5) E-mails between Echo Studios' executives and counsel regarding additional ways to profit from the disease. (6) Funds being illegally transmitted to and from offshore accounts belonging to Brier-Burton. (7) Additionally, there is an informant in each of the companies to corroborate

these findings, an Audio Engineer within Echo Studios and a Financial Analyst within Brier-Burton Pharmaceuticals.

Conclusion:

Based on the plethora of evidence gathered by our informants, we at the Federal Bureau of Investigations believe there is probable cause for a search warrant, wire taps, computer forensics intrusions for all properties and premises associated with Echo Studios Corporation to further investigate Echo Studio Corporation's conspiracy with Brier-Burton Pharmaceuticals in violation of the crimes of global and domestic terrorism, money laundering, mail fraud, and Racketeer Influenced and Corrupt Organization (RICO) Act charges.

Echo Studios is accused of being knowledgeable and complicit in the spread of the nerve agent, acting as the pharmaceuticals' marketing and public relations arm in producing reality shows related to celebrities with the illness, Cerebral Nervorum. This warrants the immediate investigation into Echo Studios, those responsible, and their involvement in these crimes.

-Casey Wickstrom

Trials and Tribulations

December 3, 2040 – Trial of Echo Studios' Executives

"State your name."

"Casey Wickstrom."

"Do you swear to tell the truth, the whole truth, and nothing but the truth, so help you God under the pains and penalties of perjury?

"I do."

"First, tell us a little about your experience and what your team uncovered in this investigation."

"I am the Special Agent in Charge at the DC Field Office. I've been with the FBI for over twenty years. This case was first brought to my attention when an IT Systems Administrator from Brier-Burton contacted our office through our public hotline and made a conscientious choice to report what he uncovered to our agency.

He provided us correspondences and files that showed us Brier-Burton Pharmaceuticals created and dispersed a nerve agent that has infected over a hundred thousand people and resulted in several thousand deaths worldwide for the purpose of profit.

Of course, all of you know, the case with Brier-Burton was already successfully tried, and those responsible were found guilty and sentenced last month. But through that investigation, we uncovered enough evidence and had probable cause to investigate Echo Studio's involvement with Brier-Burton in the spreading of this deadly nerve agent.

It started out innocent enough where the studio would produce reality TV shows centered on celebrities and the process they would undergo for CRISPR treatment for the disease. But here is where they start to get a little more ambitious and nefarious.

The studio executives got wind of the nerve agent being produced at Brier-Burton, which led to the purchase of hundreds of thousands of shares of Brier-Burton from a shell company which has been proven to belong to Echo Studios. Additionally, the studio would receive information on potential patients they could use for upcoming reality shows, the first two which were never aired. All of this is documented in e-mail provided by the informants in addition to our undercover agent's recordings which I will get into next.

In early July, the FBI was able to infiltrate Echo Studios, Special Agent Ellie Pearson, better known as 'Ellie Harris' in the TV show, "The Invasion." Agent Pearson was first assigned as a temporary accountant in the studio's headquarters to investigate their financials for any irregularities without prejudice. From my side of the overall investigation, I was trying to determine if there was a link between Echo and Brier-Burton. The effort became fruitless, at least from the workstation Agent Pearson had intruded with permission from a judge.

However, within the first day, she was asked by the Studio's human resources department to either leave employment with the studio or sign on to become a cast member on one of their upcoming shows. She was told by the studios that she happens to be a close match to the description of their desired co-star for the show.

We almost pulled the plug on the investigation into Echo Studios until we were contacted by another informant within the company that provided the missing piece of the puzzle into their finances. In light of the new information, we kept Agent Pearson undercover through the filming of the show to continue the investigation.

We received intel that the nerve agent was being produced on site within the studios, we tasked Agent Pearson to investigate and find evidence. Her cover was nearly blown, however, thinking on her feet, she was able to convince the studio that she was under the influence of alcohol and in love with the main character, 'Michael,' which caused a near breach of a non-disclosure agreement with her and the studio.

During the deposition for breach of contract with Echo Studios, Agent Pearson was able to place two audio transmitting devices, bugs if you will. They provided the nail in the coffin we needed for Echo's role with Brier-

Burton in spreading and profiting from this worldwide disease. One was placed in the conference room and the other on Erik Martin, the studio's general counsel. You have already seen the e-mails and heard the audio during Agent Pearson's testimony yesterday."

"Agent Wickstrom, who did you have on the inside of each company? Who was it that ultimately tipped you off after Agent Pearson couldn't find anything in Echo's finances that kept your investigation intact when you were about to shut it down? This may have an effect on the credibility and reliability of the evidence that the prosecution has provided for the jury to examine."

"I can partially answer that for you your honor… Two of the witnesses were crucial in bringing down this worldwide conspiracy but are now fearful for their lives as well their families. The written testimonies and evidence provided by the two informants, the audio engineer and IT administrator, should be credible and compelling enough. I won't be entering their names into public record even though their identities have been changed in witness protection.

However, an additional witness was brave enough to come forward and put her name on the line. Miss Walker worked as a financial analyst with Brier-Burton Pharmaceuticals for over six years. In those years, Miss Walker's responsibilities were to determine the cost of operations for the company's research and development branch, collect operational data, identify trends and make recommendations to management to maximize profit.

After a few years with the company, she started to notice some irregular, possibly fraudulent payments attributed to R&D to a few offshore shell companies. Upon closer examination, she discovered that these shell companies were linked to Echo Studios.

She chose not to inquire further for fear of losing her job. Her husband Michael was diagnosed with Cerebral Nervorum a few years before, making her the sole breadwinner of the household. Understandably, she did not want to risk her only means to support herself and pay for her husband's rising medical costs.

A few more years pass, Eve Walker is approached by Echo Studios to enter her husband Michael into a reality show, triggering her to remember her discovery a few years back. Eve Walker initially turned them down as that is what her husband would have done. My investigators suspect that this triggered Brier-Burton to let her go as a forcing function to put her husband Michael on the show. This is when she came forward to our office and passed along what she knew to our investigators which triggered our continued investigation into the studios. We granted her immunity from any prosecution for her involvement in exchange for her cooperation.

We asked Eve to play along as if she had no option other than to enter her husband into the show with the promises of money and medical expenses. This would buy Agent Pearson time to gather more evidence and more time for another part of our task force to investigate the pharmaceutical company in conjunction with the studios. Never in our wildest imagination did we think that they produced this nerve agent that wreaked havoc on the world. At worst, we thought they were profiteers with inside knowledge of a terrible situation… our investigation has proven their involvement beyond financial crimes. They knowingly created this problem to profit from it on several fronts.

In addition to the e-mails provided by Brier-Burton's IT Administrator, the audio provided by Agent Pearson's undercover work, we also have Eve's testimony to corroborate the evidence laid out against them. ”

"Would Echo Studios like to cross-examine the witness?"

"No your honor… we would however like to reiterate for the record that the audio recordings that Agent Wickstrom's team played for the jury yesterday was fabricated. No such conversations took place. The defense rests."

……

Agent Wickstrom exits the courthouse and down the steps to make his way to his vehicle, not before dozens of reporters and cameramen swarm him as he is a few steps away from his car. "Agent Wickstrom, Agent Wickstrom, you helped put away some very bad people who would have gotten away with the murder of thousands of innocent people in a multi-billion dollar heist. If it wasn't for you and your team, more lives could have been lost over the last few of months, is there anything you would like to say to those involved with this crime, or the victims?"

"Today, we showed the world that no one is above the law and no one is beyond reproach. Justice was served today. Money or status does not preclude one from facing consequences, especially when so many have physically, emotionally, and financially suffered as a result."

"Sir, sir! Your team's work over the last couple of years saved the lives of tens of thousands of people worldwide, if not for the work you all put in, a cure may not have been found for many more years later, care to make a statement?"

"No comment."

A reporter shouts over everyone, in a slow and deliberate manner and asks, "What about the defense insisting that the audio files that your agents produced were fabricated, what do you have to say about those allegations?"

Without a word or even a glance to the reporter who asked the question, Agent Wickstrom steps into the backseat of the black sedan and the driver takes him away.

The flashing bulbs create a wall of light on the black vehicle, but for a fraction of a second, Agent Wickstrom's silhouette can be seen through the tinted window looking forward.

As the car pulls away, Wickstrom pulls his phone out from his pocket to make a call. The phone rings a few times as he stares out the tinted windows at the gaggle of reporters and photographers, trying to snap one last photo of the man who led the team that brought to justice those responsible for one of biggest conspiracies the world had ever faced.

"Hello?"

"Hey, it's Agent Wickstrom, this is a secure line. I don't know if you're watching the news right now, but we got them, and partly thanks to you Gordon. Even with mountains of evidence, sometimes the judge and jury need to hear the words spoken from the perpetrators themselves, especially when going up against with a company with such a high profile brand. Your country... actually, the world, owes you an insurmountable debt of gratitude."

"I have no recollection of what you're talking about... but thank you for the call sir... in case you called and were wondering, those files on my end are destroyed."

"I don't know what you're talking about either, good day, and again, thank you."

…..

March 10, 2042 – Time 1400hrs

Session #15 – Michael and Eve Walker

-Begin Message-

"Okay, I've started the recording... Welcome to your last session, we've come a long way in rebuilding your marriage and your relationship. We can't let the extreme factors of what happened to you two destroy what you have built since you were kids. I'm happy to see how you both have progressed. Eve mentioned something in the lobby, apparently you guys have some news?"

"Yes! First, we would like to thank you for guiding us through this rough patch and really showing us what's important. Eve, you want to tell him?"

"We're due mid-June! We've gotten through the worst a couple of years ago and we want to share our love with a little one!" You've helped us so much, to put things in perspective. Working through those feelings was difficult at first, but getting through it with some guidance from you... we've only become stronger for it."

"That's great! Congratulations! I didn't do anything but listen. You guys did all of the heavy lifting around here. All I did was ask the right questions, and really, ALL of the blame for the trouble in your marriage belonged to those two awful companies. Once we were able to pinpoint that, everything seemed to fall into place with a little bit of elbow grease. What's next for you two?"

"Well, now that I'm officially cured and there haven't been any recurring episodes for the last few months, there's no reason to be close to the city anymore. I think we're going to move somewhere far away, with no connection to the outside world. We just want to live in peace and raise our child."

"That sounds like a great plan. If there's nothing else, I believe this is goodbye. Congratulations on the little one on the way, it has been a pleasure getting to know you two over the last year."

"Thank you doctor, really, for all you've done for us, goodbye."

-End Message-

Author's Note

This work to me was truly a labor of love. Writing is my passion and something I fervently pursued over the last couple of years. This journey has been quite the emotional roller coaster of an experience and I wouldn't change a thing.

A little about me, as you can tell I'm kind of a science fiction geek and love all things that push the limits of how we perceive things and ideas of what our future may look like with our present course. For fun, I like to read, write, golf, play volleyball, and go to the occasional sporting event and watch stand-up comedians. I studied English Literature and Law, Societies, & Justice at the University of Washington.

Thank you for reading my debut novel! I hope you enjoyed the wild ride reading as I did to write it! If you liked the book, please kindly leave a review on Amazon, Goodreads, and spread the word!

Like my Facebook Page at, <u>Chris Chau – Author</u>, to stay up to date on the latest news for Patient 3 and other upcoming projects underway. This is also where I'll do signed copy giveaways, announce Reddit "Ask Me Anything" sessions and much more!

38236079R00194